Prison Wars

An Inside Account of How the Apocalypse Happened

By

Martin Sanger

Compiled by
John, K. Press, Ph.D.
For Social Books

Prison Wars

Editor's Preface . . . i

Chapter One – First Impressions . . . 1
Chapter Two – Press Conference . . . 15
Chapter Three – Home Life . . . 30
Chapter Four – Prison Negotiations . . . 45
Chapter Five – The Ethicists . . . 66
Chapter Six – The Games Begin . . . 86
Chapter Seven – The Day After . . . 105
Chapter Eight – The Triumvirate Meets . . . 123
Chapter Nine – The Movement Rises . . . 143
Chapter Ten – Party On! . . . 162
Chapter Eleven – Wipe Out . . . 182
Chapter Twelve – Judgment Day . . . 210
Chapter Thirteen – Born Again . . . 235

Editor's preface:

A prison guard sold us the first twelve chapters of this manuscript. Social Books, the publisher, had decided to compile information on Prison Wars with the intention of releasing a definitive account for posterity. When it was safe to do so, one of our first efforts was to contact whomever might be left at Martin Sanger's prison. It was upon visiting the prison facilities that we got word of the existence of this manuscript. We quickly began attempts to secure it.

We have no independent corroboration of the veracity of the accounts herein. But this manuscript surfaced only twelve days after the final Prison Wars games took place. The difficulty of fabricating such a detailed and personal account in so short an amount of time seems to validate its authenticity.

A gentleman brought us Chapter Thirteen five days after we secured and began publicizing the manuscript we had found in the prison. Martin Sanger did not bring it to us. The man who brought it to us was extremely guarded about how he happened upon it. Like the prison guards before him, he demanded cash and anonymity.

Not having publicized that there were only twelve chapters in the original manuscript, the additional chapter being numbered 'thirteen,' lends further credence to the authenticity of this manuscript. Furthermore, the continuity in writing styles indicates that Martin Sanger wrote all the chapters.

As of yet, Martin Sanger's whereabouts are unknown. We publicly admit to the publishing the manuscript without his permission. Even so, throughout the text the author reasserts that he wrote this chronicle for the benefit of posterity. If authentic, we have no doubt that Mr. Sanger would want the contents disseminated.

When found, all of the contents herein had already been typed. Except for formatting, and correcting the more egregious punctuation and spelling errors (undoubtedly due to the haste of the writing), the manuscript has been published without alterations. We at Social Books believe that, after this preface, Martin Sanger wrote all of the contents herein.

John Kenneth Press, Ph.D.
Social Books
San Luis Obispo, California
July, 2023

CHAPTER ONE – FIRST IMPRESSIONS

I first met Quentin Longus as a junior staff writer working for *Fortune magazine* in 2020. I had been assigned to interview the top twenty young venture capitalists in America. Quentin the ninth I profiled.

Quentin immediately stood out from the rest of that crowd. To begin with, he had a devilish surfer dude look. When I first met him his blonde hair was, in fact, long enough to hang over his shoulders. It would have completely obscured his vision had it not been combed into a part and held back by his ears.

Those of you who have only known of Quentin since he became famous would scarcely recognize him. But that is what makes my account of our destruction so compelling. I knew him from the beginning.

Of course the last time I saw him he sported his well-known short hair with the elongated wave on the front. I never liked that style. And the skinnier he got the less I liked it. Paradoxically, that cut made him look like a blond Hitler at the same time that his thinness reminded me of NAZI concentration camp survivors.

Having grown up in Los Angeles and residing in the rich L.A. suburb of Malibu, Quentin's stringy long blond hair wasn't extraordinary. But Quentin stood out from his fellow entrepreneurs because had an extraordinary non-physical personal beauty.

Quentin had the tranquility of an enlightened person who has no worries because they do not judge the moment. His smile was exceptionally kind. It put me at ease at a level that challenged my self-concerned, serious feeling about my life, missions and work. He radiated a sense of reassurance that I took for spiritual depth.

All of the other venture capitalists seemed to merit the common derisive label of 'vulture capitalists.' Aware of the prestige a profile in *Fortune magazine* carries, most of them sought to market themselves. It probably reflects the dichotomies of our democratic and capitalistic society that those I profiled either tried to market themselves as bigwigs or tried to appear very commonplace and humble. But, their hunger to be famous united them all. None were comfortable with themselves.

Where I saw panic, Quentin saw possibilities. On that first day, he got my editor to agree letting me cover Prison Wars and convinced me that my boss wouldn't mind if I returned to headquarters a day late.

My first reaction to such suggestions was to generate a list of reasons why it couldn't happen. But, Quentin's enthusiasm about possibilities even captured my hard-ass editor. And though most people, knowing a later version of Quentin, would find this hard to believe, he was able to get people to sign on to his agendas because he was a thoroughly relaxed person.

Quentin made me feel that panic over my nervousness and worries about my deadline and budget were completely unnecessary. His calm was, again, transformative. Being around him was like being around a guru. Everything was a game. And for every problem there was a creative solution that, after he thought of it, he would simply manifest. No sweat, no problem.

It was as if Quentin was a best-selling fiction writer who assumed that no matter what plot twists he backed himself into, a fabulous ending would appear, he'd write it, and it would be wildly popular. No worries dude! How wrong he was.

For the very few of you who haven't seen me, I am an average looking white male. I have brown eyes and wavy brown hair. My driver's license lists me at 5' 10". I'm probably closer to 5' 9". Since the time when I first met Quentin, I've lost a good thirty-five pounds. Partying and stress have been good for my figure! Still I am a big man. I worked out a lot in my youth. When I met Quentin, having some muscles, I was one of those guys who could kid themselves that they weren't fat, but if they gained another five pounds they'd be undeniably large.

As a modern writer I compare everything to television and films. The Longus' home resembled one of those perfect homes that rich people always had in movies and television shows of the 1970s.

Picture the driveway, long and curving. The front of the main house literally had plantation pillars. In this seventies film, a woman with blowing luxuriant hair would drive a long red convertible up the driveway. Only, in reality, the Longus home had an SUV, a Mercedes, and a BMW in front of their home.

Quentin actually told me on the day we met that he had something huge in mind. Had I known what he had in mind and what kind of a path it was going to take me down, I would have run and hid myself. Had I known I would have shook in panic and vomited out my remorse.

But sitting on patio furniture, behind his six bedroom Malibu home I could scarcely guess that we would plunge into the bowels of hell over the next two years. At the time, I just felt happy to be interviewing him and stunned when I found out that he had read a lot of my work!

"Mr. Sanger, I like your writing. It has an air of panic about it." Quentin had a light blue sweat suit and tennis shoes on. In these clothes and with his demeanor he couldn't say "panic" in a way that really conveyed the essence of the word.

"Gee, thanks, I guess." You can imagine how much this remark unsettled me. No other interviewee had ever read my writing before I visited, much less analyzed it.

"No. I really like it. The sense of panic means that you are conscientious. And still, while faced with panic, your writing remains coherent. That's because, at heart, you know that you're basically competent."

"Basically competent. . . thanks again." I nervously replied, unsure of where this was going.

"No. No. Don't get me wrong. I *really* liked it." At that moment I saw Quentin Longus' wide grin for the first time. It was captivating - all teeth. And it was accompanied by smile lines and a light in his eyes that nearly actually sparkled.

"When I read your work, I felt that you had potential that was just waiting for a good story. And Marty, what I'm about to embark upon will be revolutionary. I'd like somebody to document my upcoming venture full-time. I think you're the guy for it."

"I'm extremely flattered."

"But....?" His half-question probed the hesitancy on my part.

"But..." I continued finishing the sentence he started, while thinking about the accuracy of the intuition he had about my hesitation. "But I've worked my butt off to get where I am, I've just met you and I have no idea who you are or what your intentions are or what you're talking about, really."

"Of course, I guessed you'd be reluctant because you don't know who I am. That is natural. That's why I'd like you to live here, at this house, with my family."

"What! Aren't you being a little forward for our first date?" He had just gotten my attention, but in the wrong way. My confidence in him plummeted. But facially, my humorous attempt to defray the tension wasn't accompanied by a smile, but, rather, a look of slight nausea. His smile just increased a bit on the sides.

"I mean, isn't that offer just a little extreme and impulsive?" I asked with a blend of seriousness and coyness.

Showing some self-awareness, I forced a smile meant to mirror Quentin's gamey spirit.

"Yes. But not as impulsive as you think, Marty." He cocked his head a little to the side and paused. "Can I call you Marty, Mr. Sanger?"

"Sure."

"Marty, I do my research. I know your background and have read a lot of your writing. I've even read the film reviews you did with that guy Tom McDonnell for your high school newspaper."

"You read that?"

"Yep. I've read that and a lot more."

"Wow. Geez, strange," his references made me blurt out. I hadn't thought about Tommy McD for a while and Quentin knew about him. "I thought this was going to be all about you today. I'm a little taken aback."

"Yep, it probably is a little unexpected for ya huh?" His smile was as bright and wide as the Cheshire cat's sans cat. "But this isn't a job interview. You've already got the job. If and when you want it, it's yours. I really like your writing. It is very conversational. We'll work on taking that overly professional panicked aspect out. That'll come with time."

A laughing quizzical confused tone came out of me in my elongated one word response, "Okaaay."

"Yep. I've read you stuff and like it. And though we've just met, I've already pegged you as being that nice guy your columns convey in real life. I like your energy."

"Thanks again, but..."

"Look I know this is a bit extreme and I expected it come as a bit of a shock. So why don't you think it over. I know that I'm a good judge of character," He smiled and leaned forward and squinted. Then after a brief pause, Quentin finished the thought with a broad smile, "Even though I may not be a good judge of writing." He had a great sense of dry humor and could blend it with seriousness.

Quentin lowered his arched eyebrows and went back into a more serious mode. "But character is just as important to me . . . even more important, than writing ability. And I think we could hang together. We could be good friends."

He reclined as his smile stretched and eyes brightened to an improbable amount. I blushed profusely at the intimacy of the statement as I nervously smiled.

"Thanks. I don't know what to say."

"I know it's sudden. Why not think it over? In the meantime, I want you to cover my press conference next month for Fortune. It'll be the on the second Friday at the Sunset Hyatt."

"I don't know if I can get the time off or the assignment."

"Okay. Rule number one is to relax. There are no problems, only solutions."

"John Lennon." I misattributed the anonymous 1960s era quote.

"Oh, really? I thought my therapist made it up."

"Oh, so you have a therapist."

"Yeah."

"I can keep that off the record."

"That's okay, don't. But please call him my 'spiritual trainer.'" Quentin cocked his head and said to himself, "I love saying that."

Bringing his focus back to me he continued, "But, regardless of what you decide concerning my offer, I want to tell you a little life secret."

"Okay, shoot." I said with the earnestness and tone of a reporter.

"It's all about the dream. And we have nothing to fear, but fear itself. I know who said that!" We smiled together at our new inside joke. "And you cannot let fear stop you from making your dreams realities. Be a 'yes' to life and its possibilities. That's how I got this house, my family, everything."

Quentin seemed a little hokey to me. I, who had worked so hard my entire life to get where I was, resented the glibness of the rich and spiritual. But smiling was fostering a contagious dynamic between us. He was charming.

"I know it sounds very Malibu. But that's who lives here in these expensive homes - dreamers. And I think you know that and understand the power of dreams. You, a guy with nearly no family members, who rose from a single – parent, lower middle-class background; You, a guy from a home of no academic distinction who graduated from Yale with honors. You, Marty, must know about dreams."

"Wow! Your research continues to amaze." I really was impressed.

"And, I like the fact that you're not upset. I know you've researched me too. But there must be a certain feeling of violation when a stranger researches and draws conclusions about you without permission."

"No. That's quite all right. It's flattering."

"I love that! Many people would be incensed and defensive. But you have nothing to hide. You're very open. That's why this opportunity would be perfect for you. You're a surfer, for sure."

"You put a lot of stock in dreams and spiritual concerns."

"Right-ee-oo! You can believe that. And I sense that you know that the dream precedes the reality and that belief is way more than half the battle. The rest is just sweat. But you've done it. Your dream of being a reporter has come true. And now I'm just asking you to believe in a bigger dream."

Wow. This laid back motherfucker was smooth. Whether or not I was totally convinced or not, (I wasn't), he had my interest.
"Okay. Well you probably guessed that I'd need time to think about it. But I will be at your press conference for sure, if I can get the assignment."

"Why wouldn't you?"

"I'm a junior staffer. It sounds like a big story. But it costs money to get people like me to locations."

"Hold on!" Quentin stood up and walked into the house, reached over a bar, and got a phone. From outside the house I could hear him having a conversation. What a guy! What a situation! I was both stunned and nervously exhilarated. This situation was very out of the ordinary.

I was getting the feeling that he'd pay me whatever I asked, but I… Quentin came back out onto the patio.

"Well?" I asked, suspecting, but not fully having the requisite faith to believe it."

"I just got off the phone with your boss." He really did it!

"Mr. Lockley?"

"That's right. I told him I'd be willing to have you picked up in a private jet at the airport nearest your home office if he would let you cover my event. I promised exclusive first interviews for *Fortune magazine* on the announcement, if he wanted it, and to pay for your salary for the weeks you worked on the project."

"You've got to be kidding me!"

"No I'm not. I'm really serious. I just don't get worried. When other peoples' worries stop them, I listen to them. I find out what they'd need to relax and double it. That way I can focus on dreams of wondrous things rather than fears. And your presence is one of those wondrous things. He agreed to everything as long as everything you wrote about during the time you're away belonged to *Fortune magazine*'s parent company. I told him that was no problem."

"Wow." I was saying that a lot and felt kind of stupid for it.

"Wow is right! So your boss says you'll be at that press conference. So you will at least do that for me, eh?"

"Sounds like a done deal."

"Definitely. You won't lose your job. He's happy. I'm happy. And I hope you're happy about it too and that all is well."

"I think it is." My inflection implied the definite yes my words didn't.

"Feel that buzz? That is the excitement of living on the edge. Don't worry. Be excited. Relax and enjoy.

"Let's play tennis!" Quentin exclaimed after the slightest pause.

When I told him, near the end of our tennis games, that I had to leave to catch my flight back to Omaha that night, he laughed and said I had a lot to learn. A private limousine was going to pick me up for an already booked flight the next day.

"Your boss won't mind. Trust me. After the deal I just worked out with him, just tell him the truth and don't worry." At this point, having seen his ability to assuage my boss' worries, I didn't. For the very first time, I allowed myself the freedom to brush off my normal nervousness about my boss' state of mind.

"Let's go for lunch. I know a place on the beach."

This was fantastic. My article profiling young entrepreneurs would have at least one installment with a strong element of private scoop. At lunch I continued the interview.

"How do you stay so calm?" I asked as the blond slender waitress placed my omelet in front of me. After she was convinced that all was well she left and I continued, "You're not like the other entrepreneurs I've met. You're calmer. It's in your breath, if you'll permit me a writerly insight."

"With my blessings, by all means." So many of his statements were punctuated by broad smiles.

"Other entrepreneurs give off the air of being happy and self − satisfied, but they always have a deep need to be seen.

Their posture is wolf-like. They aren't really relaxed. But you seem genuinely relaxed. How do you do it?"

"Well. I do the usual. I meditate."

"Hence the breathing."

"Good writerly insight." He smiled broadly.
"I also play the saxophone to relax…" Looking back on it, this most auto-erotic of all instruments was perfect for him.

"Saxophone! Do you play in a band?"

"No. Just alone. But I was in a band in high school."

"That's not in your standard profiles?"

"I wouldn't think so."

"What was your band called?" I pushed, hoping for a usable detail.

"The Dorian Gray Romance Band."

"Nice name. Very literary."

"Thanks. Did you ever play in a band?"

"No. I'm not that kind of artist. But," I continued with growing confidence, "This is, finally, not your interview of me, but my interview of you." My jokes only brought smirks, he was the master of broad smile evocation. "You meditate, play sax, and, and what else accounts for your calm?"

"I'm not petty. I don't get caught up in the drama of life. I see all the business machinations I get involved in like television shows or a movie. It's just entertainment. We all die sooner or later. There is no need to get too wrapped up in any of this stuff."

"So you have a detachment from the world." I probed.

"I guess so, if you want to put it that way. I never thought about it that way. It sounds kind of negative the way you put it.

"I don't think of it as negative. I realize that every moment is blessed and that this moment of being alive is the greatest success one could ever have. I constantly celebrate the miracle of life. I lean into life, no matter what comes my way."

He paused and closed his eyes. This was the first time I had seen this habit.

"Yeah, maybe I'm somewhat detached from everything except my family. That is the one thing that I take as a vital concern, that I really sweat about the outcome of. But even then . . ." His smile and shrug expressed his calm about their well – being too.

"Right on!" I exclaimed. "A sax playing Buddhist with a therapist, that's just the sort of thing that makes good copy." Then I caught myself. "Oh yeah, spiritual trainer. I'll remember to print the right one. Don't worry."

"I don't." He shrugged and smiled broadly and I believed him.

Such was my first encounter with Quentin Longus. He was magnetic, I wanted to be around him. It felt like it must feel to have a guru. And I mean that sincerely. I am skeptical of such things generally. But he made it all seem real. His restful demeanor was genuine. He looked you in the eyes with a sort intensity that made you feel like you could open up to and trust him. He had an immense and transformative presence.

As would be expected, he beat me badly in tennis. I'm sure his beating me partially resulted from my not being an experienced tennis player. But it also reflected his inner calm. When he made a stupid mistake, he didn't get flustered. His strokes and serves were done with amazing grace. His cultivated calm permeated him, his business efforts, and his tennis completely.

On that very day, Quentin taught me that who we are and how our lives come out are intimately connected. He would later tell me that how you do one thing is how you do everything. Frantic people get frantic results. Focused people get exactly what they are after. And I felt (perhaps due to my ever present insecurity) that I had much, much more to learn from him.

His having mentioned the possibility of working with him made me feel both lucky and nervous. I was anxious that it not fall-through. But, I told myself, even if I should never meet this man again, I would never forget his presence. That smile of his could calm people going down in a crashing plane. And since I often felt like I was going down in flames . . .

Quentin brought mayhem upon America. History will regard him as a super villain. It will position him somewhere between Benedict Arnold and Genghis Khan on the infamy scale. That's the reason why this historical record is so important.

Few knew the inner workings of this man. None but those who had spent time with him privately could grasp the true nature of his soul before the rise of Prison Wars. I trailed him through every significant phase of the Prison Wars venture. As what we did led to total disaster, my being positioned so closely to him made writing this account both an act of redemption and a moral necessity.

Perhaps Quentin served as an unwitting alchemist. On that day he partially transformed me into a luxury-expecting tennis player. He taught me not to worry. I believe his spirit was then entirely free from bad intentions. He lived in bliss and thought of nothing else. And so perhaps his life, and its impact on us, should change the way we normally quip about ignorance; Ignorance is bliss, but it can lead to hell.

CHAPTER TWO – PRESS CONFERENCE

I told all my friends (both of my friends) and my colleagues about my meeting with Quentin and how excited I was about it. But between the time of our first encounter and the press conference we only spoke twice.

A few days after I returned to Omaha, Quentin called to tell me of the logistics; which hotel, flight, limo company etc. were to escort me. And right before my departure date, he called again to confirm that I was coming.

Though I had Quentin's number I was too nervous about accidentally blowing my opportunity to call him. Both times he called me the same dynamic applied. In disbelief, and not wanting this to fall through, I tried to sound unexcited and businesslike.

Quentin treated me like an old friend. He apologized for not contacting me more often. He had been really busy getting final negotiations and logistics ready for the big night and promised we'd have some real quality time to talk after the press conference.

"Sounds great," was all I could say. My head and heart had to process both the fear of blowing this opportunity and tremendous excitement. This emotional balancing act percolated under every word.

Though I was honored and felt his warmth from our first handshake, trusting is hard for me. After each call I felt jaded, evil, and dirty. He had love and trust while I had skepticism. Had the world made me so gun shy of people? Was it my upbringing? It was almost unnerving to talk with him. My lack of love became more apparent to me each time. It was if I were being readied for a therapeutic immersion I might not be able to handle. That period filled me with the type of tension that must precede religious conversions.

I was intrigued by the potential of our relationship. Not having many connections with people--and those just being with run-of-the-mill folk -- friendship with him seemed like a rare and strange blessing. Like a beggar confronting Jesus, I wasn't sure why I was worthy of such attention.

Looking back, perhaps he chose me because I was average. It is easier to trust folks that haven't swum with big sharks. Perhaps it was out of an admiration for my writing. But I've never thought my writing was that special. Perhaps he just enjoyed bestowing blessings on good people that seemed to need love.

Such were the sorts of questions that besieged my worried brain in the weeks preceding the big event. Even after the limo picked me up, after I flew for a second time in his private jet, and I was dropped off in front of the Sunset Hyatt, I could barely believe that this was happening to me.

The Wilshire Beverly was the normal place for large corporate announcements in Los Angeles. Both of my previous assignments covering mergers were held there. The Hyatt on the Sunset Strip in Hollywood had an entirely different atmosphere. In retrospect, choosing it was a stroke of genius. The rich-meets-poor, party-infused atmosphere of this adult playground was perfect for the juvenile spectacle being announced.

The Sunset Strip is Hollywood's hottest street. This was the first time I had seen it at night. The whole thing is television. Though it was night, the street was lit as brightly as a movie set. The sidewalks were full of women that looked like supermodels. All of the guys looked like they are top-of-the-chart rock stars. Never had I seen such a concentration of people wearing tight, vinyl and leather pants.

The excitement builds in the Sunset Hyatt elevator. How fantastic you are is measured by how high you go. I remember predicting that the order of the passengers leaving. The couples all went first, then went the heavier businessmen, then went the sleek young businessmen, the scruffy partiers left and then we three hit the top.

Leaving the elevator I passed guards at a table and finally entered a large dark room with booths. I went to the wet bar in the left of the room. Drinks were on the house, but everyone was leaving five-dollar tips in the tip jar. Against the back wall there was a stage where a disc-spinner was fronted by a revolving cadre of strippers that went all the way to topless.

The topless women didn't go too well with this media crowd. The media folk looked too old to be titillated with such teenager type stuff. But they didn't disregard the strippers. They weren't shocked and outraged. They just tried to look disinterested. I suppose the odd blending of elderly and youthful thrills is now a part of our youth-worshiping culture. The media men not showing enjoyment made them appear bizarre and antiquated.

Not having anyone with me, I scanned the crowd. One guy stood out. He was tall angular, thick and dark. He had a bad-guy dartiness in his eyes and spoke to no one all night. It might have been due to my focusing on him as a character, but he appeared to take crowd pictures too often. Once or twice I actually felt my privacy was violated as he seemed to be taking pictures of me.

I was going to confront him when I noticed that there was an outside. Just how special the place I had the privilege to be in became immediately apparent as I first viewed the rooftop patio. It sported another bar and a full buffet. But beyond this it had a view to die for - a view of all the lights of Los Angeles.

Twenty-four floors below I looked down upon the jammed cars that cruised the strip. They thought that they were hot. And I realized I was in the hotspot they were dreaming of. Damn! This was it. I was in where the in-crowd was.

Looking down from this fantastic height actually put me in the mind of achieving final glamour by jumping. Now that I was finally fulfilled I didn't need to continue. The glass wall that lined the roof likely made the temptation of jumping a repeating subconscious theme to all. But it was so tall that our fulfillment would have to wait.

And there, precariously perched on a riser was Quentin. The riser was so high that it lifted him above the glass partition. Behind him shone all the lights of the city. In front of him was a small table with a pitcher of water and a glass on it.

I think he must have been waiting for me. Because as soon as he saw me and gave me an uncharacteristic thumbs-up he launched into his presentation.

"Ladies and gentlemen I am ready to proceed. If I may have your attention I'd like to start by thanking you for coming here this evening. I hope you've had a good time thus far. And again, thank you for coming.

"Ladies and gentleman, what you are about to hear about may disturb you. It may excite you. It may make you think that I am a madman. But it will happen.

"What I am about to announce will be the single most important development in the history of media. I am not joking or exaggerating. Take me seriously. The contracts have been signed. The legalities have been checked. We are set to go in approximately three months.

"Please hold your questions until the end of my announcement. But know that Prison Wars are for real. ESPN has already bought the broadcast rights.

"Prison Wars are what they sound like. Gladiator style games using prisoners as gladiators. We will have various battles in the courtyards of prisons. These battles will result in injury and perhaps death for some of the participants. The fascinating essence of all sport will be shown raw in Prison Wars.

"Each battle will have different rules. They will be creative in costume and setting. Each contest will be a different spectacle. Each will require intense athletic training and ability. And, as it will be a real battle to the death, you won't be able to turn away from it whether you want to or not."

Murmurs among the journalists were getting loud. And several journalists started to vie for his attention. "Mr. Longus, Mr. Longus"

"Please no questions until the end of my announcement. I believe my presentation will answer many of the questions you have. And if you have others at the end of my presentation, I will answer them then." He smiled with an imperial sense of self-satisfaction that quieted the crowd.

"You may be wondering how we can get away with such a brutal spectacle. We are employing the same legal contracts that are used in other sports. Fights in hockey and other sporting events aren't punished criminally. Such altercations are within the jurisdiction of the sponsoring league. We have used the same business model. Our contracts require that participants waive their rights to prosecute those that inflict injuries upon them.

"The league is responsible for penalizing inappropriate behaviors. But we won't." Quentin chortled with his mouth close for a moment.

"Giving the spectator everything he wants, without restrictions, is our mission. We plan to do so in a way that cannot be surpassed. We will not pull punches."

Quentin sat even taller and continued.

"Legal objections aside, some folks may object to Prison Wars on moral grounds. We have taken two actions that will hopefully qualm the ethical concerns you might have.

"First of all, all games will be preceded by disclaimers, the full text of which will be available after the press conference. In addition to the usual warning that the material is inappropriate for children, the lengthy statement will note that the participants are in prison because of their brutality. The disclaimer makes the very valid point that the desperation of the participants is proof that crime doesn't pay. The best way to avoid such violence is to stay out of prison. I have every expectation that Prison Wars will be a deterrent to crime.

"Secondly, we will be donating twenty percent of the proceeds, before taxes but after expenses, to the State's general fund. In addition, ten percent of the profits shall be put aside for payment of the contest participants themselves. In consultation with the Governor of our great State of California, we have arranged for forty percent of the proceeds going to the State to be earmarked for education. Fifteen percent of the State's funds will help the State Penal System.

"Prison Wars will be what we call a win-win-win-win situation. Prisoners will win. The Attorney General's office has agreed to adjust the terms of the participant's sentencing conditions in recognition of their positive and valiant contributions to society. The winners will also receive considerable revenues.

"Children will win. The projected income will allow a reduction in the teacher-to-student ratio in our State. This will serve to keep kids out of prison and increase their ability to lead our State out of its current economic decline.

"Society will win. Contributing to the General Fund and covering some of the costs of the Penal System will go a long way to alleviating our State's perennial budget crisis. The prisoners will be paying their debt to society by paying societies' debts. Who knows? We may even live to see it resulting in a tax cut."

Quentin laughed silently and a couple of drunks in the audience laughed out loud.

"Society will also win morally as this will be a deterrent to crime."

"And we the viewers will win. I promise you a show that will create an unprecedented buzz. I promise you a spectacle that will be more gripping than anything you have ever seen before. This will be reality television for the modern era."

Quentin paused to survey the assembled audience. They all looked somewhat ridiculous. Their faces showed a combination of distorted reactions. Simultaneously, surprise, disbelief, continued nervous laughter from a few, confusion, and excitement occupied the viewers' faces. They wanted to talk, but couldn't. A lot of round sounds bubbled out of their mouths. It was if the reporters and guests were trying to spit out tar.

"The design of the individual events will be interactive. We are working with groups of video game designers, sports enthusiasts, television producers and the prisoners themselves to make this a test of skill that will be fun to watch.

"At the end of each contest, we will have on-line polls and discussion groups. We will implement every one of the most popular suggestions at the very next contest. And nothing . . . nothing will be off the table. Weapons, sets, costumes, different rules and gadgets will all be considered. We are proud to say that this will be the first truly interactive mass sport. Our viewers will be in control. Whatever the public wants, up to and including injury and even death, we will manifest."

Several people made spontaneous outcries. These sounds were preverbal. They sounded like proto-exclamations and wails.

Instead of continually asking folks to please quiet down, Quentin just got quiet himself. He put his index finger in front of his lips while calmly smiling and made oceanic shushing sounds. He exemplified the state he wished to see. With patience, a look of extreme bliss, and no sense of anger at the sound, he waited for the audience's sound to pass.

It took a few minutes for people to start shushing each other and for the air to be cleared again for him. And I don't think that anyone missed the fact that he waited until the sound of the cars below and the breathing of those assembled were audible before he continued.

"In short, Prison Wars will be the revolution in programming that we have all been waiting for. It will provide more financial aid to our society than all the telethons ever run combined. It will radically reform our prison system. It will provide the final leap to the collective interactive nature that television and computers have made possible. And it will take us to the extremes of reality and fantasy our psyches have always sought.

"It will be the single most important cultural event of our generation. Get ready for Prison Wars. Death is expected. Nothing will ever be the same again."

Strangely, this shocking last string of sound bytes created no reaction at all. But still there was a nearly audible sound of thoughts racing. It was very dramatic.

"I am now open to take questions. Please, for my records, state your name and the name of the news organization for whom you work." The silence broke into the familiar frenzy of journalists vying to be recognized. Looking like he was having a lot of fun, Quentin pointed at one.

"Mr. Longus, Peter Flemming, Time magazine." This man was very professional.

"Yes."

"You must be aware that these contracts will be challenged in court. Do you really expect these battles..."

"Prison Wars. Please refer to them as Prison Wars. Prison Wars will be referred to as games, not battles."

"Yes Mr. Longus. Do you really expect that these Prison Wars games will be aired? Won't the courts tie them up for years, until the project is dropped?"

"These contracts are legal. No coercion is being used. If prisoners do not wish to sign-up to participate in the Prison Wars, they don't have to. The contracts we are using are based on those that other sporting organizations use. They are fairly standard.

"Besides lawsuits require plaintiffs. The athletes that participate won't sue. If they don't want to participate, they won't. And the State won't sue as it is co-sponsoring these events.

"The network airing the program, ESPN, is a cable network. The FCC's jurisdiction over them is limited as they use no airwaves. Believe me we have had a team of lawyers investigate every possible legal objection to our project and our contracts are unassailable."

"Mr. Longus, Mr. Longus." The crowd again burst into sounding like a classroom where everybody had the answers and needs credit for answering.

"Yes you."

"Thank you Mr. Longus. Paul Salerio, ABC. It seems that this scheme, which frankly, I'm still having trouble believing isn't just a hoax of some sort, would get high ratings."

"I'm banking on it." Quentin jabbed quickly. All giggled a little press conference giggle with the addition of a nervous edge.

"It seems that this would create a sort of, race to the bottom scenario where the brutality would get out of hand."

"We will not be outdone. Besides which, we have the exclusive access to the States' prisons. For the meantime, no one has the contracts and no one else could host such events without litigious battles over copyright infringement and the assumption of a lot of liability. We plan to corner this market as long as we can. I don't see any competition on the horizon."

The crowd burst back into the cacophony of a thousand chickens clucking. "Yes, ma'am."

"Thanks. Wynonna Lippman, E! Magazine. Who will be announcing these contests? Have you lined anyone up?"

"This being a new sport, there are no experts. And I hope you understood that we are looking to be a legitimate sport. The rules we decide on will be complex and changing. As such the announcer must be capable of both rousing excitement and explaining details simultaneously.

"We are currently in negotiations with several nationally known football announcers for both play by play and color commentary. But I'm sorry I cannot give you any names yet. I can only tell you that we aren't currently interviewing anybody that you haven't heard of."

"Yes ma'am, you."

"I am shocked and angered by this…"

"Your name!"

"I will not stand on formality…"

"Okay, shoot."

"This is horrible. We're talking about human lives. You want people to die on television for entertainment??!! This is barbarous. This must be stopped."

"Thank you for your honest concern. First of all, no one will be coerced into doing anything. We must consult the prisoners themselves as to what the rules of the contests will be and how they will divide their earnings. Winning teams may have access to privileges such as alcohol, conjugal visits, nice furniture, unlimited television and various other perks. All the prisoner's premiums will come directly from proceeds of the contests, with no expense to the taxpayer. Next question."

"Gregg..."

"No! No! No! You didn't answer my question." The woman who attacked him wasn't done. "You're exposing America to horrible barbarous cruelty. It isn't civilized! This is disgusting."

"Excuse me, excuse me, excuse me." Quentin suddenly looked more serious than I had previously seen him look, "Speaking of civility, you had your turn and it is now over."

"I'm not done."

"Look miss whatever your name is, these people are criminals. These are people in hardcore lockdown. Most of them are really brutal. If several of them get hurt or killed, I won't lose a lot of sleep. In fact, I'll sleep better.

"This, again, is a win-win situation. If they get hurt paying us back I don't mind. If you live by the sword you must be prepared to die by the sword. I'd hate to see someone I loved or any law-abiding citizen hurt. But these people, they are dangerous to us."

"Gregg Hernandez, the previous..."

"Mr. Hernandez, which news agency are you with?"

"Oh, sorry. I'm with KTLA channel five here in Los Angeles. The previous questioner was right in that this proposal is pregnant with ethical problems. What would you say to those that would worry about the effect this program will have on children?"

"I have two children under the age of thirteen. They aren't who they are because of television. Their loving and strong family is the source of their values. I am hoping that they grow up to be civilized humans.

"However, as an American, I am a lover of freedom. If, when they are old enough to choose, my children choose to watch Prison Wars, I will watch it with them. Because I know my children, I have no worries that they will become criminals because of a television program."

A rage for a follow up re-erupted.

"Yes, you in the back."

"Chad Auster, Fox. Sir I think that there is no doubt that such programming will be very popular, but don't you think that it will have a deleterious effect on our culture as a whole? Isn't it crossing a line that shouldn't be crossed in the interest of the public good?"

"I don't think that it will have a deleterious effect. I don't think that I am capable of committing brutal acts of aggression, just as I don't think that you are." He smiled broadly, but like William F. Buckley one got the impression that this smile was meant to mask hatred. If not brutal acts, a that moment all could believe that Quentin was capable of hate. He put his head down and briefly closed his eyes, as though he was trying to remember something. Then, nodding his head, he came back beaming and relaxed again.

"Mr. Auster, people are born the way they are. I don't think my son and daughter will end up in Prison. It won't be much more violent than the video games that kids play today. My kids play those games and they aren't violent. After they're done with their games they are just as sweet as ever." His smile went back to its original, natural warmth.

"That said, no, I don't think this will make for suitable viewing for young children. If my boy wants to watch it when he gets a little older we'll watch it together. I'll explain what it is and that these bad things are happening to bad people. I think, were my children anything but sweet and well raised, it could even serve as a great deterrent to criminal activity to them.

"But, I would definitely recommend parental discretion.

"One last question. Yes you in the green hair!" His broad grin didn't evoke the resonance with his audience that it had before.

"Justin Geller, MTV"

"Yes Mr. Geller, love your shows, watcha think?"

"Well, it sounds pretty rad!"

"Thank you."

"But, Mr. Longus, do you really think that mainstream sponsors are going buy advertising segments for such a program? Major sponsors are easily dissuaded."

"Well, ESPN has already bought onto the concept. They're major. And let me tell you something you already know. Though corporations talk about corporate responsibility etc, it is just hypocrisy. They are following the money trail just like everyone else. As they would put it, 'They have a responsibility to their stock holders.' I think that they cannot afford to miss out on this prime target audience, males between the ages of 18 and 35. If beer, fast food and truck companies want to be popular, and they do, they'll come around.

"Ladies and gentlemen that concludes the press conference. Thank you very much for coming. I am going to be leaving the building, but I invite you to stay until the closing time of one a.m. Again our disclaimer is on the table near the elevator, and I hope you give us some good copy. Enjoy the view and consumables."

At that Quentin looked over at me and made the gesture of putting a phone to his head and mouthed, "Call me," and was busily escorted away. Many people saw him gesture to me and I, for the first time in my life, momentarily became the center of attention.

Looking back on it, I am surprised at how quickly I adjusted to the other side of reporter's inquiries. I had been on the querying side of many of these feeding frenzies. It had always seemed very serious. But looking at all of these petitioners, they appeared comical. I felt a sense of superiority and power as I played bigwig.

As I had seen many folks do I told them that I was not authorized to give them further information. I wanted to keep them interested by giving tidbits. I told them my name and that I was Quentin's official publicist. But they quickly figured out that they already had a huge story and that I wasn't going to share my scoop.

I've never seen a press conference clear out so quickly. This was a hot item and folks were all rushing to their outlets to make their report. My article due date, *Fortune Magazine* being a monthly, was weeks away. But I left quickly too.

I left because I realized I had a lot of thinking to do. No, it was worse than that. I was dizzy with confused feelings. My first reaction to Prison Wars was terror and repulsion. The terror of the idea mixed with the lingering rush of the attention I had received, pride in the way I handled myself, total disbelief that this was happening and a million questions about where this might lead, all fought with each other for attention in my thoughts.

The nearly painful sensation that there wasn't room enough in my head, heart and stomach for all of these conflicting impulses didn't die down for hours. Finally, I told myself that if I didn't take this opportunity, someone else would take it. I reasoned that leaving it would be running away from the biggest opportunity I would ever run into. As a human, I couldn't be a part of this adventure. But as a journalist, I had to go where the action was.

That was a fateful night. As a person who could see the potentially destructive effects and morally questionable nature of

Prison Wars, perhaps I should have stood for my principles. I cannot deny the fact that I sold out my morals for opportunity. I had no idea how horrible the outcome would be, but anyone with any sense could tell that it wasn't a good development for our culture.

As it turned out, my personal writing ability and lingering residue of common sense are what have enabled this very report. Saying that I foresaw my ability to write against this tragedy with intimate knowledge, and thus provide a moral worth to my actions, as a justification of my efforts, would be a lie. I just plain sold out my morals for opportunity.

I have blood on my hands. My failure to distinguish between infamy and fame, my lack of shame, by making money off of horror, the words I wrote and spoke without thinking about the ultimate implications of my words, all implicate me. All of these things have tattooed my hands with indelible guilt that makes my failure to kill myself an affront to decency.

But, ultimately, for this report to have accomplished any good you have to look at the blood on your own hands. Did you watch Prison Wars? Did you fight with people who did? How many times have you sold out your morals for convenience?

Anyhow, you didn't know. I didn't know. But, I pray that whatever social order finally emerges from the chaos that now engulfs us will be cognizant of the importance of distinguishing between a healthy culture and a pathological one. I hope they tell their children about what happened to us.

CHAPTER THREE – HOME LIFE

I pretty much stayed up all night watching television. Prison Wars was the top story on every network within an hour. All night long, it dominated the news channel talk shows.

Callers asked all the questions you'd expect. Less than half of those who called in considered it a good idea. Of the supporters, about ninety-nine percent were male. More than half of the anchors editorialized their disapproval and said we ought to do what we could to stop it. A significant number of people, I'm glad to report, expressed alarm.

It was predictable that everyone would want to know more about the man behind the program. Some networks had slapped together bios of Quentin. Many, I'm proud to say, quoted my original profile of Quentin in *Fortune magazine*. As will happen, his old associates and supposed lovers showed up to spill dirt.

It was now apparent why he was cultivating me as a publicist. Speculation was rampant for the next few days. Who could believe that someone could pull off such a seemingly impossible arrangement? Surely this person was perverse. But just as certainly he must have been both rich and a genius (a combination that provides fascination for both men and women).

In fact, Quentin's life had been rather unremarkable. He went to the same local high school, Palisades High, that his children were slated to go to. His picture in his senior year yearbook wasn't distinguishable from all the other blonde, shoulder length, stringy haired boys of his generation and neighborhood.

At UCLA he majored in business and finance and graduated in the middle of his class. He did, he claimed, "Enough to not get kicked out."

Following Quentin's undistinguished graduation, he started his own venture capital company. His company did have the strange distinction of mostly funding the development of products for the toy market. His company, 'Play On,' developed the "Radio Doll" and the "Kiddie Credit Cards Buying Clubs." Other than that, his career had been entirely pedestrian.

In response to all of the vitriolic condemnation of him as the incarnation of evil, I had to produce sympathetic humanized depictions of him. This homespun-style spin about him was primarily intended to protect his family from attack. He really did worry about them being vilified.

But more practically, he saw his wholesome image as the best defense he had against his critics. I don't think he anticipated the strength of the opposition to Prison Wars. He was visibly shaken by the hostile responses at the press conference.

His remarks about the inheritability of evil didn't play well in the media. His flip remarks about the fate of the prisoners didn't convince people that he cared much for individual lives. Prison Wars incensed all the human rights groups at once. His rich children not going to jail put the spotlight on the fact that the prisons are mostly filled with people that come from poverty.

The only shining light in his series of responses at the first press conference were those about his family and taking personal responsibility for them. While denouncing the plan, due to the sanctity of life, a few right-leaning commentators agreed that family cohesion should be the basis of our morals. And, even Prison Wars' critics could see that his love for his family was real.

Creating positive spin about his having a warm and tight knit family wasn't too hard to do. He had as normal and happy a family life as I had ever witnessed. His wife, Melissa, and he had been married 13 years when I met him. Their older son, Justin was a sixth grade soccer player and Samantha was a normal third grader with a passion for ballet lessons. They were very close to the ideal American family.

Life had always been easy for Quentin. No major setbacks had marred his life. Well fed and cared for his entire life, he never had occasion to even develop a mean streak or an instinct for protection. His was a stress-free existence. And this ease and uncomplicated sense of well-being pervaded the feeling of his family.

Quentin's laugh lines weren't there due to smugness and they weren't fake. People picked up on that. Early on I figured out that one source of his happiness was the extreme joy he took in small things. Quentin was truly happy. I miss and am still uplifted by thinking of how much pleasure he would derive from his habit of picking up little items and looking at them.

But I correct myself – they weren't little things to him. Quentin liked to breathe, to hear people's voices, having eyes to see snippets of life. During every conversation his demeanor silently said, "Isn't it fantastic to be alive." His presence made you aware of how little you appreciated your own existence. I planted this personal magnetism angle into nearly all articles, press releases, and inquiry responses I wrote on his behalf.

My spin job was also intended to protect Quentin's mental sanity. As I had already mentioned, his charm came from his relaxed low-key demeanor. Outside of the moments of discomfort he experienced at the press conference, I never saw him worried about anything in the early days. The crevices of his laugh lines were never covered over. He had a permanent smile.

He prized his smile even more that his projects. Quentin wanted both and expected he could have both. Unfortunately, my spin couldn't keep him from his public image. Herein, lies an interesting dynamic and lesson; don't believe the hype. It will distort you until you are completely lost. But I am getting ahead of myself.

The morning after the press conference, when I arrived at Quentin's Malibu home, we all went on a beach excursion. It was a family only, no business allowed, beach trip. But he did have a personal goal that he snuck into the day. As his main publicity agent Quentin felt I had to know him and his family well. This was essential to my being able to paint a picture of him as a family man.

But, Quentin wasn't simply being scheming or manipulative. He was, as I have indicated, one of the kindest and most spiritually generous people I ever met. I think he could tell that I was lonely. My family had never been tight. I think that he knew that I needed a family and he wanted to help me be happy; to have a sense of belonging in the universe.

It wasn't just me. Wherever he went he seemed to key into people's deep need for love and recognition. Knowing him made one realize how lonely Americans are. Our professionalism hid a lot of pain. A large part of his charisma and power over people came from his extraordinary warmth to perfect strangers. A surprising amount of folks are easily manipulated because they are starved for common friendship.

Beyond it just being Quentin's nature to be loving, he hoped that by making me a part of the family, he would be able to conduct business without having strangers on his property. I was to be that fine line between his personal and professional life. Having no children or close family of my own, I was really happy about this part of my assignment. I felt like an adopted puppy.

The day after the press conference, a limo came to my hotel and dropped me off at Quentin and Melissa's place. It was fun and unnerving to be in a limousine. I was really conscious that people must be looking at my vehicle and wondering who rode inside. My first inclination was to roll down the window, lean out and proclaim, "It's me, it's me! I get to be in a limousine!" But that would be silly. So I kept the windows rolled up and sealed myself off from view.

Being resolved just to take my seat in the limo and quietly reflect on the night before morphed into self-scrutiny. I started asking myself, 'Why am I in a limousine?' 'Am I special?' 'Different?' 'Aren't I just that little guy from Nebraska?'

Since I didn't describe it before, let me describe Malibu now. For those of you who don't know, Malibu is an idyllic community on the coast of the Pacific Ocean, Northwest of Los Angeles. Though definitely in the mix of Los Angeles, Malibu is cut off from it in many ways.

For one thing, it is a part of Los Angeles where the air is clean. It doesn't strike one as a place where commerce happens at all. Facing a marvelous quasi-private beach, it feels like a tropical island paradise. Every home in Malibu has the perfection of homes in Better Homes and Gardens or Architectural Digest. Malibu is the sort of place that so lacks a dark side that it almost manifests one by an inconspicuous absence.

And yet Malibu doesn't give you that foreboding sense other rich suburbs have. That's because it is permeated with a very homespun, country nuance. Ostentatious homes tend to make us not-so-rich folks to feel like we should know our place. In many rich communities I am ever so slightly, but consciously, aware that if I don't comport myself well, if I am not on my best behavior, I may be taken for a criminal or member of a lower order and possibly arrested. Malibu doesn't create the sense of paranoia other suburbs do.

When I arrived Quentin and Melissa were having coffee on the back porch of their home. The white lattice woodwork and well-placed ivy is one of the reasons my description is so apropos. Their having enough money to create as great an approximation of heaven as they wished didn't result anything but good taste and a nice home. I felt very comfortable.

As I approached, Quentin came up and embraced me! Melissa politely stood up and gave me a not too strong handshake.

Melissa is a beautiful woman. She had a one-piece bathing suit with a plaid shirt tied around her waist. Her beauty is that of the Malibu country-style natural sort. Her auburn hair is full, and it bounced all the way down to her chest. Her eyes are so light brown that her pupils really stand out. And you can tell that she spends a lot of time in the sun. But being slightly wrinkled by the sun only added to her rustic wholesomeness

"So. You are Marty!" She smiled, shook her head, and emphasized several words via pacing, as though I was a really pleasant surprise. "Quent has really taken a shine to you."

"Looks that way." My reply was accompanied by a somewhat nervous glance at Quentin. His smile was reassuring and they held hands.

"You must be a pretty great guy then." She said staring right into my eyes.

"Aww, gee shucks." My comfort level at receiving love wasn't all that high and Melissa was really direct about relationship dynamics. That was a direct extension of her country robustness.

It really felt awkward to me. Awkwardly, as if to deflect it, I returned the compliment, "And he being such a good judge of character, I must also then be in the company of a really special lady."

I realized that she had only been smiling with her eyes as the full compliment of her teeth came out.

"You work for Fortune magazine?"

"Yeah. But Quentin wants me to work for him. And with all this charm and love, I feel somewhat like I'm crawling into a spider web."

"We don't bite. We're cool people. You should think about it." Melissa offered earnestly.

"I am."

We all sat down together on their porch and had some coffee while we waited for the children. She asked and I told her about my slow rise to being a junior reporter on the Fortune staff.

"Hard work! Now that's the way, eh Quent?" She shot out with a gentle mocking and a humorous glance at his eyes with hers.

"Yes dear. Diligence and sweat are the stuff of manliness." They both laughed: he a short guffaw and she a twinkling snicker.

"I guess you guys think that's the fool's way up the ladder." I queried somewhat hurt.

"I don't think Quent's ever worked more than four hours a day. He likes ideas."

"Other people's ideas." Again they both laughed in unison.

"They do the work. He smiles at them." Their love was really evident. They spoke as one person speaking to himself. They looked at each other with big smiles. The look she normally gave him always intertwined with headshaking appreciation of his greatness. The look he gave her was always intense and somewhat silly.

"That's the hard work of the venture capitalist." He said, faking a reluctant admission with total joy and self-satisfaction.

"Speaking of hard work, where are we going today?" I had been saving that question for a time when I was feeling a need for a change in discussion. That is a little reporter trick I've developed. Always have an ace question in the hole.

"The beach, Zuma!" Their simultaneous answers were the verbal analogue to the vines interwoven on their lattice.

"But I . . ."

"But you don't have any shorts. We know, we know." She was a great motherly type. They smiled at each other and then Quentin continued their thought.

"Then go into the guesthouse, over there, and you'll find some new shorts on the bed." I turned and visually followed the path of Quentin's finger. There I saw a little white guesthouse that had previously escaped my notice.

When I turned around, they were both smiling at me like parents from a portrait. She finished their thought, "And while you're there, check out the house. That's where you'd be staying if you accepted our offer of your staying with us and working for Quentin."

What does one say to such a statement? "Oh, okay. I will. And I'll be right back."

"Take your time, families don't move according to schedule." I nodded with a crooked suppressed grin in response and headed down the path.

As I walked down to the home my head spun with questions. Were they really serious? Could I just leave my job and responsibilities back in Nebraska? What was my home going to look like? Would I be happy here with the perfect family? Was this really happening to me? I came back to my decision to jump on this opportunity that I had arrived at the night before.

The guest home opened into a nice little living room / dining room combination with an adjacent kitchen. The fixtures, chairs, and rug were nearly all white. The kitchen was separated by a bar counter with bar stools. The front windows opened up to shrubbery that largely obscured the big house. I went to the other room, but there was no exit there. Coming back, towards the entrance I spotted the hall to the bedroom. And there on the bed were red swim trunks with blue trim on a king size bed.

This was true.

When I got back up the hill, feeling somewhat embarrassed to have my white hairy legs exposed, Melissa called the kids. "Kids, come on out, were goooiiiing."

"So what dya think of the place?" One of the couple asked.

"Great. I could be happy living there." I smiled broadly. This was not a mannerism that I traditionally had in my repertoire. But I was glad to feel that I was melting into their crowd.

"Fantastic."

Then the kids came out. Justin was the oldest; He was twelve years old. Samantha was in her terrible sixes when I met her. She was a cute girl. She kept pulling her bathing suit out of her butt the whole day. She must have had a recent growth spurt.

Justin and Samantha stopped flat on their feet to stare at this ungainly looking stranger.

"Kids, this is Uncle Marty." Melissa smiled at me as she introduced me. She was mischievous. I smiled back. "Uncle Marty, this is Justin." He held his hand out for shaking. "And this is Samantha." She held her little hand out too.

"Nice to meet you both." Not having any of my own, I have always been a little uncomfortable around children. My parents divorced when I was seven and I didn't have a lot of interaction with families growing up. Family dinners and such rituals are alien to me. I'm never sure what the protocol is. The kids also stared awkwardly.

"Ready for a day of fun at the beach?" I queried with loud spontaneous enthusiasm?

"Yeaaaah." The kids cheered in response to my lame attempt at connection. They snapped out of their trances and piled into the back of the car. It was so easy! Their enthusiastic acceptance was refreshing. I had found the source of Quentin's enthusiasm. The kids, like him, made me aware of the energy lying dormant inside of me. I have been so groggy and subtly cynical for so long. Being around kids would be healthy for me.

Quentin drove and Melissa sat in the back. That left the front seat, the seat of honor, open for me.

"I know we're not supposed to discuss work, but my job so far is just to know you guys. So can I ask you when you two first met?"

"I've been in love with Quent since I was six. He took a little longer."

"I loved you too honey. We grew up together. We got married when I was a junior at UCLA and she was just going off to Indiana University. We wanted to cement our relationship before others intervened."

"There were others, when he first got to college," she spilled what must have been an often repeated little chiding between them. "But that drove him to me."

"That's right." Quentin seemed a little perturbed at having this little intimacy displayed so openly. She smiled at the little grimace he shot her via the rear view mirror. "We've known each other for maaany years."

Melissa was thirty-four when I first met her. Quentin had just turned thirty-six. They had been married for twelve years. Justin must have been born right after the wedding.

In the far back seat, Justin attacked Sam and she screamed. "Maaaaaam. Justin's hitting me!" "I am not." Melissa's combining an admonishing, "Juuuuuustin" with a stern look that had a heavy element of silliness caused him to fold his arms and turn his attention out the window. My sitting in the front had nothing to do with me as an individual. It was a family arrangement. Later I learned that Sam taunting Justin, his retaliating and her screaming for Mom's help was a perennial situation. It happened at least ten times a day.

Malibu has a lot of spectacular semi-private beachside coves. Zuma was Quentin's favorite. As we got ready to go down the path that leads to the beach, Quentin reached into the back of the van and pulled out his saxophone case.

The beach was lovely. We stayed about two hours. The kids made sand castles and swam and ran and walked. Everything they did they did together. All of us swam and played with the kids a bit. I played with them more than Melissa or Quentin. I wanted the kids to get to know me and I thought it would provide a good opportunity for Quentin and Melissa to have a little intimate romantic time.

They only sat together for about ten minutes when Quentin grabbed his saxophone and went around a cliff to where we couldn't see him. After playing a bit more, I sat down next to Melissa.

"Hey Melissa."

"Hey Marty! I think the kids like you!"

"They are so wonderful. I'm usually a little awkward around kids. I don't have a lot of experience with them. But they are very accepting."

"Oh, yeah, definitely."

"After playing with them for just a bit I figured out that my insecurities were only in my head. They are just about fun and in the moment. They have no need to judge you. We can learn a lot from children." I was trying to open up a bit and show that I could be a little sensitive and insightful in a spiritual kind of way. It was a far stretch for this boy from Nebraska.

"Bliss and peace are often accompanied by a strange lack of interest in judging others." Melissa smiled at me. Wow.

"And that is the reason that I have been trying not to judge Quentin's trip, no matter how juvenile it seems."

"Quentin's charm sort of comes from his boyish nature. There is a lot to appreciate there. He is innocent." I lamely offered in Quentin's defense.

"Yes, very much so, But there is a refusal to seem adult too. I guess the best thing to do is to accept and support others and, as you said appreciate them. I am not interested in judging others." She didn't look at me when she said this. I sensed a sort of sad distance in her that I hadn't seen before.

Just then I heard Quentin's saxophone for the first time. It was a slow, ponderous, and spiritual – full of long notes. Then he quickly broke into odds and ends of half-remembered rock tunes.

Then Mellissa offered wistfully, "The profundity of complex mature vision has a beauty that kids are too young to see, even if it is uptight."

As I stared at the ocean I felt the waves trying to wear down my constant inner-dialogue about saying the right thing. As the waves pulled back after a crash they dragged a lot of pebbles back with them. As I wrestled for a reply, I fancied that they were collectively saying "shhhhhhhh."

"I know what you mean." I offered after a bit.

"I believe that you do." She said with her eyes seemingly focused on the horizon. After a brief pause she turned her eyes to me. "Why do you think that Quent is doing this latest project?"

"I don't know him well enough to even start to speculate."

"But as a man - I don't talk with many men - what is it that makes men so unable to just settle? We have peace and food and all we need here."

"Melissa," I said feeling a bit like I was auditioning to be a replacement husband, "It sounds like underneath your not wanting to judge, you're not in favor of Prison Wars."

"Well maybe I just don't understand it. I want him to do what he needs to do. He is happy when he is successful, feeling like big stuff, and driving a new project. I just don't get it. That's all."

I thought out loud, "We all have a need to be appreciated and useful. And many men feel the need to aspire to greatness and be top dog. We don't rest well at the bottom. I know I'd like to achieve a lot more before I die."

"Pissing in the ocean." Melissa said wistfully. "We, mark our spot. The waves have a sadness that we should savor. I love it. It's a great tool getting centered, for being in the moment. Waves bring us close to the essence of what it is to be alive."

That was the first time I ever had an inkling of being in love with Melissa. It was the only time that I ever heard Quentin play the sax. He said he did it to get a sense of peace. But it just sounded like random stuff to me. You could almost hear him thinking that he wanted to get his chops back and play in a band again in the melodies.

After a couple more minutes he came walking around the cove, sax in hand, with a big smile on his face. He had had fun. When he got there, Melissa asked him if they could take a walk. He said "Sure".

Quentin asked me to watch his sax and the kids and they took off. Walking down the beach she kind of went forward and he kept stopping to try skipping stones that he'd found over the waves.

The kids and I played. I was getting to know them.

Melissa had a more concerned mind than Quentin. Still, despite the contrast, she loved him immensely and he her. I could see it; as they walked back they held hands.

Driving back we had an upsetting incident. Someone was waiting with a camera already poised for us as we drove into the driveway.

"That guy was at the press conference! I saw him at the press conference." I exclaimed as the recognition registered.

"Quent, stop and tell him to buzz off. He shouldn't be in our space like that." Melissa demanded.

"No!" He replied curtly. Then he softened, "I think that might just be a part of our life for now." As we went into the driveway the kid's heads followed the tall gentleman in tweed as if they were radar locked on a target.

"Its not cool! It's not cool at all." She said.

"Lets keep our cool." Quentin's reply was almost a whisper to himself. As Melissa pouted a little he continued out loud. "Look honey it has been a perfect day. We've had fun, haven't we kids?"

"Yeeaaaah!" They cheered with the clean enthusiasm that kids in advertisements have.

"So let's keep it happy and enjoy this perfect day. Don't let anything out there dictate your happiness or change your breathing." He stared into her eyes through the rear view mirror.

"That's just it. I don't need shit like that in my life. Our life is perfect." Melissa's eyes simultaneously communicated love, admiration and pleading. Then as if it were a matter of fact assertion she said "I love you." With this she grabbed his shoulder.

"I love you too babe." Quentin replied with a tiny blush.

That was the first night that I ever at spent at their home. We had dinner and watched some television with the kids. It was a lot of fun. I was, of course, self-conscious of the fact that I was a newbie in their family. I had to observe to know who went where when and who did the dishes, decided what to watch, broke the evening up and so forth. But everyone expected this much awkwardness. And there were many moments when I just enjoyed what we were doing in the moment.

As the weeks wore on, I got to add my own suggestions to the routines. Justin and I played cards to decide who got the big chair during our nightly forty-five minutes of reading. It soon became routine for me to make Samantha laugh by saying I didn't see something she wanted me to pass at the dinner table. In short I really became a member of their family.

When I think back to what has been lost, I always come back to those nights we spent together.

I was able to write in my new place. Quentin and I played tennis nearly every day. We often had a fire in the fireplace. We drank a lot of coffee on the porch. And the kids were a source of endless fascination to me. As I mentioned, my home life growing up wasn't too great. These early days were the most contented I had ever had.

CHAPTER FOUR – PRISON NEGOTIATIONS

I picked Quentin up outside of his therapist's office in Melissa's SUV. "How was the session?"

"Good."

It was a terse answer. I sensed that things hadn't gone too well. I had to calculate. We were close, but our history wasn't deep. On the one hand I knew that he was really accessible, friendly and open with me. On the other hand, I did have to remember that he was my employer. If I pissed him off I would jeopardize what was turning into one of the most interesting adventures of my life.

I was feeling lucky, but proceeded cautiously.

"No need to mention anything you don't want to mention. But I'd say it doesn't sound like it went too well." I ventured.

"It didn't." He looked a little sad and I gave him an empathetic look. "He's given me a lot to think about. I don't really want to talk about it."

"Okay." I said. We drove silently for about five minutes. It was kind of somber.

"Okay." He said energetically as if he'd just switched brains. "Here's the agenda for today. We've negotiated basic agreements with the prisons, but we haven't negotiated with the prisoners themselves. Today we will pitch it to them in person." He paused, "They've all heard about Prison Wars."

"Everyone has." I said self-satisfied.

"Yes. Everyone has. But now they are going to want to know what's in it for them. It will be a combination of a bargaining session and a pep rally."

"Wow."

"Wow is right." Quentin echoed.

"I've never been in a prison before."

"I've never been in one before or negotiated with a group of prisoners before. I am just trusting in myself that I'll be able to pull it off."

"You must be scared." I said in reporter interview mode.

"Uh…Excited is the word I like for that feeling. It will be great fun." Though his thoughts were interior, he beamed like a mischievous child on the outside. It was an old habit that concern couldn't dull.

When I added, "If the guards do their jobs," we both laughed. The laugh vented not a little bit of nervousness. How crazy was this? I was driving into a prison to negotiate them doing battle with each other. I could hardly believe it.

"What's my role in all this?" I put forward.

"Well primarily moral support. It's good to have a friend along for such an adventure." He said without looking at me.
"Thanks." My reply got no acknowledgement.

"And secondarily to write press releases about it. You will be the only media allowed on the premises. As the prisoners are hard to access, and the prison personnel have signed affidavits saying they won't talk about this event in any way, positive or negative, until after the first airing, you will be the spinmeister."

"Got it."

"Just be a fly on the wall during negotiations. Afterwards, I want you to start writing accounts that make it sound like just another program. We want to hype it. But, I'm afraid of ethicists or whomever, interfering, getting a last minute injunction. We've taken way more heat than I thought we would on this project.

"These negotiations are secret. The news about them will be kept under wraps until just a day or so before airtime.

"Even then, we want to make it sound like just another sporting event."

"Gotcha." This was my first real business assignment from Quentin so I tried to sound business like. "I would imagine I should also make it a priority to sort out who is who in the audience."

"Precisely. Keep track of quotables, also get the names of those who seem like they'd give good media interviews."

"Can I get exclusive interviews afterwards?"

"Yes. You'll have ten minutes with eight people of your choice."

"Wow. Again, I am impressed with your planning."

"Dreams need details." He said, still without turning his eyes towards me. He was looking at the road and into the future.

I provided a bit of distraction. "I know how to do this, this is my area of expertise. Don't worry about it. I'll choose them, interview them and get all that dramatic stuff that makes for good stories from their records."

"Yeah." He said considering and agreeing, still without looking at me, "You can get all the details of their legal situations and records from the prison officials after the interviews."

"Got it boss! Only they don't have records."

"No?!" He sensed the set-up and urged me to continue without a whole lot of humor.

"No. They have player stats."

"Excellent." His response contained no humor. With that I started to think to myself about my assignment. I must have been doing my nervous gesture where I tighten my lips and squint, because Quentin figured out that I was nervous.

He finally broke his intense stare at the road to glance at me.

"Marty, I have total faith in you. I chose you due to your personal qualities, but also due to your writing style. You have the tone we need naturally. If for no other reason than trusting my successful track record at picking winners, you should have confidence in yourself.

"You are a really good writer. I have no fear or doubt about your abilities. Take pride."

Seeing that his pep talk didn't work, he intervened further. "Marty I want you to say it, 'I am a good writer.'"

"I am a good writer;"

"Okay. Now say it twenty times to yourself silently. Its one of the things I do with my spiritual advisor. You saw me decide that today was going to be fun when I first got in the car. It works. Do it. You can trust me."

The fact that he didn't seem to be having any fun didn't reassure me, but I got absorbed in my work and forgot about my nerves. By the time we arrived I had a whole list of questions entered into my i-throttle and a little spreadsheet set up to put the answers in.

When we finally saw the huge, cold, imposing, cinder block prison fortress, we both gulped audibly and looked at each other. My nervousness had returned full force.

After getting through the gate and pulling up to the waiting officials, Quentin turned to me and said, "Confidence Marty. Relax." Seeing my breathing was still constricted he said, "Marty let's have a sense of drama and some fun in there! Breath! Are you ready for some memorable fun?"

"Yeeaah." I cheered just like Justin does.

"Okay. Here comes a lot of memorable fun."

We were padded down for weapons and went down several long corridors. The walls echoed. Due to their thickness, not even sounds escaped these corridors. The prison was also very cold. The smell alternated between smelling like fresh paint and a locker room. Only later did I fully absorb what a strange odor combination that was. For the most part, I was in an adrenaline filled sort of haze.

At the final door, the warden, who looked way too much like Don Knotts to be real, blurted out with an ill-fitting military style grunt, "Don't worry about the inmates. Anyone that tries to start a fight or attack you will be promptly beaten and rushed back into their cell, if not shot."

Egads. This guy wasn't kidding either. He wasn't Don Knotts. It became almost impossible to imagine him laughing about anything. That must have been his prison face. No one could live like that full-time.

"Anyhow, they know why you're here and have been looking forward to it for a while. They won't blow their only opportunity to negotiate about the only privileges they're ever likely to get. Even these animals will probably be able to keep it together for this."

Ouch. Ugly.

On the other side of the final door lay the main hall of the prison. A stage and bleachers full of prisoners awaited us. It would have looked like an opera house, but the bleachers were pure metal folding chairs and the balconies were jail cells. The bleachers were divided into three parts. There were two seated people in front of each cell. It was an ordered and packed house. The repetitive nature of the patterns made it seem like the prison went up for infinity. We were in the heart of a maximum security State prison.

The Warden showed us to our metal folding chairs on the stage and then proceeded to walk to the lone microphone that waited for him front and center.

"Prisoners please quiet down." As could have been predicted, the microphone produced a little feedback as the warden started to speak.

"Hey ya' animals shut up or we're goin' for lock down." I'm not quite sure what that meant, but it silenced everyone rapidly.

"What we have here is a very unusual situation. We have a man that has come here to negotiate with you concerning a program that you have all been informed of."

The warden was completely immobile as he spoke. I could only see him from behind. But having spoken to him and heard his voice, I'm sure his steel eyes were focusing tightly on the inmates' eyes. He seemed to have memorized his speech and the paper in his hand was dead still. This man didn't have any nervousness in his person. I suppose he learned that nervousness was a luxury he couldn't afford a long time ago.

"I do want to remind you that this opportunity is strictly voluntary. No coercion by me or any representatives of the State or its institutions has applied any pressure whatsoever concerning the choices or commitments you shall make or actions you might take as a result of this meeting."

I was impressed. But I should have guessed that he'd be good at memorizing legal formalisms to the letter.

"The purpose of this meeting is to negotiate prizes and terms. All of the provisions will have to be ratified by the lawyers. Any and all agreements that you enter into will be strictly between you and Longus Enterprises as represented today by,

Mr. Longus and Mr. Sanger." As he said our names he pointed behind his back to each of us without turning his head around at all.

"So, Animals, that means we have no responsibility for anything that happens to you. And you are totally free not to participate in Prison Wars. Though personally you know how I feel about your being injured."

A small grumble that was magnified by the room's cavernous concrete acoustics filled the hall.

"Here are the provisions with in which we are able to negotiate. These are the limits on what can be given away by Mr. Longus and his organization.

"First of all, the program cannot cost the State any money. All set up costs will be borne by Mr. Longus and his organization, Longus Enterprises.

"Forty percent of the profits after costs and before taxes have been designated for education. Fifteen percent of the profits after costs and before taxes will go to the State correctional system. And finally, ten percent of the profits after costs and before taxes can go to remuneration - that means payment animals - of prisoners, of you; that is, towards buying you what you might want.

"Secondly, all proceeds go to the winners. They will not be shared.

Thirdly, all rights may be maintained, but the cost of those rights will come out of the balance of your ten percent. For example, if we need to provide medical attention to the losers, that cost will be subtracted from the monies the winners would have received. If you decide to provide no medical attention then no money comes out of the pot of the winners.

"Fourth, all monies that would have been spent annually on those who do not survive the games shall revert to the pot of monies that are allocated for the prisoners. So if it costs thirty thousand a year to house and feed one of you animals and that person dies in the games, their thirty thousand a year will go to the winners."

These provisions, which I was hearing for the first time, encouraged cruelty and punished pity.

"Lastly, your sentences cannot be altered, only the provisions for them. If you win, your incarceration needn't be on site, but you will in no way or manner be free to go beyond the walls of whatever housing situation you earn. All the costs of the creation, of your new housing situations will be born by you. That is the costs will all come out of the ten percent of the proceeds that will be going to you. If they are off site, the extra security measures and personnel will have to be borne by you.

"We now come to the question and answer portion of the presentation.

"You will need to have the microphone to speak. Some of you will have trouble abiding by the rules. Look, take a good look, at the extra security, posted around here today. If any of you beasts gives us any trouble or is disruptive you will have your beastly ass taken out of here by being shot or clubbed until it is easy for us to take you out of here. If it becomes difficult for us to take you out of here, due to prisoner interference then we will shoot until it becomes easy for us. Cappiche?

"There will be a lot of cameras rolling when the games happen. There aren't any cameras rolling now.

"Mr. Longus."

Once done, the Warden walked backwards to his seat and his eyes never stopped scanning the prisoners. I saw no indication that he even heard anything that Quentin said after he introduced him.

The contrast between Quentin and the Warden were quite clear and deep. Quentin strode to his position like a candidate in a town hall meeting. He was formal, yet casual. He approached the folding chair next to the microphone, but only really used it as a prop. He started sitting but quickly stood up. At one point he put a foot up on it. But he never sat back down.

"Thank you warden." Quentin's smirk and slight shake of his head was meant to distance him from the warden. "And thank you for leaving your cells to come hear the general outlines of my proposals." Humor, golden. This was the public Quentin. No seriousness could be detected. All was a fun inside joke. Life was great.

"Later you can meet in small groups and hammer out details. But today, I want to inform you of what kind of opportunities and dreams you might want to consider as you go into those meetings.

"Men, you have heard what we cannot negotiate. I want to now talk to you about what we can negotiate. Basically we can negotiate the format of the contests and the way that your reward money will be spent." His slow firm nod at this juncture reminded me of a gesture a football coach would make. Quentin was masterful.

"First I want to talk to you about the formats of the games. You can negotiate, in fact I'd hope you'd help design, the format of the games. But as you do so I would ask you to remember some things as you do. We can have safe battles. We can have two men come out and box with gloves on for fifteen rounds. The problem is that we won't attract many viewers that way.

"Your collective take will be ten percent of the profits. So when making suggestions, think of what you yourselves would like to see on television. Think of what a lot of people would pay to watch.

"I also want you to think without any limits. Without limits means anything goes. We have a blank go ahead from the State within the confines of what your warden has discussed with you.

"You can use any weapons you desire. We can use any rules you desire. It can involve killing, it can involve rounds. It can involve multiple teams. It can involve sets, barricades, whatever. Whatever you want is yours. The set up costs are mine. You, my colleagues, are the executive producers of this show. Whatever you'd like to see, we'll have. Be imaginative. Let's put on a show!"

At that quite a bit of rumbling emerged. Quentin signaled the warden to remain seated almost before he started to stand up. Quentin just looked around the audience and nodded.

"I also want you to be imaginative in terms of envisioning how you will use your earnings. Gentlemen, ten percent means at least twenty million. You not only are getting ten percent of the original profits, you get ten percent of the proceeds resulting from rebroadcasts for the two months following the broadcast.

"Now the direct merchandising rights around the games themselves belong to Longus Enterprises. But you will retain the right to exploit your own name and image. Some of you, gentlemen will become international superstars – we'll say criminal stars. You will become as big as any professional athlete out there. And you know what comes with fame. You will be able to shoot advertisements, markets lines of clothing, make music videos, whatever."

Now Quentin paused and nodded his head a bunch of times as if to affirm their growing understanding while the sound of audience grumble once again rose and subsided. He turned and smiled at me and made some gestures to point out folks out in the audience.

"With enormous sums of money in your mind, you should envision getting out of this rat hole. As the kindly warden mentioned, you cannot be free. But, I don't know," he paused to model the act of thinking he wished them to engage in, "you might rather be imprisoned in a sixteen room mansion with servants."

At that there was quite a bit of laughing that turned into hooting. Not deterred by Quentin's gestures this time, the warden stood up and made a gesture that caused a platoon of about ten guards to split off and go up either side of the bleachers. They stopped and put their weapons in the ready position.

"It's okay warden. It's okay. No one is leaving yet." The audience laughed as Quentin smiled at him. "Okay, men," he told the crowd with nonchalance, "Let's respect the institution."

"You, cannot go free, but you might like to have a 40 acre ranch and invite a couple dozen of your old friends over.

"If the women are okay with it, you might want to have a girlfriend or two over to your new million dollar mansion. Now that's a kind of prison lifestyle even I could get into.

"So think of game design that will attract the largest possible audience, think of the revenues, and think about how you'd like to spend them.

"With that said, are there any questions?" Hands immediately lunged into the air.

The warden was already on the way to the microphone. "When given permission, you can come forward and speak at the central microphone, one at a time. Anyone approaching the microphone without permission will be subject to lockdown. Lockdown in solitary. Do you understand me animals? Lockdown!"

"Number One Zero Two Three Five come forward. He spoke this out as a quarterback calling a play from the line of scrimmage.

The first person to speak that day was Freddie Jackson. Yes, *the* Freddie Jackson.

"Yes sir. My name is Jackson, Freddie Jackson." Jackson was an incredibly large black man with a geri-curl style hairdo. Needless to say, he was in blue prison duds.

"Mr. Jackson." Quentin smartly engaged him as the business partner he hoped they would be.

"Are you sayin' that we kin' get the hell outta here?"

"Yes. If you as a winner want to buy homes and live in them, that's what you can do."

The warden took the microphone back.
"But remember you gotta pay for the guards and security systems that'll keep you animals away from the general public. Next, number Two Se-"

Quentin interrupted with a hand gesture meant to dull the rudeness of the interruption, "The warden is correct. The cost of hiring and equipping guards and your residences with security systems that are tied into the penal system would be borne by you." He paused dramatically, and looked at the warden. "But with millions, I think you can hire some guards."

Quentin smiled a broad smile and ever so slightly gestured at the warden. Quentin was really currying favor with the inmates at his expense. I was worried that he may go too far. Then Quentin put his hand on the warden's shoulder. "Sir, Mr. Warden, would it be alright with you if Mr. Jackson was allowed to ask any follow-up questions he might have."

"Very well." By deferring to the warden for permission he kept him in the game. Wow. Quentin's finesse was impressive.

"Mr. Jackson." Now, in turn, Quentin was deferring to the prisoner again. Showing folks respect and care was one of Quentin's greatest skills. I had seen him treat strangers and employees like best friends. Now he was treating everyone like the professional business partners he wanted them to be.
"Say some faggot motha fucker gets his ass all blasted to shit. And I'm standin' over that sorry ass mother fucker with a gun on national television. Are you saying that I can just straight out execute him with impunity N shit?"

"If you agree to those terms in advance, the State has allowed you a special sporting exemption to cover that action. It will be like boxing. You aren't allowed to hit another person, right? But in a boxing match you are. It's the same thing here. You will all have to sign a waiver in advance. And this waiver will stipulate, say, that you will not sue the State for any injuries, life threatening or not, that result from the games. So, in short the answer to your question, Mr. Jackson, is yes."

"Now then!" The warden was a little bit peeved and venting his authority. "Next will be number Two Seven Six Three Nine."

"I just want to say in front of every body."

"Your name sir?"
"Sorry sir, Jim Turner sir. I just wanna say in front of everybody, that this sounds like the opportunity of a lifetime and I

am gonna smoke your sissy faggot nigger asses crispy and the Mexican thirteen barrio's pussy asses too."

With that serious disturbance erupted and I got very nervous. And several inmates started to fight. But the guards on the sidelines fired their weapons straight up and that immediately stopped much of the noise. Still two separate fights continued. Guards moved in with stun guns. I had never seen a taser used before, but it was ugly. The men hit the ground and twitched and drooled for a good twenty seconds. Towards the end they were clubbed in the head and dragged away. A man was shot and bleeding. The crowd grew still.

The warden took the microphone. "Okay you animals, that's it. Show's over, I don't care how many goddamn questions you have."

With calm restored, Quentin reclaimed the microphone and summarized, "Thanks to all of you for listening, and I hope, participating. I look forward to receiving your proposals. My assistant, Mr. Sanger, would like to interview the two gentlemen who spoke today and a few others. We will be dropping off contracts for you to read and some proposals for game ideas this week. Take a week to tell us which ones are your favorites and what modifications you'd like to see. Again thank you for your time."

It turned out that the wardens had complied with a request Quentin had made to compile a list of troublemakers / leaders. The prison warden salivated at the concept of having them fight each other to death. These were the 'animals' that the warden hated most. Quentin realized that these folks had already selected themselves as leaders. They would provide the celebrity core for our new sport.

I also asked if I might interview the people who had been fighting. Two of the people on the lists were involved in the fights. At first the warden wasn't going to let me go ahead with my interviews of them. He said that there could be no hint of a reward for disobedience. Quentin argued and the warden relented.

Chapter Four

As per the original plan, I waited to the side of the stage for those I was to interview to congregate. When the prisoners assembled they segregated racially. Each pod kept its distance from the others. And nasty grunts were thrown from each group to the other. The grunts seemed to balance each other out. I was sure that if any group had dared to add an extra grunt we would enter an escalation that would end in riot and death.

The more prisoners that approached me for interviewing the more nervous I got. Seeing this, the guards formed a circle around me and took me to a secure room where I could interview the prisoners in privacy. Even though ten or so guards stayed in the room with me I was nervous. Each prisoner was easily larger than the guards who nervously petted their guns as they looked on.

This was the first time that I had been really close to prisoners. Prisoners are scary. On television, prisoners are all clean-shaven. Though occasionally hostile, TV convicts are usually shown as intelligent and disgruntled, perhaps chagrinned, about their captivity.

Not only are these guys huge and thick and tattooed, but they ooze a negativity that is hard to explain. It isn't just the scary oppression of the prison environment. They had been so angry for so long that a chemical cloud of hatred actually surrounded them – you can smell it.

A few of the prisoners had good looks. But that isn't the source of their charisma. Their eyes uniformly intimidate. Even when they smile, their eyes intimidate. This, combined with a constantly threatening posture gives them an intense aura. These men were truly free in that they could never be controlled, only restrained. There was no knowing what they would do. You sense continuously that these men are not afraid to die and take you with them. To look at them is to confront all of your fears.

Each and every one of them had the ability to completely dominate your attention. These men clearly had enough star power to be famous.

It was under these conditions, at this meeting, that I first met Freddie Jackson face-to-face. You know him as a celebrity. I

---

can tell you that in person he is way more menacing than on television. As friendly as we seemed when appearing on television together, I was always afraid of him.

The thing that immediately separated him from his peers was his insistence on speaking. You don't interview Freddie Jackson. He talks about what he needs to talk about. Whether that happens to coincide with what you want to hear about or not is irrelevant.

He is a genius. The gangs of every race respected that fact. For the three games he participated in he not only invented the plays based on a disciplined study of the parameters of the game, but he taught his team many signals so that he could call them on the fly. A strategic application of his genius was behind every aspect of his meteoric multifaceted rise to international fame.

Freddie asked me a lot of interesting logistical questions. He asked me if these games were going to happen inside prisons or football stadiums. He asked me details about the distribution of the proceeds. He asked me if this first game would just be between people within the prison he was in. He was making plans.

He also told me a bit about himself. He said that he had been thrown out of the Marines. He previously ran a tri-city crack ring. His father had been killed in a drive by. He said that he had recorded six rap music tracks.

But, unfortunately, his story didn't stand out as more tragic than the others'. In fact with two rapes and four robberies on his record, which he failed to mention, the feeling of awe I felt didn't alter the feeling of disgust. His final crime had been killing a cop when they raided his home.

Though not his life story, what did stand out was that he was very consciously feeding me sound bytes. He checked to confirm that I was getting fodder for announcers. All gangsters deal in bravado. The others just trash talked. He gave me details that he thought would help position him as a commodity for the general public. He understood that this was an interview for a celebrity / leader position. He understood the dynamics afoot immediately.

After I got the warden to agree to send me files on each of the prisoners I had interviewed, I left. Quentin was leaning on the car outside when I emerged and smiling broadly. The intensely concentrating Quentin of the ride up was, thankfully, gone.

"Did we have fun in there or what?" I told you that was going to be great. Hey! Whatddya say we go out for drinks, eh? Let's celebrate a job well done.

Like the day, the evening was also milestone for me. It was the first time I went to the Skybar. This haunt is about two blocks west of the Hyatt (where the original Prison Wars press conference had been held). The Skybar is a very exclusive bar on the Sunset Strip. You have to know someone who is connected or be known by the public to get in. It is on the ninth floor of the Metropolitan building. Like the Hyatt's roof, it is half indoors and half outdoors. Unlike the Hyatt, the outdoors half features a large swimming pool.

Half the women there on any given night are working. Learning that later burst my bubble a bit. Their drinks are half off, unless a man is buying. The house uses them to up the ratio of women to men. Ultimately, many of the women are looking for Johns, film producers or sugar daddies. And regardless of your interactions with them, they are largely model quality beauties.

Still, the Skybar has an air of class about it. The women don't dress in a trashy manner. The men you meet there have generally accomplished something. It is a hive of film industry movers and shakers. And even if you aren't one, just having gotten into the Skybar gives you and edge in the dating scene. But that won't automatically get you all the way with a high percentage of the women there. You are in competition with some big players.

I've seen celebrities there, but saying who would break the code. Silence and privacy for the clientele is one of the most important attributes that the Skybar offers. If nothing else, it is a place where, even if you go bottom fishing with the sleazy partiers, no one will ever divulge your secret. And if that isn't enough, there are a lot of scene skating women there that are just into good times. 'Will have fun for fun,' might be their motto.

This was the first time that I had ever really hung out with Quentin at night. And it proved to be an interesting night from the get go.

Almost as soon as we sat down, we were approached by a fairly short and sleazy looking young lady. And to my surprise, Quentin knew her.

"Marty, Sindy. Sindy, Marty." He had his head down as he introduced her.

"Nice ta meet cha'. It's Sindy with an 'S'" she informed me.

"Wow I don't think I've ever heard of anyone spelling it that way before." I usually don't talk to women with as much assurance as I did with her, but she was young seemingly dumb and not the hottest number in the vicinity. I had no reason to expect anything could or would happen between us or to be intimidated.

"Can I sit down?" She purred flirtatiously.

"Not now Sindy." Quentin said, "Marty and I really need to talk."

"Oh, okay." She showed no emotions, only attention in anticipation of her next order.

It looked like no order might come when Quentin said, "But go get a drink or two on my tab and maybe I'll see you later." He paused again. "Actually, Sindy, could you order four Patriots for our table while you're over there and have them sent our way?" She nodded and skedaddled in the direction of the bar.

"Wow. What a great place. I feel fortunate to know you Quentin. I've not quite sure why, but you've changed the path of my life."

"Nothing doing. You're a great person and you've already done a great deal for me and my family that you don't even realize."

"Like . . ?" The waitress dropped four frothy red, white, and blue drinks on our table.

"Like, for one thing, Melissa worries less about me when you're around. She trusts you and so if I'm out late with you she doesn't get worried or suspicious." I removed all doubt that I was going to interrupt his flow or had any interest in doing anything but listening to him by taking a drink at the very instance in which I might have spoken. It was a good move.

"The reason I'm stressed when I leave my life coach is that all we seem to do these days is talk about my problems with Melissa. I mean don't get me wrong, I love Melissa to death. You can see that when we're together, right?"

As I nodded I started to pick up my drink again.

"But we've been together since I was a kid. And I don't know if you've noticed, but I'm a powerful motherfucker. And we're different. I like to go out. I love staying home with the kids and all, but I just, I like to go out and meet people and have drinks and she gets worried when I do.

My spiritual trainer is always on me to do affirmations about each moment, to love my life the way it is, limitations and all. And I do realize that I have the best life. And I don't want to do anything bad. But after a night like tonight, I like to go out and..."

Just then Sindy came back. "Quentin can I talk to you by the pool in private for a minute." Quentin just shrugged his shoulder in comical wonderment and they went off.

While they were gone I looked around this freaky scene. I wondered where it had been all my life. Anyhow, I am me. And there is no way that I am one of these mover and shaker cowboy – junkie – hipster types. I just don't move like that. I don't think like that. I'm an information junkie nerd. I do news and print, not hot talk and wild irrelevancies.

Quentin came back alone. Shrugging his shoulder, he said, "She wanted to borrow some money. I lent her some. What's happening now?"

"I'm just looking at this scene and feeling like a foreigner. I'm a Nebraska boy. I've never been too social or socially smooth."

"Nonsense. You, my friend, can do anything you want. If you wanted any woman in here you could get her. I know I could. I can get any woman I see. I could have all of them at once. That's how I do all my business, I get an idea and I just make it so. And that's why I'm stuck, because I know that, without a doubt, I could do anything or have anything I can imagine. I'm a badass to the level where I'm about to revolutionize the world of T.V. You think I couldn't get seven women to go to Maui with me for the weekend?

"I'm just blocked by circumstances. That's okay. I have all that I need and I love now. I have never cheated on Melissa. Don't think that I have. These women mean nothing to me. I just flirt with them for the fun of it. Please don't misunderstand and take my conversations with them to mean more. I know that Melissa is my love and all is better in imagination and nothing beats the pure love of my…"

"Okay Quentin I get it." He was protesting too much. I was disappointed. My eyes said that I believed him even though I didn't.

"The point is, you are my friend, so you are hot. You're magic." He skimmed out of the previous topic. "You're not here by accident. And if I can rock the world, and manifest anything I can imagine, certainly you can get a girl to share her love energy with you.

"Hey hey hey." Quentin flagged down a girl. "Hey. I'd like you to meet a good friend of mine. What's your name?"

"Lindsey."

"Lindsey this is Marty. Marty, Lindsey. We're putting on a television show together that is going to change the world. And right now, he's writing about me for *Fortune magazine*. Anyhow, Marty is pretty shy and I told him that it isn't impossible that a girl like you would be into a guy like him. Isn't that so?"

"He's a definite possibility."

"Please sit down."

"When she sat down, Quentin said, "Okay Marty, here is a couple hundred dollars. I'm going to go home now." He tossed three hundred dollars down on the table. "Don't worry about the tab, I already told them you're with me. Lindsey, he's a great guy. Ask him about his life and tell him about yours. I haven't touched either of my drinks, they're both yours or whatever else you want you can have." He directed his eyes straight at me and punctuated the previous sentence by saying, "That's a rule."

"Stay here with her Marty. I won't take no as an answer from either of you. Give me the keys to the SUV and take a taxi home and I'll see you in the morning."

I handed the keys over with a look of someone who was sort of being tricked, helped, and abandoned all at the same time.

We both gave a 'good night' to Quentin and quick as a jack rabbit, he scurried out of the bar. Wow. I felt speechless. And yet, Lindsey and I spoke for about an hour. She couldn't believe that I had interviewed prisoners earlier that same day. My life had become something to talk about, a selling point.

I walked her to her car. And we kissed there for about five minutes! It was more action than I'd gotten in about a year. I took a taxi back home and crashed out.

CHAPTER FIVE – THE ETHICISTS

Quentin was not a dumb man, just impatient of learning. He had no more than twenty books in his home and most of those were unread gifts and impulse purchases. As many businessmen, he wanted to know where the pedal hit the metal. The bottom line was, after all, the bottom line.

After being publically attacked at the press conference in which he announced Prison Wars, Quentin convened a group of ethicists to coach him. He fully well expected that after the first Prison Wars contest the criticism would explode. He needed to be able to respond intelligently to the charges that would be leveled against him and his enterprise.

His reasons for convening a group of ethicists wasn't, however, purely a calculated business maneuver. He also needed help thinking through what the troubling aspects of Prison Wars meant to him personally. If you've read this far, you realize that he was, despite what the media reports would have you believe, a real person with a family.

The meeting didn't go well. I could easily blame the ethicists. Their combative style didn't endear them to him. They didn't sense his fragility. Despite his power and confidence, he didn't like to be confused, belittled, and mocked. I never saw him in deeper confusion and frustration than at this meeting.

More so, I think that the ethicists' transparent maneuvering for power disappointed him. Quentin was a good judge of character. He didn't get to where he was by letting people put things over on him. Sensing their hypocrisy probably furthered his unwillingness to listen. He didn't trust that these ethicists were ethical.

Like most of us, Quentin was a mundane creature of habit; he liked things to be easy. He was very much a consumer in this way. I'm not sure what emotional, practical or intellectual resolutions he wanted from this meeting. But I'm sure he wanted a simple solution. Beyond that, just knowing that a person with advanced degrees had worked out the details would totally assuage his conscience.

But above all, I blame Dr. Les Christensen. At least that self-serving pig was honest about his depravity. I realize those sentences contradict each other. But, his level of depravity was subtler than it should have been. His depravity would have been less costly to us all had it not been so refined.

I'll let the record explain that.

The ethics meeting took place about a week after the prison negotiations. Quentin had, I found out later, actually set up the ethics meeting before the press conference. Quentin thought ahead. He should have thought more deeply. The ethics meeting, however, was something that he had realized would have to be done.

We went to the meeting in his limousine. Had I thought about the level of privilege I was being exposed to I probably would have been less blasé about the whole thing. Doing? Not much. Off to meet with the world's leading ethicists, in a limo with the world's most controversial billionaire. What an amazing experience.

What kept me level headed was the closeness that I felt with Quentin and work. We had both been working hard in the intervening days. I was writing articles for, placing editorials in, and send letters to, newspapers and magazines concerning Prison Wars. Now, simultaneously, I had to come up with fifteen professional profiles for contestants and announcers. These needed to be ready at least a week before the first Prison Wars games.

And between our respective toils, Quentin and I hung out together. We played tennis mostly every day. Sometimes I'd go swim as he played sax. Actually, since my work could all be done at home, I was around more than he was. But he was almost always there for dinner. We had become good friends. Being with him lost all its aura of drama. I had a friend in this adventure. In a way, for the time being, Quentin had become my best friend.

Quentin said that he had meetings away from his home to separate his work from his private space. I don't know when he got in at night. Melissa's not complaining led me to believe that he was home at normal hours. Suspicions aside, I admired his dedication to keeping his private space stress free. It certainly made for a comfortable home life.

Quentin arranged for the ethicist meeting to take place at the Beverly Wilshire. He thought its conservative reputation would help it attract more staid expertise. Actually he needn't have worried. Money and the thought of influence on someone important was usually enough to get whomever we wanted to show up anywhere. We held the meeting at a prestigious locale to set a serious tone, but for a chance to meet the man behind the most talked about controversy of the age these ethicists would have come to a McDonalds.

When we entered the conference room the lively conversation stopped. Comfortable wasn't the way I would describe the room. The hotel had done all it could to create a comfortable space for us. But there is something about long rectangular tables that creates immediate discomfort. The beige color, rectangular shape of the room and the half closed Venetian blinds made the room seem like a cross between a filing cabinet and another prison.

The sudden silence and newly focused glares of these twelve or so distinguished looking men on us was a bit unnerving. I immediately recognized several of the professors present from their punditry on television concerning Prison Wars. Everyone held their breath until Quentin broke the silence.

With characteristic charm, comedic timing, and a gesture, he asked me, "Oh my God! Marty do I still have coleslaw on my face?"

Everyone laughed and resumed breathing. The ice had been broken.

"Gentleman, don't let me stop your conversation. We'll start in about five minutes." With that the sound of a crowd bartering in a market revived. Quentin broke free of me and started to work the room. As I was with him, I had a bit of celebrity and commenced to work the room in my own way.

About eight of the men present had tweed jackets on. The average age hovered around fifty. All but two were white men. The few younger members were more likely to just have collared shirts and jeans on. Quentin and I fit in better with the younger set. Great minds dress alike!

More than their names, I remember their universities. Not one of them introduced themselves without mentioning the name of their university. I suppose that had a significance that I wasn't privy to.

After about ten minutes, Quentin called the meeting to order.

"Gentleman, gentleman, if we may, let's focus as a group. Everyone please take a seat and we will begin."

After the collective of individuals, collected themselves, Quentin continued fulfilling the role of MC.

"I think you all know each other, and you all know me."

He gave one of his charmer grins. For the first time I realized what distinguished it from his real smile; he showed more teeth when he smiled in public.

"I think the only unknown in the group is my friend and publicist, Marty. Everyone, Marty. Marty, everyone." He snickered through his teeth with the others as I did a small queen like wave with my wrist.

"Before we begin I'd like to thank Professor Royce for organizing this get together. Thank you Professor Royce."

Quentin used a dramatic pause to focus his thoughts and turn the mood solemn.

"Gentlemen, I have gathered you all here out of respect for your profession. You are also here because I need to learn about ethics. Partially, this need comes out of a desire for personal growth. But it also grows out of a need, frankly, to be able to articulate coherent rationales and defenses of my games in front of a national audience.

"To these ends, I would appreciate it if you would each give me your frank thoughts for and against Prison Wars."

The twelve men around the table squirmed a little uneasily.

"We can either proceed individually or we can have discussion. I leave the choice up to your collective professional discretion."

"If I might sir..."

"Yes. Professor Bentham. Please, each of you. Speak as freely and liberally as you want to."

"Yes. Professor Bentham, UCLA. I just want to say that we, . . . I think I speak for all of us, . . . appreciate your convening us. Your proposed program raises many contentious issues that we need to look at as a society. I appreciate your taking the involved issues seriously enough to convene professional ethicists before proceeding. Furthermore, I'd like to say that truly hope that we may be of some guidance and assistance to you."

"Jesus, what an obsequious ass-kisser you are Bentham." Burst Professor James.

"Gentlemen, Gentlemen," Professor Royce asserted his authority. "How can ethicists teach ethics if they do not maintain a respectful toleration for opposing views?"

"Sorry, I should tolerate your being an obsequious ass-kisser." James replied. My adrenaline rushed a bit. I liked this guy. "I forgot that we're in mixed company."

Everyone frowned in silence with averted eyes. And when the peer pressure got too hard, James repeated himself with a shrug and a playful sarcastic exasperation you might hear from a fourteen year-old girl.

"Saaawree!"

Professor Royce made a good effort to create a shared and efficient protocol for the community.

"Let's go person by person. When a person has finished with their statement, we'll allow questions." Without pausing for a vote or general assent Royce chose, "Professor Green, Michigan University."

"Thank you." Professor Green changed his posture radically. He leaned over the table and perched himself on his right forearm.

"The problem here is that we must assert a complex answer to a simple question. It is a matter of explaining the tenets of idealism. For this to take place I must be permitted the time required to put forward some proofs."

"Please." Quentin invited him with a grin.

"First of all the nature of the universe is to expand. Stop me if you disagree or if I've lost you. The nature of the universe is to expand. And there is also a direction seen in the tendency of life to creep into matter and out of matter. For example, mankind is mind in matter. When mind realizes itself.... Just a moment." He was overriding Quentin's raised hand.

"When we see that mind goes into matter it presents us with a value system. One more minute," He waved Quentin off again, "I'm almost done.

"As we accept life to be positive, we can see that the movement away from conscious life fostering is a negative. Therefore, from an idealist position, I would argue that it contradicts the natural tendency of the world towards idealism to proceed with the fleshly ambitions of Prison Wars.

"Mr. Longus?" Green recognized Quentin at last.

"No. No. You answered my question. I was wondering if your argument was for or against the idea of Prison Wars. You're against it. Any questions for him?"

Quentin was trying to be officious, but it was clear that he was over his head. He didn't really get anything that the professor had said. I'm not entirely sure anyone did.

While feigning neutrality, a hint of irritation crept into Quentin's voice. He was relying on getting an answer that he could use at a press conference to support Prison Wars from this meeting. That first answer didn't make it seem like it would go over well with the media.

"Professor Green, um, Bill James. And, during my previous rude outburst I forgot to mention, Harvard. The problem with your conception is that it is airy fairy." Thinking his crudeness would buy him credibility with the non-academic world, Professor James looked to Quentin for approval as he said this. Quentin showed the thinnest smile I'd ever seen him make. Perhaps herein he'd find the justifications he needed. Professor James continued confidently.

"What we need is a solid material ethical system to work with, that folks can disagree with Prison Wars from. And I don't think that your average Joe is going to follow the argument Professor Green just made.

"Perhaps our natural aversion to cruelty being a part of our neuro-anatomical make-up would be a stronger basis of condemnation."

"We are against it because it doesn't feel right is your basic argument?" Green replied.

"Well not just that. I mean that it doesn't fit with the neuro-anatomy we have evolved, but essentially, yeah." James shot back.

Professor Green protested, "How can you start by saying my argument is too airy-fairy and then start with talk of neuro-anatomy and evolutionary programming? That is not down-to-earth it's a fairy tale, a just-so story.

"And you cannot get ought from is. As I reported in Philosophy Quarterly's Winter issue on the resurgence of idealism, not being able to get ought from is, is the main problem for your thesis."

"Perhaps you are right. Perhaps, I'm only gratuitously showing the backing to my argument. But I don't argue for truth with a capital 'T' like you. And the point is, if you are going to argue against Prison Wars, you would do well to go against it at the visceral level. Exploit people's natural revulsion." James suggested.

"James you have no morals!" Professor Mugabe, the only black professor, interjected to back up Green. "If it feels bad you're against it, if it feels good you're for it. What an animal you are. Oh," He stopped, and remembering himself added, "Professor Mugabe, New York University."

"That's right I am an embodied animal. You are an embodied animal too." James shot back angrily.

"And more. You are also more than an animal." Mugabe said matter-of-factly.

"Get this guy a time machine; let's bring him up to our age. Neuroscience is here." James asserted defensively.

"Well speaking of time machines, did you know Mr. Longus," Mugabe said turning directly to Quentin and smiling, "that long ago on the continent of Africa and here in the Americas man lived in absolute harmony with his environment. And . . . "

"Oh Jesus," James uttered with exaggerated exasperation, "here we go again back to fairy land."

"Well it is true," Mugabe insisted! "There were no diseases or hate until the white man and his culture came and I believe that Prison Wars is the culmination of the abomination that is white civilization!"

At that a small and timid professor spoke, "I am Professor Rorty of Cambridge." He cleared his throat. "As all of my very influential books argue, I am sure that history has nothing to do with anything. We simply need to enact a thought experiment where you see if a room full of anonymous people not knowing where they stand in society, would vote for Prison Wars."

Quentin belted out, "Well, I am no philosopher, but some would be for the games and some against them."

"But," Rorty raised his voice in a small attempt to reach normal volume, "the catch is, if I didn't make it clear, the people deciding would not know if they themselves would end up participants in Prison Wars. If you had to be in Prison Wars you couldn't possibly agree with it!"

"BS the people fighting in Prison Wars want to be in Prison Wars!" Quentin shot back with twice Rorty's volume. "I know them. Furthermore, there is no way I'd end up in prison."

Slamming the table repeatedly, Mugabe insisted, "This very choice presupposes the oppressive white world as the only choice we can meditate on.   Why doesn't your thought experiment compare that alternative to the non-white world of harmony and feminist ecological . . . "

"You stupid racist demagogue!" Professor Kress of Hillsdale College interjected. "Your inaccurate racist philosophy makes me want to . . . "
"Gentlemen, gentlemen," Professor Royce tried to stop this downward spiral's momentum. "We are hearing reasons, not hurling insults. Mutual respect is the cornerstone of discussion."

"Please gentlemen." Quentin was taking the floor. "What of my arguments that I've made that Prison Wars will be good for the economy? These prisoners are paying their debt to society? No water there?"
This question was met with a general grumbling.

"Okay. Why is it wrong? Explain that to me."

"Sir. With all due respect, oh Professor Tim Paine of the University of Pennsylvania, it should be really clear to you why killing for the economy is wrong. I mean, as the kids said when I was young, '*Hello*'."

Hurt, Quentin looked them in the eyes and pleaded, "Okay. I don't need to be taunted and disrespected. I have built an empire that is valuable. I have done lots for many. And these people aren't just people. These are killers and criminals that don't have a lot of redeeming value as far as I can see. What is their value?"

"They are humans." Professor Paine said softly. "And all humans are created equal."

"All humans are valuable? No matter what they've done? You all believe in that? 'Cause I don't believe in it. I think they are more valuable dead than alive. Valuable to society. If one of them had raped your sister you'd change your mind." Quentin's assertiveness rose as his respect for these men declined.

Showing some deference Paine nodded slightly as he continued, "You've got to understand that all people are created equal and have the same rights. Doctors and bums, legislaturos and the people, they are all the same.
"And these people's lives are not over. We do not know for sure that they may not provide value to the world yet.

"Furthermore, what if they aren't guilty?" Professor Angela Rand interjected without giving her name or affiliation, "Unless the case is completely clear, we must always worry about the group condemning the individual unjustly? Could you imagine being innocent and condemned to fight to the death for your freedom? Is that moral? Can you imagine yourself being in such a situation? The victim of a mob?"

"No I can't. I've never been to jail. And furthermore, a lot of people who have been brought up in bad situations haven't been to jail. And even those who didn't "do it" were likely contributors. Talk to them, these are bad eggs!" Quentin had had such debates before and had already developed a small arsenal of rebuttals.

The entry of Pat Arnold, a Professor with a Southern drawl, seemed to calm the room for a second. "Paine, we should gaze beyond the individual and, as you so precariously perch him, his atomized interchangeability. Nor, Mizzz Rand, does your reification of the individual considah the deleterious and pernicious impact of debasing individuals through the cultaah (culture).

"At the risk of sounding too Christian for you gentlemen and you Mizz Rand, manners make civilization. And we cannot talk of an individual extracted from this cultural milieu.

"Idealism or neuroscience or anonymous people without a scratch of history voting, do not, as I wrote long ago, respect the earned grand stature of our Christian and Athenian based western inheritance'.

"Within the context of this real world, we as a collective must recognize crime. We must punish the wicked. But in striving to live up to our ideals, to be true to the best in our heritage and not descend into the anaachy of nihilism, we must avoid the crassness and crudeness of the philistine in taste."

"Are you calling me a philistine?" Quentin nearly shouted.

"Oh no sir," Professor Arnold said with no affect of sarcasm short of a small batting of the eyes and twinge of the lips just past the conclusion of his remark, "As I hold condescension a sin and judgment a transgression, I am of no doubt but that you aare a man of many refinements."

I held my breath fearing that Quentin would see this remark for the obvious insult that it was. But Quentin seemed assuaged by it and only blinked a little faster than normal. He was a distracted cauldron.

Everyone went silent. Finally Professor Green broke the silence by reasserting himself. "Again, I do not completely disagree with Professor Arnold's goals, but as my review of his collected works in the Journal of Metaphysical Science explained, his only grounding his ethics in our evolving culture, makes him a relativist.

"As a Platonist, I assert that we need absolute and eternal basis of morals grounded in the unshakable and proven realm of beauty. Yes, we must recognize and cultivate a relationship with the realm of beauty."

Quentin was on the defensive. "Cultivate a relationship with the realm of beauty? I'm in the real world with criminals and traffic signs and ..."

"Su, you aare quite right. Our situation is in the world of worldly predicaments." Answered Arnold in full repose and drawl, "And Professor Green's desire to loftily escape to a realm of beauty grows from a fear of reading history, as the necessary interpretation would distract his full focus from that pointed pinnacle of unity he so solipsistically aspires towards." And as before the very end of the last word of his sentence was punctuated via a small eye gesture and a hint of a smile.

Green got angry. "It is sad to be so bound by this sordid world. I'd rather be a blind idealist than be bitter and defile such a chunk of my spirit with the filth of this earth. I am talking about the realm of ultimate good and beauty."

"Well, where the hell do you live? All of you!!" Everyone could tell that this was Quentin's goodbye speech. "Welcome to our world. All of you, Green is in the sky, Mugabe is in Africa, Rorty you have your strange thought experiments that happen nowhere and, and, . . ." Quentin sputtered out and caught his breath.

"Most of you aren't talking because your taking notes. Are you doing it to help the discussion or because you want to make profit off of this conversation? You don't care. You're going to go back on television and reap glory off of Prison Wars just like me, just like the viewers, just like the rest of society. Only you guys, you ethicists," and he put the quotation gesture around the word 'ethicists,' "are major hypocrites about it!"

I had never seen Quentin so without hope. He was not only pissed off but disappointed. His eyes looked downward, he seemed dejected. He wasn't acting out of a strategic angle either, he had nowhere to go with these folks who he had hoped could speak in his language to his media situation.

"Has anyone got any other stupid reasons that Prison Wars is wrong? Is there anyone here that is for Prison Wars?" After the briefest silence he capped the event, "Okay Marty lets get the hell out of here."

Once outside Quentin was clearly still agitated, "Perhaps I am just too dumb to understand. Perhaps good and evil are beyond me."

"Those guys were no help at all." I echoed. After he handed out so much rage, my reactive tendency was to assume the posture of a sycophant and try to placate him.

Twenty feet from the limo we heard someone calling us, "Mr. Longus! Mr. Longus." It was one of the professors.

We turned around to see one of the elder tweed-wearing professors running after us, with his briefcase in hand and tie waving off the rear of his shoulder. He leaned so far forward as he ran it looked as though he would fall over. He had incredibly broad shoulders. And though he raised his knees too high, he ran pretty well for a guy in his fifties with dress shoes on.

When he got to us he was clearly hurting for air. "Mr. Longus. Mr. Longus." He was having trouble standing and violently trying to catch his breath.

"Take your time friend. Catch your breath." Though upset, Quentin could always reset to a generous charmer who offered friendship and listened to people from their point of view.

While waiting for him to catch his breath, I took my first good long look at the now infamous Professor Christensen.

Skinny and tan to the point of being withered, he had the look of a lizard with a goatee. You could easily imagine his intestinal tract. He always made me think back to dissecting frogs in my junior high school biology lab. His overflowing white eyebrows and slightly-long salt and pepper hair contrasted with his weather beaten bronze skin. For a professor he seemed kind of gruff.

After he got his breath he stated his purpose. "Mr. Longus I'm sorry we weren't much help to you. Within our small profession there are a lot of political forces going on that you don't know about and so the professors were more concerned with attacking each other than addressing your concerns."

Quentin looked a bit impatient but was still listening.

"If I can talk to you privately I think I may be of help to you. I can give you the justifications you need to simply and convincingly explain why Prison Wars is ethical."

"Can you give it to me standing? Because I'm going to have to give quick intelligible defenses for my program, on television, right after Prison Wars airs."

"Yes."

"Good man, let's hear it." Quentin crossed his arms and looked at me seeking acknowledgement of his ability to pull rank and give orders.

"Quickly put, ethicists like that will be the downfall of our society. We are getting soft. We need an infusion of manly values if we are not going to fall like Rome. Prison Wars will improve our nation's character. That is a positive national character argument with muscle."

"I like it." Quentin, though guardedly, finally smiled again a little.

"Here's another. There are codes of life other than ours. Prisoners have their own code of life. And those who love diversity must respect the Prisoner's inherently noble value system. And in civilization that values diversity, the prisoners too have a right to express themselves and live out their dreams. They have a right to partake in Prison Wars. That is the diversity argument."

"And there's the related rights argument. It parallels the diversity argument but relies on the word "rights." We average Americans also have a right to happiness. If watching Prison Wars is happiness, we have a right to it. Prison Wars is our right. That is the rights argument."

"Excellent." Quentin now really focused in on our new acquaintance. "Any more?"

"Well, I have been watching your television appearances Mr. Longus, and you need to go more on the attack economically. Ask your opponents if they can close the deficit. Ask them which one they will cut, education or police. And if they don't answer, don't let up. 'Education or police?', 'Education or police?' Repeat this angrily. You're the savior of children; they need to defend themselves from the charge of immorality."

"Excellent. Why didn't you speak up in the meeting?"

"As I said, there were a lot of hidden political forces going on in that room. For me it was better to meet you in the parking lot. Besides, I was enjoying their bungling implosions too much to interrupt."

Quentin's face had gone into pure concentration, but then he snapped back to the public smile. "You enjoyed that, eh?"

"Very much! I could laugh at those pompous clowns attacking each other all night long."

"Well speaking of all night long, we were just going to go out and get a drink. And . . . . I'm sorry, but I've forgotten your name. Professor..."

"Professor Christensen. But please, if I may call you Quentin, I'll let you call me Les. Is it a deal?"

"It's a deal."

I guessed that if I were to be introduced I'd have to do it myself, "That deal needed more bargaining Quentin, you could have held out for more." I smiled though miffed at being on the outside of their conversation. I put on what was probably an obviously false smile and offered my hand to Les. And, I shook it a little harder than necessary.

"Marty Sanger," I offered, "Since you're a friend of Quentin's, you can call me Marty."

"So, Les." Quentin interrupted our developing catfight. "You'll join us for drinks then?"

"With pleasure."

"We'll all go in the limo." The ethicist's face lit up. There is no one who doesn't get excited the first time they get to enter a limo. And I think that Quentin realized he was giving someone a treat when he let them ride in it.

"Sam, our driver, will take you back to your car here whenever you're ready to go." The three of us piled in. Instead of our normal positions of facing each other, Quentin and I sat side by side. Les sat across from us, alone. This was the first time I ever felt like the limo was too small. Les was already cramping my style.

"Sam, take us to the Skybar please." Sam, our chauffer, nodded, closed the separation glass and started to drive.

"Quentin." Les said, sort of brushing me aside. "I almost blanch at calling you that because I see big things for you. You don't realize it, but you could end up being a significant figure in world history."

'Oh brother' I thought to myself, 'this one's a loon.' I dared a look at Quentin to see if he had the same inkling. But Quentin was silently smiling and looking directly at Les.

"Quentin, I think I can provide you with all the ammunition you need to defend yourself against your enemies and even develop a philosophy of Quentin. Once developed, this philosophy could give you some followers and you may be able to mobilize a bit of a posse to back you up."

"I'm not sure I need a posse Les. But you are intriguing. Please continue."

"Yes. I'm sorry. I have a tendency to get a head of myself. I have a short term plan to resolve your immediate problem. We can start on memorizing the arguments that I gave you outside. And then, as you have time, we can investigate nuances and evidence for these arguments. We can spend as little or as much time on it as you'd like. But I can get you ready for your television appearances fairly quickly. I'd like to be your personal philosophical manager."

'I guess I could still be his personal buddy and publicist if not his manager.' I thought to myself, again feeling more than a tinge of proprietary jealousy. But it wasn't just personal. To the extent that I could separate out my feelings, I didn't trust Les' intentions from the beginning.

Quentin and I made gestures towards each other that seemed to say, 'Well isn't that interesting?' Sensing that I must be a bit put off Quentin said, "I need approval from my best friend before I accept a personal anything."

Wow! Quentin had never called me his best friend before. I'm sure he had many and was overly warm. But it was a great feeling to be called that by him.

"If I can be in on the training sessions, I'd be happy to have you talk with Mr. Longus." I smiled broadly. "I'm curious about something, Les."

"Good!" Les seemed to pay a bit more attention to me after I was called Quentin's best friend.

"You just threw out three separate reasons for Prison Wars being ethical. Do you actually believe in any of them or are you just filling a position?"

"Excellent question Marty! You choose your friends well Quentin. The truth is that I could have given you any number of ethical justifications to validate Prison War's morality. And while many choose their beliefs based on evidence, some also choose them based on implications. Needless to say, not to worry, I have a lot of evidence for each of these arguments."

"So you don't believe in any of them, you're just getting a job."

"Ouch. No, I'm not as banal as that. The truth is, that my beliefs are very complicated. I don't think I can fully explain them in a limo ride to a bar. I have a lot of visions about sociology and political philosophy. But I do see truth as somewhat constructed and instrumental. The subject these days is, in a sense, caught in a belief web, as passive, seemingly active, and ultimately prefabricated..."
Quentin must have shot him a glazed and tense look, because Les seemed like he was about embark upon a lecture when Les attentively let the last words sit as a conclusion.
Les then changed tracks.
"The beauty about television is that it doesn't have enough time for deep reasons. So you can have your backing or not have it. It doesn't matter. It is a medium of assertions. So we can get by with just repeating a few simple arguments. In such a context the sound bite is the subject; the personality is the argument."

"Hmnn, I never thought about it like that." Quentin announced. And this was the first time that Les and I ever shared a smidgen of bonding. Our eyes caught each other's laughing at Quentin's lack of depth.

We didn't spend a lot of time together at the Skybar. I saw Lindsey and we talked for a drink. Sindy, as before, came out of the shadows and interrupted Quentin and Les. Quentin sent her away and not long afterwards came to ask me if I wanted to share a taxi home with him. I did.

That evening our basic dynamics became apparent. Les and Quentin, on some level, couldn't make a connection. Quentin was impatient with any of the theory behind Les' ideas. And Les, who only drank a Coca-Cola, wasn't really interested in bars or small talk. After that night, I was never jealous of their potential for closeness again.

Furthermore, Les and I developed some rapport. In retrospect, it is embarrassing that without Les I never would have figured out that Quentin was impatient with theoretical explanations. But, I like ideas well enough to discuss them. So occasionally Les and I would bond via the exclusivity of our club.

But appreciating ideas didn't get us all that close. For one thing, Les was much more into ideas than I. When we discussed ideas he usually took the position of the teacher. For another thing, without fully knowing why, I instinctively disagreed with much that he said.

I wish that I had learned more about philosophy in my life. If so, I might have been able to have stopped Les. I didn't even have a basic vocabulary with which to discuss the issues he raised. And I always knew that, before I had raised objections, Les had already thought long and hard about those I was raising.

As it was, I was happy to learn from him, and he respected my willingness to learn. But I was never the initiator of the topics we discussed. Our bonding was always over the esteem that came from my visiting his exclusive realm.

My first impression of Les was that he was nuts. His ideas and visions were too over the top. But that was an error. Just because someone is nuts doesn't mean that you shouldn't take them seriously.

Here is a philosophical truth that I learned: power creates sanity. Once you're in power, you establish the norms. Then those that disagree with you are nuts. Always be afraid of genius lunatics in close proximity to power. If you value your life, get intellectually prepared to do battle with them.

CHAPTER SIX – GAMES BEGIN

I am describing these tournaments for future generations. Future generations, and a very few people alive in our time, may have no other way of knowing what the Prison Wars games were all about. There are lessons within the descriptions of the content. They may contain more valuable lessons then actually watching the footage.

The description is meant to be anthropological, not titillating. Please read it with a sense of pain. If you read it with glee you will be as guilty as any killer in it. You will have become the worst kind of mass murderer – the spectator without conscience, complicit in the destruction of civilization.

The stadium seemed huge to me. Having it outside of the confines of the prison yard was a marketing necessity we couldn't get around. Prison yards just proved to be too small and too hard to work in. This was pay per view, but it was live too. 46,000 fans packed the Los Angeles Coliseum. This coliseum was the one used by the football team, the Los Angeles Marauders. It was also the one that Muhammad Ali had long ago lit an Olympic torch in.

The stadium had been outfitted with vigilance towers for the security of the audience. We also had one hundred and fifty-two cameras set up. In fact, there more cameras than any other single sporting event in history.

The games were interactive. Afterwards the fans were to choose on-line and via phone which of the formats to abandon and which to keep. We shattered the record for most website hits received in a twenty-four hour period, week, and month.

All of the normal sports trappings were there. We had the talking booth of three commentators, ala Monday Night Football. There were pre-game interviews featuring each of the players I had profiled. Their bios were advanced to the media with full criminal records and crime descriptions. The announcers just had to replace their normal sports statistics with crime statistics. It was a rather painless transition for them.

Again, the fine line I spoke of in this chapter's opening was crossed too often. It was never clear whether the crime descriptions, lurid in detail, were there to build up revulsion or admiration.

We wanted the public to get a blood lust for the death of these SOBs. Included amongst the contenders were the worst of the worst: murderers, rapists, drug runners, and child molesters. The battling inmates being evil gave us moral cover. Hopefully you hated them then as much as you hate Prison Wars now.

These gruesome profiles also created a sense of awe. It gave the participants a level of magnetism that completely overshadowed fake TV wrestlers and run-of-the-mill cage fighters. These potential criminal stars had allure of being from a totally different moral system. Their from-the-street looks gave them a nobility of nature that our clunky, chunky law-abiding population doesn't have. These were humans who had seen the heart of darkness. They were dangerous and had no fear of death. There was no hesitation in their actions.

The crime re-enactments of the first Prison Wars were toned down. I thought that important. I fought for it. Perhaps that is one way in which I can say to have been a good influence on this destructive episode in our species' longevity. Cowardly enough, my argument was that we wanted to give the FCC as little ammunition as possible to use against us. What I was really thinking was that it was going to encourage people to commit crimes like those being announced. I was scared.

Take Freddie Jackson, via reenactment they showed his hometown – gangster cars moving in a blurred punctuated slow motion down a boulevard at night. But when it showed him committing his murder it was just as implicit; a gun going off, the leaning side of a man in slow motion with trailing effects and sirens. The whole scene played out with melodramatic sad hip-hop music. It was designed to make you feel the pain of the tough streets and what it did to him. It was a deterrent.

But two of his other crimes had been a rape. And perhaps it was just me, but the depictions of these attacks were morally ambivalent.   The woman was, thankfully, plain. She didn't really make your blood rise much. She also didn't have on the slinky clothes that later girls always had on during rape re-enactment segments.

She was wearing jeans, and a plaid shirt, as I recall. And she was walking down a street at night. It looked, again, like downtown anywhere. The area itself was scary. The one shot I cannot forget was her turning around and staring at the car. It froze on her face and she had a real look of fear on it. It was as if the entire female species' epochs of cumulative victimization and collective wounds were on this girl's face. She was pale with fear. Thankfully, her stringy dirt blonde hair and bad skin made it apparent that she was a real human, not a television actor.

As they showed her being lifted into the car, you could hear Freddie Jackson's voice-over, "I just saw her N I wanted her.   You know it was Satiday night and we was bored. She looked like we could have a good time wit her. We decided we wud. I'm real sorry for any pain that I caused her *an* her family." The announcer's voice-over concluded the cut-away segment. "Horrible, heinous crimes and individual. Let's hope he gets what he deserves tonight."

They didn't show the real victim of this crime, just an actor. Later episodes included the cutaways to the victims in attendance, especially if they had been maimed in the attempt. They would always hold signs that called for revenge. With anger and tears the announcers would solemnly "hope they get what they came for." For the rape victim of this first game they just said, "The young lady in question, declined to attend, apparently the rape messed her up really badly."

Powerful stuff.

We arrived early that morning. We were there for preparations, talking with producers, cameramen, set designers, announcers, the players - everybody. I had seen Quentin the father, the friend and night owl. But this was the first time that I saw Quentin the business executive in full bloom. He also had his now famous short hair cut with a little extra length in the front combed over. His voice deepened and he smiled much less in this role. He wore a casual light grey-blue suit because he was going to be making the public introductions later. But his demeanor had taken on tinges of mafia-in-pinstripes assuredness.

We sat in a box very close to the fifty-yard line. For security reasons Quentin had bulletproof glass mounted along the wall that separated the players from the audience. About half an hour before the games began, Melissa came. She left the kids at home because of the violence and also because no one under eighteen was allowed in. And just as the games were about to begin Les showed up. I hadn't seen Les around since the first night we met and had forgotten that he might show up.

Quentin didn't really relax until the spectacular was over. But you'd never have known it from his opening speech. During the anthem he stood with his hand over his heart and sang loudly. He was on the big screen twice during part of the anthem. Realizing that I might be on the screen too during the game, I elevated my pantomime of volume when I saw him up there.

It was inspiring to see that the prisoners instinctively stood up and put their hand over their hearts for the anthem. None of them were bad Americans. They knew what to do in stadium games during the anthem.

Anthem over, Quentin drove a golf cart over to the microphone abandoned by the black woman who excelled in the current emphasis on holding the word 'free' in the last sentence of the national anthem as long as possible. She stood behind him as he spoke.

"Ladies and Gentlemen, we are gathered here today for some very solemn games." Steam came out of his mouth, dragon style, with each breath. "Some will die today…and some will live.

"Solemn yes; but a celebration also.

"Today is a day of celebration for the State, whose coffers will be stuffed by this event, providing educational funds for your children and mine. And we couldn't have raised this much money for education without you. We thank you for that.

"Today we also celebrate our freedom. We celebrate our freedom from the petty legal constraints that have tied up our social systems for so many years. This is America, the land of the free. Today's event is a celebration of that democratic freedom we hold so dear.

"Today is also a great day of celebration for the participants. Just like us, many of them have dreamed their entire lives of being in a major sporting event. And today they get to leave their cells and show us what they are made of. Though it is made of a rough street code, today we also celebrate their freedom to live their version of the American dream.

"The prisoners have written most of the rules of this game. But due to my coaxing, they have also agreed to look up into the audience before they make a kill. And if you think the person has fought valiantly - valiantly enough to deserve a second chance at life and possible celebrity - please put your thumbs up and applaud wildly. The contestant will be swept out of the competition and be resurrected to play another day.

"But, if you feel that the person should be put to death, and you've read their rap sheets, their lives outside of today were an abomination; If you think their performance here was also an abomination, boo, hiss, and put your thumbs down and he'll be dispatched. This is democracy. The call is yours!"

Les, in the booth with me, lip-synched some of these words as they left Quentin's mouth. He smirked as he smiled, Quentin that is. I hadn't realized that they had met since I last saw Les. It was then that I also realized that the influence that Les was starting to have over Quentin. He had succeeded in becoming his personal philosophical trainer.

"One last thing, you will notice that the teams are often divided by race. That is not our doing. That's just the way it works in Prison. The prisoners have chosen their own teams. Please try not to be lowly like them. Don't let race influence your decision for life or death. Call 'em as you see 'em.

"With all of that said, let's bring out the contestants, start this celebration, and let the Prison Wars games begin!"

The crowd went wild as the splashy instrumental techno-rock music played across all 300 speakers housed in the stadium. Quentin and the singer got into the cart and drove off. I had never heard such noise and cheering before. It was deafening.

The stage was already set for the first round. Blocks were scattered around the field, as you might find blocks on a child's floor. These blocks, however, were made of brick and between 5 and 12 feet long. Some of them were stacked in order to provide a climbing surface. Others were so thin that you could barely get shelter behind them.

Each player was announced as they came out. They got their proverbial day in the sun. For many of them, the only thing they had ever wished for, the only profession they had seriously dreamed of was being a professional athlete. Well they got the full treatment; Lights, announcers and a stadium. Their American dream had come true.

One team was dressed as police and the other as gangsters. I wasn't there for the coin toss to see who would get to wear what. But I bet there was a lot of jeering when one group got assigned the police uniforms. Then again, prisoners may just see dressing as a cop or gangster as wearing the cool costumes of equally dangerous and cool gangs.

I remember when we learned the results of the coin toss Quentin exclaimed "Yes!" enthusiastically. Seeing my perplexed face, he leaned over to me and bluntly explained, "The fans will enjoy being in the minds of white police fighting black gangsters much more than the opposite. I was hoping for that."

Each team had fifteen players. As per all modern mass sporting events, the costumes had the names of the player and numbers on the back. This helps the fans and announcers distinguish the otherwise interchangeable players.

This whole event was ripe for sociologists. I would have loved to know the demographic make-up of the audience and players. What would happen to crime statistics the following day? I was sure the American Civil Liberties Union, who were looking for ways to stop Prison Wars, would undertake racial counting to see if there was bias in who got the thumbs-up and who got the thumbs-down.

"Ladies and Gentleman let's make some noise." The invisible stadium announcer's sonorous voice said to the accompaniment of light changes. "The first round of Prison Wars' Cops and Robbers game is about to begin."

"And ready, and set, and goooooooooooo." The way he said it was to become an obnoxious catchphrase used by many across the country in the coming months.

Starting in the lower left corner of the stadium, the criminal team had to get into the "police station" on the upper right side. The police had to raid the "drug den" on the lower left side of the field. The entrances to both were pretty wide. Neither team could hide. Both had to come out and fight.

Freddie Jackson was the head of the black criminals. Their colors were modeled on those of the Los Angeles gang called the Crips. He was going against Jim Turner and his all white 'police.' In fact, all but two of the police had been violently initiated into the prison system's infamous Aryan Brotherhood prison gang.

Freddie Jackson said, in pre-game interviews, that he was going to create a manned tube up the middle left to protect aggressive runners in a bid to get to the 'police station quickly.' So it surprised everyone, including the police, when most of his men flanked out to the right wall. Jackson only sent three players to the left wall to keep the police concerned about their right flank. Turner's team apparently caught off guard, five of Jackson's Crips nearly got through the no-gun zone before they were checked by gunfire.

As per all the games, the middle of the field, from the offensive thirty-five yard line to the defensive thirty-five yard line, was a no-gun territory. That meant that you could neither shoot from or into that portion of the field. The penalty for violating this rule was three shots at you by the police. These real live police guards served as the ultimate referees.

The no-gun zone between the thirty-yard lines was littered with knives, maces, mace, brass knuckles clubs, broken bottles, trashcans and an imaginative assortment of other instruments that could be used in a fight. The no-gun zone was always where the best action took place. Outside of the no-gun zone, there were guns, but there was also a heavy proliferation of barricades to hide behind as you progressed towards or defended your goal.

As the bulk of Freddie's crew was streaming up the right and the police reacted to stop them. Gunfire rang out and two men were shot. Chris Petersen, number 25 of the police and Andrew Butler number 36 of the criminals became the first fatalities of the Prison Wars games. But Butler did not die immediately.

Butler had left the right wall with four other men to spread the rear. Freddie Jackson led from the second spot up the right wall group. Under fire Freddie Jackson fell back and got his wounded man, Butler. He put him on his shoulders and ran him further out towards the middle of the field to a three-foot high and six-foot wide trapezoid block. He perched him behind a barricade so that he could be a sniper, or at least make folks nervous. But the important point from the vantage point of the fans was that Jackson had returned to get Butler to safety.

Jim Turner paid no attention to his dying comrade in arms. He let him lay exposed and get shot repeatedly. Jackson's demonstrating a street ethic of solidarity, by way of contrast, bought him a lot of allegiance from the fans.

We were in the middle of the shooting free zone in a protection box in the front row. We knew we were on television and so had to keep cheering. But we were all anxious to see the audience's reaction to the first kills. We were glad that they were body shots rather than gruesome headshots.

The crowd around us seemed to be polarized between the 'can looks' and the 'can't looks.' The 'can looks' kept on prodding the 'can't looks' to look. All three of us were 'can looks.'

Those who averted their eyes were in the minority. Being in the minority is uncomfortable, but in an arena dominated by men, being squeamish has even more stigma attached to it. Thus the pressure to conquer one's disgust, along with the desensitization of repeated exposure to gore, significantly reprogrammed the audience members.

Quentin seemed to be a bit squeamish at first. But he had to fight through such tendencies as they were bad for business. And once he got the gist of it, he was cheering as loudly as anyone else in the crowd.

With the first headshot, which was shown and re-shown on the East side big screen, the stadium let out a collective "Eeeewww." It was a bizarre spectacle. The cheers were mixed with gasps and murmurs when it was replayed. But as soon as the gore was off the big screen, the engrossed fans started cheering for the live action again.

We, through my publicity, bios and countless faxes, had tried to get the fans to have favorites. It had worked. There were people in the audience with "We 'heart' Freddie" and "Go Jim" signs scattered through out the stadium.

The police team that ran down the middle to forestall Freddie Jackson's announced fun up the middle, soon found them selves sandwiched in between two groups of criminals. They were in a bind. If they ran at the Crips on the right wall, would overwhelm them. But if they ran at the three isolated Crips on the left wall, the Crips on the right wall would have had free reign.

Turner, speaking through his headset microphone, ordered five of his men to "get the niggers in the right." This remark, like the others, was broadcast. Then he ordered, "Tom, Craig, Big Dog, secure the [police] station back to the station. Everyone else, was to defensively hold the Police station's sides.

Jim Turner hadn't written any real plays. If he lived to see it, he would have some plays written for the next time.

But, containing the few gangsters on the left wall proved to be harder than anticipated. And to the joy of the sponsors and creators alike, the games soon devolved into several simultaneous situations.

The three isolated Crips held five police in check with gun shots. Then the stalemate was broken when Freddie barked out "six, three, and five, spread left attack five. Twelve, four and ten up center to station." At this three of the Crips who had flared out in the rear, ran up field shooting at the five police trying to pin down the isolated Crips. And Crips twelve and ten went up the middle to pin the police closer to the station. In the scrimmage, one of the police holding the three isolated Crips in check was shot, two ran away to hide in the upper left corner. One of the remaining three kept repeating, "man down, man down."

But no plan, no reaction came from Turner. His men in the left sector were now outnumbered by those holding the left wall and those who had gone up field to harass the police had a fairly clear view of the station. But Turner could not take pressure off the right wall to aid them as that line of Crips flared from the middle and advanced.

Freddie yelled, "Four treasure streak." And a brave criminal streaked through the no – gun zone towards the goal end when a policeman on the right flank shot him. This being a violation of the no-gun rule, three simultaneous shots ran out from different police towers. The police violator of the no-gun zone rule was shot in the leg and torso. Two criminal-policeman started running to his aid.

The shooting angered the crowd. Loud noises of disapproval were broken by the calming reassurance of the announcer. "Giles Police number eleven, in violation of shooting someone in the no-gun zone. Penalty, three shots." This explained the first breech of game space by an outside force.

Everyone knew and understood that the penalty for shooting anyone in the gun-free zone was being shot by guards in the towers three times. But the crowd seemed to either favor the white police or resented the interference from an outside power.

Freddie Jackson yelled, "twenty-two, seven attack three left" and two criminals ran to attack the remaining police officers isolated on the left. Though he was now less likely to be shot in a gun-free zone, a Crip aggressor ran at the defensive minded isolated flank policemen like he was running for his life. Simultaneously, three criminals converged on the two police tending their shot comrade, Turner, the leader of the police, yelled out "Jack, Craig, Little Bill, Fred, Jon Jon, back up Tim and Paul." When the streaking men all intercepted each other in the no-gun zone, a great melee began.

At this Jackson, with his eyes on the prize, countered, "nine and two run at treasure." Turner yelled, "Jack and Craig, go back to the station. Big Tom and Snake, go up the middle. These criminals knew each other. Thus the use of names allowed the Crips to know who was where. The repetition of names also made Turner's changing his mind and getting defensive obvious. His partial retreat to the station combined with sending two men up the middle seemed confused. It also gave the Crips numbers in the field.

Furious fighting in the no-gun zone broke out. There were three fantastic battles going on. The announcers were going crazy, they didn't know what to cover. "Turner is holding his own, Robertson stabbed but still fighting. King of the Crips is running from the right and hoping to attack Benning.

Then with a burst of excitement the color commentator exclaimed, "Oh from nowhere, O'Neil took Benning out with a metal pole! He's got a cinder block. Now he's looking to the audience for direction. No clear direction from the audience, oh that's gotta hurt! Right in the head."

That did turn out to be one of our disappointments. First of all, it was really hard for the players to discern whether the crowd had mostly gone thumbs up or thumbs down. And, anyhow, the contestants seemed to interpret everything as a condemnation. Though never disavowed officially, the real-time audience input had very little meaning from the beginning.

O'Neil looked up at the audience, remained quizzical for a split second and continued crushing Benning's head with four blows from a cinder block.

Jackson and another Crip advanced into back of the police gun zone, where the end zone would be for football, gathered ammunition and took cover. He ordered "Ten sniper right south treasure." With that, the Crips had snipers on both sides of the Police Station. There was no fear of running out of weapons, as they laid scattered around the gun zone. But the weapons were not always close together. Getting to them once you'd run out of ammunition could expose you to danger.

The Police guarding the station began shoting. The brick walls worked to great effect. When hit by a bullet a cloud of dust would emerge. Jackson wasn't directly hit, but a piece of flying brick cut his face. A close up showed that he was panting and glaring like nothing had happened, though blood stained the right of his jaw, in the immediate aftermath. This was a tough man pumped up on adrenaline.

The white Turner and black O' Neil were circling each other with wooden baseball bats in the no-gun zone, when a shot hit Turner's arm and made him drop the bat. It came from the injured man that Jackson had helped to a perch. He was immediately shot for violating the no-gun zone law. But he was already dying and this gambit doomed Turner.

Turner blocked the first bat swing with his right arm, but the force must have broken it. He kept his mangled arm elevated in a defensive posture, but he could not stop O'Neil from making the decisive blow to the head. Turner started twitching uncontrollably, but three more measured blows to the head left him completely still and presumably dead.

Without a leader and having lost so many men that they had now become a minority, the four remaining police in the no-gun zone retreated back to the gun zone to ward attackers off with guns. But Freddie and his fellow Crip had taken the back wall. Other Crips were making their way to the bottom of the Police shooting area. And the Crips now had several men on the right wall in the Police shooting area. The Police who had retreated were surrounded. The others were pinned at the station. A shoot out ensued.

Two fights continued in the no – gun zone. But the action had advanced to the Police side of the field. The game was nearly over. Covered by his firing comrades, Jackson cautiously crept across the top of the field towards the police station as his right flank shooters advanced. As the gunfire grew heavy and a hand held rocket blew up a barricade in front of the police station and another took out part of the police station door. At that, the remaining Police ran back into the station disqualifying themselves from further participation.

Freddie, firing forward, ran across the thresh hold into the police station. Jackson's gang won! And for the first time Jackson did his emblematic pump-up-the-noise motion - jumping and waving his arms, as the bright spot lights created white reflective areas on his black face.

"Goddamn that was good." Quentin said to himself while indulging in his own contorting victory dance. "Yeah!" Les was too busy cheering to hear him. I leaned back in my chair, pumped my fists in the air and laughed in astonishment, "you actually did it you crazy motherfucker you. Whooo – hoooo!!"

Quentin stopped for a second and looked at me, "We did it!" And he then went back into his contorting and jumping. I stood and joined the general cheering. It was a moment of celebration that was famously flashed on the big screen and reproduced when we started to achieve celebrity as a group.

In the moments following, I was standing and looking out at the cheering crowd when I saw the photographer I had seen at the press conference and outside of our Malibu home on the day we had gone to the beach. Rather than the crowd, his creepy attention was on us. I didn't want to upset Quentin, so I didn't point the photographer out to him.

Jackson became an international celebrity after this game. All of his remaining teammates acknowledged him as the team leader. And his having gone back to prop up his wounded comrade made him seem somewhat, believe it or not, compassionate. Well, if not compassionate to the other team, he was at least seen as loyal to his own. This image was bolstered by the well-publicized fact that he spent a significant part of his own personal winnings getting hospital attention for injured survivors, both black and white.

That night was totally fun. Quentin had set up a street party in Hollywood to celebrate. It was a huge mob scene. There were probably twenty thousand people there. Five blocks had been cleared off from traffic and the weather was beautiful.

Other than the large amount of vendors selling food, drinks and souvenirs, the entertainment centered on a large stage that featured bands until midnight.

But the bands were stopped whenever Quentin did one of his numerous television interviews from the side of the stage. The television programs were projected onto a huge screen behind the stage. It created a cool effect. You could see an extremely large image of Quentin behind him whenever he appeared on television.

The audio system, being designed for a band, was great. It meant that, not only could we see Quentin's twice, during the interviews, but a large loud echo accompanied his voice. Better yet he had a large cheering section. And it was hard to hear those who challenged the Prison Wars games and Quentin during these interviews over all the booing.

The first interview was with CNN. It is always weird to see programming in a different context. Case in point, the projection behind Quentin during one interview started with an advertisement for floor cleaner. It got huge laughs from the audience. After the advertisement came the familiar CNN theme music, a little update from the newsroom and finally, Ed Snyder.

Snyder introduced the segment with some footage from the contest. The crowd made much the same excited noises that it had when it saw the floor cleaner. Then Mr. Snyder introduced the speakers.

"Discussing this sporting event this evening, I have three guests. The first is the creator of Prison Wars, Mr. Quentin Longus who joins us from a street party in Hollywood." When Quentin's head appeared it was accompanied by cheering. It was natural from our vantage point, but looked funny on the screen when Quentin smiled and waived past the camera filming him to the crowd and said "Hello Amigos."

"Also joining us is Professor Arnold, an ethicist from Stanford University." I remembered him from our ethics meeting when they projected his head. "And from Sacramento California we are joined by Congressman Jaime Fuentes of Los Angeles from Sacramento."

"Congressman Fuentes, we'll start with you. You have been an outspoken critic of Prison Wars in the State Assembly. What are your reasons for not liking these apparently popular new games?"

"Sir, the American dream is being perverted by these games. We're concerned about a sport that glorifies criminals. These are not people that should be glorified in any way."

"Are you worried that children will follow in their footsteps?"

"Exactly."

"Mr. Longus, do you have a response?"

"Certainly, Mr. Snyder. Congressman, I don't know who you are to tell others how to live." The whole crowd made a big 'wooooo' sound like television audiences upon hearing something juicy. Quentin smiled to acknowledge the crowd. "Sure, these are hardened killers and criminals; they live by a different code. But that doesn't mean they aren't great by their own values. Did you watch the games?"

"Yes, but. . ."

"Well you can't tell me that Freddie Jackson is an amazing person. Could you have done the same? No way. The man is incredible. And did you see him go back after his fallen team member? I mean damn!!!!"

The crowd started chanting, "Fredd-ie, Fredd-ie, Fredd-ie, Fredd-y." Following someone's eyes, I saw Les on the stage actually leading the chant. 'Brilliant.' 'Brilliant.' I thought.

Mr. Snyder asked that Quentin control the crowd. "Okay. Okay." Quentin said winking at them, smiling broadly, and feigning that didn't love their rowdiness on his behalf.

"With all due respect to Mr. Jackson and yourself sir." the Congressman intervened, "Mr. Jackson is a rapist, a criminal and a bad man."

"I'm not saying that he should be free. But within his own code he is a hero. And he should be given, just as you have been, the right to excel at what he's good at. He's locked up. What else do you want? Let him live his dreams as the criminal star he is."
At the moment I thought how catchy of Quentin to use the phrase "criminal star." Later I found out that Les planted these words in his mouth piece, Quentin. And as Quentin finished his sentence, Les started the crowd to chanting, "Let Freddie dream, let Freddie dream, let Freddie dream."

"Mr. Longus. Mr. Longus. Please, the crowd. I think the point that he's trying to make is that people shouldn't profit off being evil."

"Does that mean that the State won't be cashing the checks from Prison Wars? Congressman Fuentes, will you cash the check? Will you cash the check?"

"Well, it isn't. . ."

"Cash that check. Cash that check. Cash that check." The audience started under Les' direction.

"It isn't. . ."

"Mr. Longus, the crowd."

"Sorry. But they're actually the Congressman's constituents. I for one believe that politicians should listen to their constituencies. Even if the crowd is loud, I believe in democracy."

"Demo-cra-cy. demo-cra-cy. demo-cra-cy . . ." Quentin closed his eyes momentarily as a broad, toothless, triumphal version of his smile stretched across his face. He reopened his eyes and signaled the crowd to quiet down.

"Thank you for quieting them down." Snyder moderated. "Professor Arnold, you have been an outspoken critic of Prison Wars, indeed you've got a book coming out on the topic. Professor Arnold, what is your take on this event?"

"Well, Mr. Snyder," Arnold launched with his enigmatic and slow southern accent, "Prison Wars is wrong in so many ways that I don't rightly know whea to begin. But, for one, I do worry about the influence that idolizing horrible criminals will have on children and general cultura."

"Professor," CNN's moderator asked, "would you argue that children will commit crimes to get into jail in order to participate in Prison Wars?"

Arnold continued, "It isn't that. The deleterious undertow has a deeper pull. This event will undoubtedly confuse the foundations upon which children build their pillars of good and evil. And, forbiddingly, civilization rests upon a civilized, refined, and cultivated, appreciation of order and beauty.

"What about the influence on morals, Mr. Longus? You can't think that there are good lessons for children in Prison Wars?"

Quentin leaned forward and bubbled, "Who is Mr. Arnold to say what is beautiful and what isn't. I think that Prison Wars was really beautiful. Holding a wounded comrade is beautiful. A slow motion replay of a fight can rival any painting in beauty."

Excited into a normal pace of speaking, Arnold shot back, "Violence degrades the soul. Plato taught the West, the soul is beautiful, intellect occupies a higher realm than body, the reverence of animal beatings makes us ugly."

"To you. But you don't have to participate. Tell you what, you read books or do what ever you want to do, let us do what we want. We'll leave you alone and leave us free, okay?"

"I cannot leave you free," Arnold snarled in condescension, "I am a part of a nation, a civilization, that you are making ugly."

"If you say Prison Wars is ugly then I guess I love ugly."

"Ug-ly, ug-ly, ug-ly, ug-ly. . ." Les led and the crowd broke into a huge celebratory cheer.

"Mr. Longus, can't you please control the crowd?"

"Sorry. They have a mind and loves of their own. We have a real party going on here." At that, Les got the whole crowd to cheer and scream. "I'm really sorry," Quentin continued with a tall smile and a wicked encouraging look at the crowd. "I don't know what's gotten into them."
At that the crowd burst out laughing and it lowered the noise volume.

"Thank you."

"Professor Arnold, Mr. Longus has a point. Why is it that your idea of fun should be his?"

"They are having a rollick, but murder isn't levity, it's depravity. We punish it because it is synonymous with brutality. It offends us. Broadcasting murder as fun tears us asunder from refinement."

"Yes that is your twisted vision, but the country is us." Quentin shot back.

The crowd roared, "The country is us, the country is us, the country is us." It was now obvious to anyone watching that these slogans had been rehearsed in advance

"Okay, that's all the time we have for this segment. Thanks to all of you for joining us tonight. Mr. Longus congratulations on your success and enjoy your party in L.A."

"Thank you." Quentin nodded as if receiving an award and an inside joke at the same time. And at that, the band on stage played a punk-pop number and the crowd went wild. The other interviews, on other major networks, went similarly. Significantly, Arnold came back for these later interviews, but the Congressman suddenly had another commitment.

I was a little miffed at being left out of setting up this stunt, but I had to admire Les' work. It was a fantastic bit of theatrics. By the next day, "Cash that Check," "Let Freddie Dream," "Criminal Star," and "The country is Us" t-shirts were being sold on the Prison Wars' website.

Quentin, Les, and I went to the Skybar at about one in the morning. Lindsey was there waiting for me. I'm not sure when I lost track of Quentin and Les, but I did. That wasn't a bad thing though. Lindsey and I had a great time. We went to several after hour bars and parties. I finally said good-bye to her from a Malibu house party and stumbled home.

CHAPTER SEVEN – THE DAY AFTER

I got home some time after five in the morning. I tried to watch some of the coverage on television when I got home, but I was too dizzy. I woke up about 2 in the afternoon and felt there was hell to pay. My head hurt. I stayed curled up in bed, basically, till about four in the afternoon, when there was a knock on the door.

"Come in!"

It was Quentin and he looked about as bad as I felt. But he seemed perky.

"Quentin! Hey, ole buddy, how the hell are you? You look like shit."

"Thanks!" His old smile of confidence was still reassuring. "How'd ya do last night?"

"Do? Okay. Lindsey and I went out. We ended up at a party not too far from here. I walked home."

"Well did you finally fuck her?"

"No." I said with obvious resentment at the phrasing of the question. "What happened to you?"

"I went out with Sindy and Les. We had a great time. But it sounds like you did too." He didn't sit down, he just kept pacing. He was making me a bit nervous.

"Sit down, ya' going anywhere?"

"No. I've just got a lot on my mind." He sat down briefly and then got up again.

"You do look a little tense." I observed.

"I'm not. I'm fine. Have you got a beer?"

"This early?"

"What is this, the third degree? I just want a beer. I am still celebrating! Is that such a crime?"

"No. No. Not at all. So what's the world saying?"

"You didn't see the paper today?"

"No. I tried to watch some coverage when I got home, but . . . and I just really woke up when you knocked." He didn't really seem to hear me as he was lost in his own thoughts. Considering what his thoughts were about jarred me into realizing why he was so far away and changed my tone immediately.

"Wow Quentin! Wow! We really did it. It wasn't a dream. It happened. It was magnificent. You were magnificent. I'm so proud of you. This is unbelievable."

"Thanks." Quentin said putting his attention back on me. "And I think this is only the beginning." He smiled a distracted half smile I hadn't seen before and sat down.

"Look at this." Quentin handed me the newspaper and I surveyed the headline, 'Prison Wars Ignite Furor and Fans.' He took the paper back and silently skimming the front-page article, Quentin startled me by yelling.
"Fucking nosey bodies!"

"Who?" I inquired somewhat in shock.

"This organization, 'Mothers Against Prison Wars,' they suck." Quentin cursed demonically.

I was afraid to offer my true feelings on this issue. He was a fairly loving father. Certainly he had to see that this sort of thing would seem less than wholesome to some. I put my assertive feelings into an oblique protest.

"Are you surprised? Didn't you realize that these kinds of groups would form to protest us? I thought you'd like it as free publicity."

"Yeah, it is publicity." His smile this time was for himself. His eyes did not peer outward, but fixed only on themselves. It was as if this dialogue was competing with others inside of his head.

"But couldn't they think of a better name? They sound lesbian."

"Quentin mothers don't sound lesbian to me!"

"Well why do they have to split off the female viewing audience? Why must it be a feminist thing? This will create more divisiveness than I want. In a battle between the sexes men will lose. Women will tell men not to watch if they want some. That'll kill us."

"Or men will become more assertive and assume their sense of power. That would be something like Les would want." I offered.

"Yeah. But Les is a philosopher. I'm a businessman. I want ratings."

Tired, with Les on my mind, I did not see the writing on the wall and offered my first impression. "Well just speaking as a human, who wants to live in a world divided between the sexes?

That connection is one of the most important things men have. It is our major civilizing force."

Though distracted, Quentin was clearly agitated.

"Quentin…" I hesitatingly ventured, "Did you see this whole thing as a promoter of civic values?"

"No." He paused and his entire being seemed to go inside. His chin hit his chest and he actually went a bit cross-eyed. "I thought it would wake people up to think about right and wrong. I thought it'd be fun and make me money. It would be a great adventure. But I didn't think a lot about possible bad outcomes. It's just TV you know."

Wow! It was then that I finally realized that Quentin wasn't a guru. His living in the moment had a strong element of not thinking too broadly. He was just a big surfer kid. How could any adult not think through the implications of such an undertaking?

For a moment I felt a little superior to Quentin. My Graduate degree was in Journalism. I had a clue about civics. The world was not a toy to me. I finally understood the source of his tranquility and success. He wasn't tranquil - as I had thought, - out of some sort of metaphysical realization. He was a rich kid whose stupidity had allowed him to actualize his dreams. That was the source of his calm. There was no deep understanding behind his zen.

"Just T.V.? Quentin don't you know that the T.V. is the major formulator of values in America today?"

"Hey smart guy don't tell me about values. I have a loving family that I'm close to. If you know so much about values, how come you never talk of your family without a sense of anger and spite?"

'Oh Yeah.' I remembered. 'He also got where he is by having a keen sense of people.'

"Ouch." I protested to his first-ever nasty zinger aimed at me.

"Hey sorry about that." He said through a slight panting. "But you shouldn't get smug with me. I'm not some little idiot kid. And I can smell condescension from a mile off."

"No...I'm sorry. I respect you. You are successful both personally and professionally. I should and do respect and love you."
We sat in a bit of silence for a while.

"That's okay. Look," He definitely had more aggressive direction in his voice than I'd ever heard before. He had taken his businessman demeanor home and I didn't like it. "I have an assignment for you that I think you're going to love."

"Okay." I said with a cautious sense of tentativeness.

"I want you to do some investigative reporting."

"On...?" Though the answer was clear, I wanted him to say it. I wouldn't want to be accused of having originating such a thought. So I waited for him to say it out loud.

"On that damned women's group." After about two seconds of my looking agitated and confused he added on, "That is your assignment. And, I'm sure you'll have fun doing it."

"Wow." I was exasperated.

"Wow is right! And you'll be good at it Marty." And though he was closing the deal, there didn't seem to be a choice. He was trying to strike the textbook balance of authority and being personable. I felt dejected, like an employee.

Quentin sensed my dejection and tried to reach out to me. "Marty it isn't just about TV or me anymore, it's about power."

"Power?" I did an interior eye roll. I sensed that Les-isms were imminent.

"Power. I can't explain it very well but...can't you feel it? There is a movement starting to reclaim America." Because of the little confrontation we'd just had over my condescension I kept a straight face. But I was reeling inside. Reclaim America? Had he gone mad? Was he on drugs? What was going on with him?

"To reclaim America's spirit." He continued, "We, we have become weak. There are lots of issues that we are not facing anymore because we have gotten weak and effeminate. We are, to put it not too politely, getting pussified."

"What!?"

"Pussified! Come on Marty. Can't you see what is going on? Take you for instance. You go out and you are scared to talk to women. You go out on a night of glory with Lindsey and you don't get any."

I blushed knowing it was true.

"Yeah?" I was trying to reassure him that I was listening, not being condescending and not thinking he was totally mad.

"It shouldn't be that way. That is a sign of spiritual rot. Men need to be manly. That is the essence of our being. We need to be a masculine take care of ourselves, to reassert some control over this country again.

"This group Mothers Against Prison Wars. They are symptomatic of the shrill nature of our society. They should be able to stand a little masculinity. Their children should be allowed to fight and face competition. It's bad enough they want to protect their children from real experience, from their real selves, but they want to turn all us men, our entire society into dainty little girls. That is wrong."

Wow. Too much. Les had totally bent him. He seemed like a man possessed. He was so excited about these new ideas that he was ranting.

I was totally speechless but thought I had to say something. "So that's why you want me to investigate the mother's group?"

"Yes. I want to know everything about them, especially about their leader. Her name is, it says here, Jayne Butler. If we can find any dirt on her we will use it."

Suddenly, there was a knock on the door. The light knock gave it a way. Quentin politely getting very poised cleared his throat. "Come in Melissa."

As the door swung open, Melissa's eyes, laser like, locked onto Quentin. "Quent! You're here! I was coming in to ask Marty if he'd heard from you."

Quentin looked at me with a pained look. Wow. I realized that he came to see me before he went in to see her! He turned towards her.

"Honey, we just got up. We've been passed out here for hours, then we just got up and started talking."

"Well you certainly did have a lot to talk about. God what a splash! Darling we are famous! When did you get in?"

The question was directed towards me. It was my moment of truth. What would I say? Would I lie to a woman that had been so decent to me, a woman that had been like a best friend and hostess to me, a woman that had housed me?

"About five in the morning."

In retrospect, she hadn't asked me when we had gotten in. She used the pronoun 'you'. Though she was clearly asking about both of us, the question could be interpreted to only be about me. But it was rotten. There was no excuse. There was no honesty in the answer. I lied to her.

"And you haven't left this room since?"

"No."

"Have you eaten?"

"No. Well dinner will be served in about sixty minutes. Will you join us?"

"Certainly."

"Oh Quent. It was wonderful. The kids are so excited. I wish you'd come in earlier. But we'll all share our excitement at dinner. See you there, right?"

"Of course dear. Sorry I didn't come in immediately. I didn't want to wake you. We got in late, drunk and in no mood to be quiet or go to sleep. We just talked until we passed out."

"Of course. See you inside, soon."

When the door closed we remained quiet as we listened to her feet go down the path.
"Thanks Marty. Man, I wasn't sure if I could count on you. I think you know what happened last night and I didn't want to upset her."

I'm not sure if his clandestine admission would have only referred to infidelity at this time.
"You bet Quentin," was my weak reply. I felt like a beaten man. I was bewildered. From the height of elation, I plunged down into the valley of confusion. Betrayal, guilt, confusion - everything but elation and happiness – wreaked havoc inside of my head now.
Was Quentin mad? Had I just lied to a very kind woman? Should I have made a stand? In retrospect I am proud that my job and home weren't all I considered at that moment. My

friendship with all members of the Longus family and my values system were the contenders in this psychic war.

Quentin could tell, as anyone could, that I was stunned. He calmed down. I finally felt his mania tuning down to a friendlier compassion. The old Quentin came back into focus for a second.

"Marty, I'm sorry that I just put you in that position. I know that you're feeling confused and a sense of divided loyalties."

"I'll say."

"You probably even are confused about my grand changes." For the first time since he entered the room we really looked each other in the eyes.

"I am totally changing. Les has helped me to see the world in a whole new way. It's not that I'm mad, though I had a long night of passionate venting and discussion with Les. But I'm, for the first time in my life, starting to have some ideas about society and things other than my little happy life."

"Well, I'd be happy to talk about social philosophy with you. But I think you also have to think about the individuals in the world too. Look at what you just did. You just lied to your wife. You were mean to me. I'm not your wife, but I hope I mean something to you." Little half smiles broke a bit of the tension in the room.

Finishing the sentiment, I followed, "I mean, you mean a lot to me Quentin and I'd hate to see you mess up your life. You have a lot to lose. And I don't think that Les is a particularly good influence on you."

"That's just it buddy. It isn't that I'm losing myself. For the first time I feel like I have finally found myself. A lot of the centered calm that I used to aim for came from denying my self, my desires, what I really wanted.

"For years, my spiritual trainer has been trying to get me to get in touch with my desires. And Marty, I'm going to tell you something. Remember that girl Sindy at the Skybar?"

"Yeah."

"I've had an affair with her." He instinctually looked down towards the ground.

"Oh Quentin!" Mine was an exasperation mixed with disappointment. I thought I sounded a bit like a housewife. "And you lied to me about it too."

"Yeah. Sorry about that buddy. But that's just it. I'm not sorry about the affair. It was what I wanted. I am an alpha-male and I shouldn't spend my life apologizing or rationalizing away my power.

"Men are men when they acknowledge their power. Women are attracted to power. I take care of Melissa in fine fashion. She has all she needs to play out all her womanly dreams. But she should also respect me and give me the space I need for me to be the man that I have finally come to accept that I am."

He looked to me for understanding. I was silent. He let me have my silent space.

"Are you going to tell Melissa about this new vision of yours?"

"Well like you've said, you're a good friend. You know us as a couple as well as anyone else. And I trust you and your judgment, as I hope you're sort of trusting me with my endeavors. And because I trust you I want to know what you think I should tell Melissa. I'm not the man she married. I'm changing. But I don't want to hurt her. I don't want to hurt anybody. But I have to be me. So do I tell her?"

"I don't know Quentin. To be honest with you, I'm not sure I'm really in sympathy with this new you. It seems kind of juvenile, very juvenile. That was hard for me to say and I hope that you recognize that it took courage. But I felt I needed to say that. I'm your friend. I think this whole thing smells a bit."

At that he looked a little perturbed, but got out a "Thanks. I know you're a good friend."

My counter thought was also spoken, "But I also know that I can't stop you. I mean, you're your own man. I can argue with you, but it'll probably just piss you off and drive us farther apart. So what the hell can I do?"

"You can trust me. You are welcome to come along for the ride of your life. But you're right. I'm finding a whole new me, I am in a spectacular place in my life, and I'm not going to throw it away. No way. I'm having too much fun. Was that Prison Wars game a blast or what?"

"It was a tad bit gruesome for my taste. But the rally and parties and hanging out afterwards. . . Ya it was a hell of a blast."

"It was huge!" Quentin insisted.

"Yeah it was! Capital F – U - N fun!" I enthused to show I wasn't a total downer.

"You bet it was. And for you to deny that is to deny a part of yourself. You're a nerd. I know that." I shot him a pained look. "What? Only you get to give brutally honest shots? You're a nerd and that isn't bad. But you're also a man. And, you know it was a rush being in the center of that thing. And if you thought it was fun being with me, imagine what it must be like to be me.

"Honestly, I don't want to lose an opportunity and I know you don't either. And I love you brother." Quentin reached across the space between us and grabbed my shoulder. He had a large presence. He was an alpha-male for sure.

"So I hope that you follow me along on my ride, even kicking or screaming. I need real friends around me that can be brutally honest with me." Without waiting for assent or reciprocal affirmations of brotherly love, he threw out the question again.

"So what about Melissa? What do I tell her?"

"What do you suppose will happen if you tell her everything?"

"Odds are she'll flip. But she's always been a bit of a devil, beneath her momliness. Perhaps she'll give it a nudge and a wink. What do you think?"

"I think she really loves you tremendously. And she won't be as complicit in losing you or seeing you hurt yourself as I might be. Life is not a game for her."

"It should be. I watch life like a play. Les read Nietzsche to me last night. Have you ever heard of him?"

"Of course." Without meaning to, I made myself aware of my feeling of superiority and drew back.

"Well, anyways, he said something like life is a tragedy for those who feel and a comedy for those who think. He also said marriage is the completion of the woman and the death of the man."

"Don't you love Melissa?"

"Of course...but a man's way. A man's way is different than a woman's way. I'm just being brutally honest."

"And your kids?"

"They should know what it is to laugh. Justin should know what it is to be a real man behaving manly."

"Well perhaps you're right. Perhaps there is a difference between manly and female love." I was maneuvering him and thinking of protecting her. "So perhaps you shouldn't tell Melissa about all this stuff now, because she, being a woman, wouldn't understand."

"Perhaps you are right. Perhaps that's the right thing, the protective thing, to do."

It was in this conversation more than any other I ever had that I sealed my fate. Worse than that, I sealed Quentin and Melissa's fate, and possibly that of the whole country.
What could I have done differently? I don't know.
I could have been a more forceful advocate of an alternative ethical system. But I'm still not trained in ethics. I probably couldn't out argue Quentin. He was super intelligent.
Of course, the outcome of the story could have worked to counter his ethical bent. But, the outcome hadn't happened yet. Even so, once he'd gone around the bend, once he had gone power mad and corrupt, even if Quentin had known the end, he still might have wanted to go out with guns firing in a destructive flame.
Leaving him wouldn't have helped either. I could have quit. But had I quit, he would have continued down the same path regardless. If I had done that it would have changed nothing and no one could have chronicled this important story from the inside, beginning to end, as I have.

As we entered the house for dinner, Melissa beamed. And in a sort of staccato crescendo cheer she proclaimed, "Welcome home conquering hero!" She was holding a glass and toasted him with it.

"Thanks Honey. Hi." Quentin responded, leaning over and kissing her affectionately on the cheek. He was confident. He had none of the sheepish edge of shame for being out the entire night that he had had in the guesthouse.

"Hey Marty!"

"Hey Melissa, and hey to you little ones" I said messing up Samantha's hair a little. Being so unkempt and feeling a bit dazed gave me a bit of guilt about my being there. I felt out of place. Still it was such a warm and welcoming home I knew the awkwardness was unjustified.

"Hey Uncle M!" Justin offered. We'd become close enough through roughhousing, that he had given me that pet name.

The kids seemed nonplussed. I don't think they knew what daddy had been doing the night before. It was Saturday, so they hadn't gotten the attention they'd be getting at school when word got around.

Dinner was beautifully arranged on a white lace tablecloth covering a perfect rectangle table. Quentin and Melissa always sat opposite each other. Justin sat next to my empty chair when we came in. Samantha sat waiting on her side alone. As usual, her chair was a little closer to Melissa's than Quentin's.

"So how was the night after the games?" Melissa began.

"Did you see it on television?" I asked by way of interception.

"I taped the coverage. After putting the kids to sleep I watched it." She was a great protective mother.

"Didn't want the kids to see dad's handiwork?" Quentin chided with a sense of accusation I hadn't expected from him.

"Not really. That program was one of the most gruesome and ghastly things I'd ever seen." Her polite but irritated voice made her less than a passive ambassador of peace.

"It was pretty brutal. Seven killed; two in cold blood." Quentin was relishing the figure in his mind.

"Horrible. It shouldn't be allowed." Melissa declared softly.

"Powerful stuff." I offered in a dopey kind of conciliatory way.

Melissa shot a look of repulsion and disappointment at me. "Let's eat."

"Hey, kiddies!" Quentin asked the kids about their schoolwork and week. Justin had gotten hurt in a soccer game.

"Well, Justin, you've just got to keep fighting. Next time you get that boy who hurt you back."

"Quent!"

"Well, he is a boy, he has to know how to fend for himself. He can't go through life being coddled. He is a boy. Boys are violent and competitive. It's in their nature."

"Nature is often violent and brutal and stupid. That doesn't mean that we should all be."

"But you can't go around your whole life suppressing it."

"Perhaps there is a happy blend," I offered. My fear of conflict was pathetic.

"Yes," Melissa said, "a happy blend." She said with a forced smile meant to reassure the kids that Mommy and Daddy were not fighting. Though perturbed, she went about her making sure that the kids all got some of each of the foods and ate what they were supposed to.
"Quent, you've been away a lot. Can you start spending more time at home? I mean the program is up and launched isn't it?"

"I'll try babe. This thing is getting larger than I thought it would."

"It *is* huge." She smiled seemingly relieved to be able to agree on something with Quentin. She seemed to cling to this moment and statement, this emphatic agreement, in a sad somewhat desperate way. She was worried about Quentin. That much was clear. But I could also see that she, as I had been, was confused about how to navigate this unanticipated change in Quentin.

Quentin was no longer a docile doting husband. He was getting willful. I felt for her. She had more, much more invested in Quentin than I. I could find another job, but she had only one family. One could almost see them negotiating for power as if in a business meeting. Quentin was always the winner in such arenas.

"How about tonight? Can you spend today here? After all it is a weekend."

"Sure Honey. I'm still really tired. Let's rest together." Quentin was a charmer and he was concerned. This wasn't an arena where he sought out being adversarial. "Marty how's your energy level?"

"Fine."

"There is a meeting of the group we spoke of this evening at the Century City Plaza Hotel. I'd like you to go. I can't, for obvious reasons, go. But bring me back useful information please." Quentin was giving me an order, showing that he was in command. He was also letting all present know that he was in the middle of something that couldn't take full holidays. It was a moving train that had it's own priorities, whether he wanted it to or not.

"Honey, Quent," Mellissa responded to the situation, "You need to get some space between you and this project. I want to spend the night and tomorrow having family time. I really need to talk with you; to be with you." She was plaintive now, bargaining for time.

He didn't look up. This was a classic power move. "Sure Honey. And I want to spend time with you and my little ones too." He made a really cute and funny look at Samantha who gave him a little girl, 'I love you' squinch with her face.

"I'm not little anymore!" protested Justin.

"Sure you're not," said Quentin with a more enthused version of a hair messing than I had earlier mustered for Samantha. And then a light beamed across his face and he exclaimed, "You're a big killer! A wonton little mischief maker."

"Quent Longus! Our boy is not a killer!"

"Sure he is Honey."

"Sure I am Mom."

"Would you kill your mommy?" Melissa drilled Justin, with a higher dose of anger and irritation than she normally puts into her playful bantering.

"Honey! Now whose being extreme? Of course he wouldn't."

"I'm sorry." Her eyes and the sides of her lips smiled over an expression that otherwise looked like it revealed a headache.

"But we'd both kill to protect Mommy. Wouldn't we killer?" Quentin looked right to his boy.

"That's right Dad. I'd kill for Mommy."

"That's it boy. Lemme see your muscles." Justin, fork in left and knife in right, flexed both his muscles and, egged on by

---

Dad, they both growled together, "Grrrrr." Sam joined in with a little "grrrr". I even grrrred a little and Melissa broke into a laugh that seemed like the beginning of weeping. But she quickly joined the rest of us, food in our smiling teeth, growling.

Quentin changed the topic and addressed me, "Will you be able to get some of that research I asked you about done this evening?"

"Yeah. I'm going to get right on it. I'll make a serious go of it tonight and tomorrow."

After eating Quentin went straight up to sleep. The next morning, we all went to the beach. Superficially, it seemed that things were better between them. But the day trip to the beach had a kind of nostalgia hanging over it. It was as if they had already lost what they had. Both Quentin and Melissa knew things would never be the same. It was a 'once more for old time's sake.'

But, being honest, because it may prove important, there was a selfish nature to the decisions I made that day. Of course my choices didn't end up being in my best interest. But at the time, I was curious, in a journalistic and salacious way to see where this whole thing was going. I gave into temptation both as a journalist and as a human.

Knowing what happened, I guess I'm, again, glad I stayed with it, because it allowed me to write this. And, if society ever gets back together again, later generations might learn from this written history. But never think for a second that that makes any of my actions all right. It doesn't even justify my lying to Melissa. I was complicit in evil.

Corruption is called corruption for a reason. It will eat at you inside and out, ravage your face, heart and, eventually, your civilization. It was on the very day after the very first Prison Wars game that I was first consciously complicit in evil. Evil is evil, even though it comes in packages of different sizes. Full dinners get eaten in bite-sized bites. And you are what you eat.

Beware of evil. Be good.

CHAPTER EIGHT – THE TRIUMVIRATE MEETS

The night of that morning beach trip Les, Quentin, and I had a really important meeting. It was the first time I got a hint of what Les' real intentions were. As we left for the meeting, Quentin promised Melissa he'd try to be home early. "Take care." Was the last thing she said to us as we left. I really loved her. Melissa Longus is a kind, strong, and a caring woman. She deserves no blame for what happened.

Sam was waiting in the limo for us at the end of the driveway. The doors were open and we got in and closed them ourselves. "To the Skybar sir?"

"To the Skybar." Quentin replied.

The journey to the Skybar is interesting. Out of Malibu, you just drive down the coastline to where Sunset hits the sea. You then go left, past the self-realization meditation center, past UCLA, past Beverly Hills, onto the seedy Sunset strip.

The route itself always seemed like an analogy to me. You leave nature and the spiritual and even sail past the pursuit of knowledge on your way to money and decadence. The ride kind of changes you. As you drive up Sunset, the famous windy boulevard, you feel like you're entering a movie. You are transformed as if sliding down the bat pole or something.

You emerge centered and ready for action.

"I've missed you Sam." I didn't think I'd ever heard Quentin give anything but directions to Sam. I had a hard time believing what I was hearing.

"Thank you sir."

They made a happy, mischievous eye contact in the rear view. Perhaps they went back farther than I had ever ventured to guess. I wasn't going to enquire. Fraternizing with help...the whole idea of help, always made me feel a little uneasy. Waiters, after all, could be your family members and there they are serving you. The wall that made them your servants always seemed contrived and artificial to me.

"And if you don't mind my saying so sir," Sam now commented, with appropriate formality, "Prison Wars kicked some serious booty."

"Thank you Sam." Quentin's tone said that'll be quite enough. He nodded, winked and pushed the button that slid the glass partition that separates the passengers and drivers into their respective places.

"God I love limos." Quentin exclaimed as he stretched his whole body into one big 'X'. "I've missed them. Do you like limos Marty?" His question almost seemed like an interview question. He wanted to know if I was going to be a full player or just a servant, another Sam.

"You bet I do." I was answering him in a way that let him know that I wasn't against him and that I wanted to be a team player. I was also searching to ascertain if I did like them and if so why.

I started to muse out loud. "I do like them Quentin." The first name sounded a little strange after his conversation with Sam. "You know what I like most about them?"

"No, what?" Quentin seemed amused and satisfied by my playing along, my acting the part he was hoping I'd play.

"I like the insular feel of them. Limos have a feeling of power that is an aphrodisiac for sure. But I think a lot of that has to do with how well protected and supplied they are. Nothing can screw with you when you're in a limo."

"Exactly. You're invulnerable in a limo. You can get whatever you want, whenever you want it and no one can touch you." As he was saying this he pushed the button that made a small bar come out of the back of the front seat. He started to mix us drinks.

"It's a sense of smug well-being that makes one feel nearly evil. And that kind of security is a rush." I affirmed.

"Yeah. It could almost corrupt you." He said as if daring me.

"How so?" I called his bluff. I was sort of hoping that the danger of corruption was an admission of vulnerability, a sign that he was going to be cautious, or might somehow reform himself.

"It's the sort of thing," Quentin continued with a determination to out cool my apparent panic, my apparent fear of the power of the limo.

"It's the sort of thing that could make you want to do evil, just to check how impervious you are. After a while that kind of danger would be a nice addiction."

At that he flashed his old smile. But it now represented a different sort of self-satisfaction. It was self-satisfaction with an implied violence.

I sort of gulped. I was pale, taken aback. Wow. What an intense monstrosity. To be with him, to play at his level, an ordinary guy like myself would have to somewhat transform himself.

Quentin had always gotten what he wanted. He had always said that he could have whatever he wanted. I had to muster up a different character inside of me to relate to him.

I could feel that I was to be cast in a different part. I wasn't sure that I could do it. I've never considered myself to be extraordinary. As a journalist I sought out and reported many stories. But I had never fancied myself an actor in one. Now I had an opportunity to be in one, to star in one.

"I have something for you Marty."

"What's that?"

"It's a gift. A token of our friendship and business relationship. It was actually Les' idea. It was his idea that you should have one." He leaned forward and took out a credit card sized little present wrapped in newspaper.

"Open it." It was obvious what it was because nothing else is credit card sized other than credit cards. It had my name, 'Marty Sanger' above the words 'Prison Wars Inc.' embossed in gold on it.

"Thanks! How extraordinarily nice of you."

"Marty, you're off salary. That's an e-ticket. You're along for the ride 'cause I want to have you along for it. That card will get you anything you want, when you want it. From your own limo rides, to helicopter rides, to women, to hotel rooms, you name it. That's your ticket."

"Wow thanks!"

"It's nothin'. I love you brother. I want you to be part of the team. I've seen that you've had some tension with Les. He's a good man. I want you to cool it with him. I want you to get on board. I want you to be part of the team.

"You along for the ride?"

Wow, Jesus. What an opportunity. Still, after all this time, I had to ask myself if this was really happening to me, a normal working class guy cum journalist. "Thanks Marty. I don't know what to say."

"Just say you're on board with us."

"I'm on board with you with pleasure. And the first round of drinks at the Skybar are on me."

Quentin smiled and leaned forward. "You're in a unique position between me and my wife and myself. Last night you showed me that you'll always be honest with me. You are a superb publicist and I believe that there is even more to you than you yourself realize right now. For all those reasons, I want you by my side on this adventure."

"I appreciate it." While I was still saying that, he nodded, smiled and winked in the way that conveyed calm warm acceptance he had always favored me with. He was an amazing guy, and I again reflected on how super lucky I was to know him. His confidence, balls, imagination, and calm under fire were amazing. "I mean I really appreciated the confidence, the card, and the friendship. And especially the confidence and the friendship."

Quentin raised his glass and we clinked them together in apparently mutual admiration.

Once parked at the Skybar, Sam opened the door without a word. As we got out, the energy of the Sunset strip seemed to pulsate. There is nothing like the night air at Sunset and Vine. We strode to the front of the line at the door in a way that we knew couldn't fail to draw gossiping, admiring attention.

Inside, not out where the pool made everything too transparent, sitting at a cozy booth, Les was waiting for us with a beautiful young lady. She had a sort of Jewish look, a wide nose, big eyes and lips that wrapped around a smile that made one's heart skip a beat. She made me feel like I was going to have a heart attack.

"Michelle, if you'll excuse us, my friends have arrived." She slid around the booth and looked me in the eyes as she smiled and skipped away.

Les rose up and he extended a firm grip to me. "Marty. How are you?"

"Great. How's things by you?"

"Superb. Couldn't be better." Les had slicked up since I'd last seen him. His hair now appeared to be gelled. He wore a dark purple shirt that was unbuttoned to his sternum and his shirtsleeves were rolled up to give him an action packed look. Somehow he looked larger. His breathing, his presence had grown. He had lost his cramped little office look.

"Good to see ya bud." Quentin started the move into seats. "What're ya drinking tonight?"

"Patriots." Les replied.

"Beautiful, we already started on tequila sunrises in the Limo. We should probably stick with them."

"Actually, Quentin, I think I'll switch to patriots in the name of congeniality." I was working the charm and trying to fit in as I never had before.

"Okay, in the name of congeniality, I will too."

"So when the waitress comes we'll all have one and one for all!" We laughed, quasi-forced laughs. I still didn't really trust Les and I didn't think I was going to. But, if he was going to be my new partner in crime, I had to get along with him.

The waitress did come (I won't describe her, just know that the waitresses at the Skybar all look like supermodels) and we ordered a round.

"So, Marty, has Quentin asked you about doing a little investigative journalism for us?"

"Mothers Against Prison Wars? Yes, Quentin asked me to look into it yesterday. And after dinner last night, I started compiling records on all of their leaders." It was a calculated bluff. I hadn't done any such thing.

"My, my. That is impressive."

"I told you he was great." Quentin and Les made a spontaneous little mini-toast to me. Quentin continued the tremendously encouraging look of pride and joy as he turned his head back towards me. "Go on."

"Well I will, I would, but I need to know what you want from me first. What's the agenda here? What do you want to know?"

"Well my astute friend," Les took the lead though, out of habit, I expected Quentin to answer. "We are on the cusp of a revolution in American culture and politics." Les being the source of Quentin's new ideas was confirmed. "We are going to launch an organization that will be on the forefront of this revitalization of our country.

The organization will be called, 'Men for Manliness.' It will start as an advocacy group for the continuation of Prison Wars, a sort of counter to 'Mothers Against Prison Wars.' But we have plans for it after that. It will mutate into an organization that will tackle a host of issues that are important to men. Issues that are important to our country."

Knowing that these men were not inept, but actually successful men; knowing that I wanted to be a part of this crew; I resolved to only stress the positive. There would be no doubts emanating from Martin Sanger. I wouldn't mention the brown shirts. I wouldn't mention civility.

"But our first priority," Les nearly returned to the tone that preceded his crescendo. In the time this took, I tried to show my agreement by finishing his thought with a hint of excitement, "...is to discredit the group against which we are fighting."

"Not exactly. We have to think strategically, otherwise we'll just look like lunatics." My guffaw stayed in my stomach. "No we must milk the animosity between our group and theirs. We want to slowly bring society to a boil by festering this controversy into a long running feud. We don't want a pyrrhic victory. We want a prolonged battle of attrition, and have people accept supporting concepts before we draw our conclusions. Conflict is good for us, conflict is fun, we must maintain it."

"Did I tell you he was good?" Quentin beamed. He was good. Some of you will have trouble believing that Les Christenson used words like 'attrition' and 'pyrrhic victories' in his normal speech, he did. He was, after all, a professor of philology. Being macho and crude was a device he used for public appearances. In conversation he was casually erudite.

"Wow. You are a strategist. You do have vision. Keeping the issues we want to address in the public eye will mean that everyone will have heard about them. You're right. We want news stories about families torn apart over this. Such stories could be as big as Prison Wars themselves." I was trying on my ability to speak like a manic apocalyptic preacher. But though louder, my ideas were small in comparison with Les'.

"Precisely. And all along, Prison Wars will be our church. It will be where we come to cleanse and energize ourselves. Our juices and understandings will flow from it. But our battles will not be confined to the stadium. No we're creating a civilization that has more of a competitive bloodlust. One in which people know their strengths, their weaknesses, and their true nature."

"I feel what you are saying." His passion actually did stir my feelings a bit. He wasn't one of the weak professors I had met earlier. This was a worthy partner. Whatever he was thinking, he was, like Quentin, thinking big. Like a moth to a flame (for selfish, not just journalistic interests), I wanted to be a part of this.

I consciously tried to reinforce his bonding to me by stealing lines I had gotten from Quentin that must have originated with Les. "Society *has* gotten very legal. Everyday people move around like little scared pawns in someone else's game. So what you're talking about is some anarchic release from the ties that bind."

"No. Not a spirit of anarchy." Les petted his goatee and rolled his eyes up and to the left as he spoke. Though I was conscious of my trying to fit in, for Les acting had become natural. "That would be extremely dangerous. Rather, we need to direct the energy we are releasing in a particular direction.

"For my vision Prison Wars is like a dream fallen from heaven. It is the perfect analog to what I wrote about in 'Blood and Technopolis[1]'. Have you read it?"

"No. To be honest, I have ..."

"No. You haven't even heard of it. I know." Les looked down as if burdened. For a moment the breath went out of him and he looked like a broken man at his end. But he revived quickly with a gleam in his eyes.

"It rolls out what I feel to be the central issue of the times, the severing of man from his nature and that of the natural world, his being turned into a passive, consumer, . . . a statistic."

Quentin butted in, "Do you see how passive people have become? They are consumers in someone else's advertisement. Prison Wars isn't about violence. It's about giving people back their voice. It's about getting them to think and feel with a fresh energetic perspective."

---

[1] Christensen, Lester. <u>Blood and Technopolis,</u> (Chapel Hill: University of North Carolina Press, 2015).

"We will give the people the ability, the permission, to shout down the status quo constrictions that hold them down." My words seemed to strike a chord with them.

"Yes." They both nodded and said simultaneously. "Yes."

"I knew you'd see it our way Marty. You don't know how good it is to have you on board one hundred percent and with us." Quentin beamed.

Les continued, "An excellent distilling; you are a quick study. Gentlemen, shall I propose a toast? To the future of the Men for Manliness campaign! Three cheers. Hip, hip – hooray! Hip, hip – hooray! Hip, hip – hooray!" We all drank deeply of our glasses.

Quentin took the next, "And to a long partnership that stirs up the world. Three cheers." Hip, hip – hooray! Hip, hip – hooray! Hip, hip – hooray! We all drank deeply of our glasses again.

And sealing the circle, I offered my own. "And to our leader who got us the forum from which to operate - Quentin! Three cheers. Hip, hip – hooray! Hip, hip – hooray! Hip, hip – hooray." We all drank until we polished off our glasses.

"Oh God, what fun!" Les worked to say, "I really haven't had fun since my youth. I've spent so many years of my life trying to figure out what's wrong with society that I haven't had much time to just enjoy nights like this. It feels good to be alive. It's exhilarating to be back to being the real me."

I was so engrossed in the fakeness of my own smile and my drink that I'd almost completely forgotten what we were talking about. Then the thread of it crept back into my head. His ideas struck me as having some merit, but the implications. . . I couldn't see where he was going with this.

"So what would you do with this energy once you've reconnected people with it?"

"Oh, I have ideas about that. But the first thing to do is to get people loud and shouting as a mob."

"Well, you've already shown your ability to do that! That night of Prison Wars. . ."

"That's true. But think about the dormant potential in such a crowd. Such a voice could shake the lawyers in the bureaus of statistical human management - that's what I've nicknamed Congress. It would be a voice that they would have to listen to with fresh ears. It is a voice that would call upon a new type of leader. Out with the soft and in with the new."

"It's like Bob Dylan's old song, the times they are a changin' 'they'll rattle your windows and bang on your doors." My speaking leaned towards singing as I got to the end of the quote. Surprisingly Les joined in on the chorus.

"For the times they are a changin'." It was the first time that Les and I ever had a mutually concocted reason to laugh together. We bonded a little on that chorus. The pronoun 'us' became appropriate for the first time (Especially as Quentin, though delighted, seemed to never have heard of the song before).

Quentin, then sealed the bond with a shrug, a quizzical look and a salute. "I'll drink to that!" We all joined him.

"So you are talking about a revitalization of democracy."

"Precisely. And yet," Les went back into his goatee fingering, this time with his eyes darting down for a second. "The mob is an unwieldy thing. It requires direction."

"Enter us!" But this seemed a bit too much to believe and got no response. Thinking perhaps that the exuberance was getting the best of me, I added a question as a tag line. "Do you envision us as some sort of triumvirate?"

"Not exactly. But it was an impressive reference. You're an intellectual of sorts Marty, you should read some of my books." I blushed a bit accordingly. "There are things that make sense for a country and things that only bring chaos. I believe every man should reclaim his own mind as a man. We can be spokespersons. But the ideas must percolate up if they are to be pursued with energy. We can suggest directions. But they will only gain a following if they strike a chord with the mass of men."

"Isn't that demagoguery?" I was back to my journalistic self.

"No, only if it consists in pandering - redistribution of wealth and all that. I'm not for that. I think in much more personal terms. I'm thinking more of letting people have a collective voice in the running of our country. A healthy amount of 'mob-ocracy' can strengthen the nation and the people in it. But I'm not into the chicken in every pot and a car in every garage pipe dreams."

"Please." I was being a tough journalist now. The evasion annoyed me. "Give me a specific."

"A specific, my dear friend," He showing his power and annoyance at my criticism, "Is Prison Wars." He snapped me out of my aggressive journalist mode and back into the role I was vying for.

Laughing at myself to make light of the exchange, I rolled my eyes up signaling that I thought I had been an idiot to miss the obvious. With a silly expression and a shrug I said, "Whoops, I forgot."
"To Prison Wars." I offered. And after that was met with approval and drinking, I offered, "To Les, a great thinker."

"And, damn good drinker." Quentin added.

"To Quentin." Les showed his hand at buttering up.

And I was very glad, when they both turned and said together, "To Marty."

We all drank and laughed.

Just then Sindy came slinking on over. I use 'slinking' so you can tell that I didn't like her very much. What was there to like? She was a shallow user, a siphon. She contributed not one positive thing to us. Whatever she says is a lie. Don't believe her or her agent's hype.

Sindy wasn't the hottest girl on the block. But she knew exactly what to do with what she had. She was manipulative. Those who have watched television know what she looked like. But you have never smelt her perfume. And she always dressed conservatively enough that you were tempted to violate her and trampy enough that you thought you might have a chance. On this night she wore a red angora sweater that cut off just above her waist line. Not having a bra was the perfect touch.

Sindy, Sindy, Sindy.

"What you fella's celebrating so loudly over here?" She had a certain wholesome quality in her skin that made the existence of her lips a miracle. By what right did these temptations intrude so suddenly into my mind? By the authority of the pouting salaciousness of the universe.

"Well, well, well, stop the presses. If it isn't Ms. Sindy with an 'S'." Les said, apparently recognizing her.

So here she was, the center of intrigue. Quentin had told me about her. Well if he had to be guilty with someone, she seemed like a person that would be easy to dismiss down the road. But what about Melissa? What of his new ambitions? Weren't they all endangered by such trivialities? There was nothing I could say without going severely against the grain.

"Isn't she lovely?" asked Les.

"Glad to see you fellas again. It's been too long. Saw you with Michelle earlier, Les. I know you're taken care of. But hows about you Mr. Drools a lot? You with anyone?" She punched me without gloves.

"Well I don't see . . ."
"Lindsey?" Quentin interjected the name. "That girl is no good for you. Has she put out yet?"

"No." I was embarrassed at his crudeness.

"You didn't want to have sex with her?" Sindy baited me.

"Yeah, but . . ."

"But nothing." Quentin interjected. "You need to lose a lot of inhibitions. Sindy, do you have any friends here tonight."

Without a word Sindy walked away with a wide swinging of the hips that couldn't have become second nature without years of practice.

I vocalized my concern. "Les, Quentin, don't you think this kind of behavior is reckless? Doesn't it do damage to our righteous cause? Won't it get in the way of our ambitions?"

Les responded, taking the lead more than I'd have liked him to. "Marty the medium is the message and we are the life. And if not for us, then for whom is our message appropriate? The weak present a danger to the strong. To lead people out of their stifled modes of living we need to stretch our own wings first. We need to embody freedom."

"Remember when I called you a nerd and told you that I think you have a fear of women?" Quentin continued the probe.

"How could I forget?"

"Well I think it's true. Sorry about that. But it's only because you were brought up in a home that was, like our society, matriarchal. I really think it would be therapeutic for you if you followed your passions without fear. Try it."

"Therapeutic? Okay sounds good."

"Oh my God! I can't believe I almost forgot to tell you guys the big news!"

"What?" We both asked.

"I graduated from therapy."

"How does one do that?" I was still smarting from the rehashing of the nerd comment.

"I punched my spiritual trainer out!"

"What?!?!"

"He said that I was getting lost and I needed to take a break from the confusing situations I had placed myself in. He told me that I had to clear the air so I could remember my true self. I told him that I'd been thinking the same exact thing, wound up and decked him."

"Wow! That is impressive!" Les exclaimed. I was totally shocked.

"I've been wanting to do that since the first time I met that asshole. It felt so good. I felt really free and whole. He was a source of a lot of anxiety for me. I feel so much better since I did that – like a new man."

And turning he said, "It was a total vindication of your philosophy Les. Thanks."

"Courage beats vulnerability." Les chimed as though repeating a slogan or a mantra.

"Literally!" I added. They looked at each other, got the joke and laughed.

Then the two turned to me. Speaking seriously, Quentin said, "Marty, you need to get in touch with your manly aspects. Hunt some women for a couple of nights and keep switching. For the first time in my life I feel like I've stopped being afraid of women. I feel free to be myself and it is empowering."

A mental image of Melissa's face, that I couldn't say anything about, popped into my head when Sindy came back with one of the most exquisite young ladies I had ever seen. She was so gorgeous I was embarrassed to look at her.
"Everyone, Sheila. Sheila, everyone. And Sheila, especially Mr. Sanger."

"Marty." I publicly insisted with an extended hand pushing through the lump of nerves in my throat.

"And if my work isn't done here I don't know how to do it. Quenty baby, come with me."

"Then I to mine." Les added. "Marty, can you cover the tab?"

I smiled and nodded in stunned silence. Quentin answered for me, "Yeah I gave him a card, as you suggested." Les gave a look of confusion that led me to believe that it wasn't his idea after all. "Take care Marty. Explore, learn and grow. And if I don't see you the rest of this evening, I'll see you back at the house when you get there. And I expect to hear some good stories."

As they left I felt like a drowning man that couldn't call out for help. But this was my hazing and I needed to survive to be a part of the team. Besides, I felt that I needed this experience, it could possibly transform me, remake me into a better, more assertive person. From a perspective totally different of that of a journalist, I needed to come back with a good story.

Sheila plunked down next to me. She had a red satin dress on. In the forties this sort of dress would have had sequins on it. Instead it just had a bow on the left, and only, shoulder straps. Ripples on the front of the dress all pointed to her nipples.

"Bet you don't get a lot of dates?" She looked empathetic, through her thick lipstick and period curled blonde hair.

"No. Not too many."

"I wanna do something. Let's role play, okay?"

"Okay. What shall our roles be?"

"I'll pretend that I'm a horny chick looking for a good time and you pretend you're a really confident and macho dude."

"Okay." I was so nervous I could die. "I'll try."

"Start." She said moving closer to me.

"Uh, I stumbled. How are you tonight?"

"Great. Don't be afraid of me. Look at my body like you appreciate it. Do it. It won't bite." I looked down shyly. "Do it till it isn't frightening anymore. Don't I have hot nipples?"

I blushed. "Don't be afraid. Describe everything hot about my body and what you want to do to it."

"Well, you do have nice sized breasts." She smiled a big smile. I had expected that kind of comment would cause a woman to hit you. I had always thought such thoughts, of course, in the presence of women. But I had never said anything like that before. I was still smiling nervously in anticipation of being slapped. Though still uncomfortable, I decided to challenge myself. "Your neck is like that of a swan."

"Did you think my legs are nice?"

"Oh so."

"Tell me what your exact thoughts are right now without censorship. Tell me what you'd like to do to me. Don't be afraid of your thoughts. I won't find them offensive."
"I'd love to lift up your skirt. I have been wondering about your underwear since I saw you."

"What do you fantasize they look like?"

"They are cotton and have little prints on them."

"Like little girl underwear." I blushed and looked away. "Why don't you put your hand in my lap, lift up my dress a bit and see what you want to see?"
I shook as my hands ran up her thigh. I slowly lifted her dress. She had red silk underwear on. "Tell me what you want me to do. You can't get what you want unless you ask for it. You know what you want. Tell me."

"I'd like to see you bend over so I can see down your dress." She bent down to where I could almost see her nipples. "I'd like you to lick your lips." She did. "I'd like you to put your hand in my lap and touch me." She did.
And though I never ever thought that I would say such a thing to a strange woman, I mustered up the nerve to ask her to come to a hotel room with me.

"Only if you'll completely dominate me and treat me like a slave." She replied.

We left and went to a special hotel. It had whips and rope and other accessories. It was a transformational experience. It was the first time in my life that I ever got exactly and everything that I wanted. That night I found the power to do things that I never thought I'd be brave enough to do. I conquered much of my fear of women.

CHAPTER NINE – THE MOVEMENT RISES

Everyone knows what happened next. Men for Manliness exploded. We filled stadiums. We redefined the meaning of relationships. We completely transformed the culture. We gained so much airtime and spoke so directly to the passions of the lower end of society that all other television seemed dead by comparison. We dominated America.

Along the way some now very infamous ideas and participants emerged.

Traditionally dictators have slowly introduced more and more unacceptable policies so that none of them seems much worse than the preceding ones. Thus the country slowly gets used to atrocities. Les also inched his way, subculture by subculture, into control of the masses. But he introduced his initiatives with an entertaining bombast. He removed America's self-control in the name of freedom. He got people addicted to change for the sake of change.

Herein lies a lesson you learned a long time ago. We should always look for the ultimate implications when considering policy. 'What if everyone did it?' is not an illegitimate question. Your third grade teacher was right, 'calling people names can lead to the holocaust'. But in this case, it would be more appropriate to say 'not telling people that they have limits can lead to a holocaust.'

This story would seem unbelievable had all of society not gone to this school of hard knocks together. I don't think anything exactly like this has ever happened before. I hope it never does again. But the lessons are hard to apply without a lot of forethought and depth of understanding.

Finally let me say, hoping that it provides a useful lesson, that this movement's success was aided and abetted by the Supreme Court nominations after 2015. We had, what was for us, a fortunate string of nominees that were all extreme advocates of State's rights. We didn't actually use any legal tactics. But, the absence of the law, the lack of willingness to enforce it, made things easier for us. Had we been seriously challenged by the government at anytime, our momentum might have been deflated.

It may seem too obvious to write just after the destruction of our society, but there is a difference between what is right and what is popular. Democratically elected governments must tell their constituencies things that they do not want to hear. They must know that they are their wards' betters. If they do nothing to stop mobs from making bad decisions, they validate them.

Les and Quentin, of course, first got onto cable news advocating Prison Wars. Other issues were initially only addressed tangentially. Les said that every time an outrageous idea was put on the air, even if there wasn't time to pursue it, even if it had no chance of being accepted, it was a victory. We planted a lot of seeds early on that bore bitter fruit later. The only vaccine I know against this is principled leadership. A leader that is willing to tell the mob unpopular truths about morals. But, that's just speculation. No one really tried and I don't know that anybody could have stopped us.

But Les did not script the corruption of society step by step. He had an understanding of masculine and feminine desires and believed in the sordid and low nature of people. He fed off corruption and just saw himself as what already existed in the average American's mind.

Les actually wrote up scripts for the particular moves and for every interview he ever had. He was like a chess player. He studied his opponent, predicted what they would say and crafted speeches around those statements. Debaters commonly do such things. But Les gained advantage by making his responses so off the wall that it left his opponents speechless.

I'll never forget the first night he went up against, the leader of Mother's Against Prison Wars, Jayne Butler. She was totally flabbergasted. It changed the tone of dialogue all across America. Les would later say that it, not only 'planted some seeds' but it 'widened some parameters.'

When asked what he had to say in response to her decrying the just aired second Prison Wars, he launched into his script.

"Jayne if you used just a little more rouge you'd be a hottie!"

"What! What does that have to do with anything?"

"The lip gloss is good, it is sexy, and you pull back on the rouge because you're subtle about being a tease. I like it."

"Oh my God. You're sick! Don't mention my make-up again, it is irrelevant and I'll thank you to stop talking about it."

"No it isn't irrelevant. It's exactly the point. Who are you to dictate what is appropriate for me to say?

"I remember the good old days when men had girlie posters up in auto shops and bars. Now you and your ilk have outlawed every male prerogative in the name of a harassment free environment.

"Yet you still try to harass me with lip gloss. I want my girlie posters back in the men's zone. You and your type have torn down the male environment, I still have a right to enjoy getting back at you by violating your sensibilities. You can leave if you want to, but you can't tell me what I can look at and speak about."

"Sir there is decency and indecency." Jayne offered flatly.

Les was very well educated. He knew about the communal nature of the early republic, the ethical precepts of civility as a palisade stopping primitive naturalism, and explanations of the mind-body dualism that are the basis of much of western morality. In fact, he's probably the one that taught me all of those concepts.

Les understood the importance of the argument Jayne was making about decency, but he also knew that historical basis for conventional morality could not be conveyed within the timeframe allowed by television segments. He consciously exploited such limits and assumptions about the goodness of nature and passion in his arguments.

"Decency! Let's be honest, your make-up is designed to control me, to manipulate me sexually. It is indecent. And I can't fire back by saying it isn't working?

"The power of man isn't his delicacy. It's his honesty and his birthright. Since when can women like you tell all men what they can and can't say? Lady, you can't control me."

His vocabulary lost all of its sheen when he was appearing in public.

"I'm speechless. You're deranged."

"I seem that way to you. But, that is because you hate men. Don't you get it? Men like to talk crudely, watch sports, have girlie posters in their workplace, and run the damned world.

"Your mothers organization may want to treat us like children. I'm deranged by your rules. Your coming on in here with all that pretty lip-gloss and telling me what I can and cannot say is offensive to me. You shouldn't be allowed to come on television and try to control men."

"Sir it is my legal right to be on television and it is an outrage for you to suggest that someone like me, a concerned mother, cannot be on television expressing my opinion."

"Legal rights, legal schmites. I'm talking about something deeper. I'm talking about reality - *Earth to you.*" His posturing as the everyman was totally contrived. Had he just been the average loudmouth he posed as, he wouldn't have had the impact he had.

Then in the Les style he went for a typical uppercut, "If you want to be a good protector of the children why aren't you home with your two little ones now?"

"Sir it is insulting that you tell me how to raise my children." She spoke that line exactly as he had scripted it.

"Well excuuuuuse me. I am a man and I think that the female view of childrearing is different from the male's and I think it is valuable. You need a man in the house to teach a boy not to be a sissy, how to fight. Instead you're on television telling me that it is offensive that I don't act like a little girl.

"The fact that you have a woman nanny raising your kids and no husband says a lot about your vision for the world."

She looked totally bewildered. In my fantasy she was wondering how he knew that she had a nanny watching her kids at the moment, in my fantasy she remembered my presence in her meetings and belatedly realized I was a spy.

Stunned, but recovering herself, she fired back, "My family life, my make-up, has nothing to do with Prison Wars!"

"It has everything to do with it. If you care about children so much, get a man. And if you hate men so much that you must penalize you son by not having one around, please let it end there and don't try to castrate the rest of the men in the world too.

"Look, you want to tell men how to think, to domesticate us, but you don't even have a man around for your little boy. You hate men. You make me sick. You're a bad woman."

Can you imagine the impact of this tactic? I can tell you that, even knowing it is coming, as I did, watching it left you stunned and confused. Viewers, the moderator, the person he's been talking to, all of them have a strong and accurate feeling that they've been ambushed. These were not the normal debating tactics.

After figuring out what was happening, the other person would often try to re-establish normalcy by returning to their traditional roles.

In this case the announcer broke in after an uncomfortable silence, "We are here to debate Prison Wars and that is the issue."

"Thank you!" Butler exclaimed.

"You're quite welcome." The moderator was happy to have been told that he had successfully re-established normality when he had so clearly lost control of the show.

"Mr. Christensen, do you then take the view that children being exposed to violence at an early age doesn't have a negative effect on their morality?"

"I would say it has a positive effect. Competition, violence and cruelty are realities. Trying to protect our sons and daughters from reality, though a noble feminine goal in theory, has the negative effect that it makes the youth, especially the boys, soft and unrealistic."

"Look at our feminized schools. They coddle because no one wants their feelings hurt. They are womanly and not brutal so boys back out of them.

"Prison Wars will help boys become men again. It is a lot better for kids than Mszz Butler's shielding her son from men."

"Aggressiveness and brutality are not qualities that I'd like to instill in my children. They should be steeped in understanding and compassion so that they can live in a society that is descent."

"La, la, la." His nastiness was intended to entertain his audience. At no time did any network threaten to stop inviting him back for more interviews. He was too fun.

"Look caring and decency are great. But remember that this world isn't a flower-scented tampon commercial. There is terrorism and we're getting our butts kicked economically.

"Our country needs to be tough and manly or it will cease to be a superpower. We can't always be striving to make a world safe for your delicate womanly aversion to hurt feelings and men, if we want to have a competitive nation we must be willing to reward the strong and fight our enemies."

Interviewers rarely got the topic back to Prison Wars when Les debated other guests.

Quentin, because he was younger, more handsome, the pinnacle of the cult of fun, and rich, made a more appealing source of admiration than Les. So Les always spoke of himself as a representative for Quentin's ideas in those early days. Only Les could convey the twisted vision he wanted to associate with Quentin and Prison Wars. And as long as Quentin said, "that's right" and "that's what I believe" he was seen to understand and stand for Les' ideas.

Meanwhile, Quentin took issues that were calculated to bring controversy and easy approval with less explanation. For example, he was the main proponent for new drinking laws. This turned out to be a very popular issue. Men had felt hampered in for years by the irrational drinking laws. In most States Mothers Against Drunk Drivers made it so you were only allowed one beer an hour.

The basic idea Quentin floated on the media circuit was that we decriminalize drunk driving from the hours of 2:45 to 5:30 in the morning. This would encourage folks to keep from drinking for forty-five minutes after two o'clock closing hours. It also recognized the fact that there aren't many people out at that time. Men went ga – ga over this change in the drinking laws. Bars and alcohol corporations supported it. Alcohol consumption went way up.

With Prison Wars and this campaign as his calling cards, Quentin instantly became a celebrity and a hero to men. The closeness of the names Mothers Against Drunk Drivers' and

Mothers Against Prison Wars' also got us a two for one victory by association. Furthermore, when Quentin scored victories against laws men hated, men felt it vindicated the whole Men for Manliness platform.

Men for Manliness also got help from an unexpected party, Freddie Jackson. Freddie became a criminal star due to Prison Wars. Les likely foresaw the corrosive impact of the rise of criminal stars in general. But he could not have foreseen how enterprising Freddie would be. He wasn't always exactly in line with us, but he was always a force, especially amongst the young, minority, and criminally inclined. We tried to connect with these natural allies. But we couldn't reach these demographics as well as Freddie.

Freddie's crimes had, again, been robbery, murder, and rape. That young people considered him a hero should have scared all adults. But America had long since stopped distinguishing between the famous and the infamous. In journalism school they told me that media used to bear responsibility for informing America. But we all knew that by the time Prison Wars started the media would have sold heroin to children for profit. Freddie was symptomatic of their willingness to push anything that would turn a buck regardless of merit.

Freddie had charisma. He was six foot three, black as night, and had gold lining on one of his teeth. I recognized his gift for gab when I first interviewed him. He had shown his leadership skills by speaking up in the first meeting we had with prisoners and in leading his team to victory. But he also had an uncanny flair for publicity and marketing.

Every time Freddie was on television he got huge ratings by saying things that dominated discussion all across America for weeks. 'Keep talkin' bitch, I love to watch your mouth move' became an American catch phrase overnight. I can only imagine the shock that many mothers must have felt the first time their son said that to them. More women should have stood up for themselves.

Freddie's charisma was also borne of his bravery and his lavish lifestyle. Most people would have been satisfied with the take from one go at Prison Wars. Not Freddie. After that second bout, he went into semi-retirement a very wealthy man. The income from Prison Wars being divided between so few folks made each of them very rich. As a leader he had contracted for a disproportionate chunk of his team's take. Freddie was an all-or-none guy who had won.

Right after his second victory Freddie bought the all white Jacksonian Mansion. If anyone else would have bought that place it just would have just been an example of excess. But Freddie was a genius, and an enterprising one at that. He ran three huge multi-national businesses out of that mansion. He had a music studio, film studio, and party enterprise that easily outshone the playboy mansion as a hotspot and moneymaker.

The State-mandated guard towers around his Jacksonian Mansion only added to his clout. When he went out in his white limo, the motorcycle police that escorted him didn't detract from his image either. Everyone the State assigned to control him ended up seemed like employees. Having police as body guards only added to his mystique. In fact, it was because so many guards surrounded him that he got the nickname, 'the Blackest President.' Nothing succeeds like success. He was huge.

Women who came to see him were invariably filmed and became recipients of royalties from his pornography subsidiary, Jacksonian Enterprises. Being under arrest and guarded, women who came to see him had implicitly consented to be with him. They couldn't complain, let alone try to send him to prison. His life sentence had made him, ironically, free. He was a prime example of the emerging model of the new male that Les was working so hard to liberate.

Linda Kellor was a total surprise. A divorced housewife in her late thirties, she started a group called "Women for Womanliness." Had we been the impetus behind that group, as so many have suspected, we would have chosen a much younger and hotter spokesperson. Linda seemed to be homegrown and pathetic in a way that you would never expect to succeed.

The look Linda wore combined sexiness and respectability. All of her outfits involved suit jackets. Les, who did end up managing Linda, provided her sexy yet respectable outfits to give her credibility. But he also found ingenious ways for her to be inappropriate. Low cut suits showed off her ample breasts. Too high skirts showed off her thin legs. And, quite often, she'd just wear a suit jacket with nothing under it.

Between her middle of the road looks and iconoclastic references to respectability, Linda apparently struck a chord with average lower-class woman who had dreams of getting ahead. If this woman could get a little power and glamour by following the Woman for Womanliness doctrine, anyone could.

Les didn't want to support Linda at first. We initially sold 'Women for Womanliness' t-shirts on our website as a kind of joke. The t-shirt models were naked outside of the t-shirt. We had no official affiliation with them. But to our surprise the shirt sales started to take off. It gave a wonderful boost to our movement to have some women publicly supporting us. These were women that were supporting us because, not despite of our overtly sexual representation of women.

Les' decision to associate with Linda Kellor publicly happened for a number of reasons. It was partially because Linda Kellor and her organization wouldn't go away even if he ignored her. It was partially because he thought he could keep her from embarrassing him by association better if he had some control over her. But the real reason he supported Linda was that Les firmly believed that democracy was the way to power; he supported grassroots efforts.

Les had always repeated that we were the midwives of democratic impulse, not the creators of it. Top - down leadership always stunk of moral control. He repeated 'we can best awaken the masses by tapping into their dreams' often. As became apparent after it was too late, he wanted to destroy America through corruption. Linda got our help and support because she was a genuine product of the unrefined, trashy masses.

Moreover, Les found Linda easy to dominate. She really believed in the natural dominance of men. Les told her one night that all sex was about dominance not pleasure. "Having your skin rubbed is not the object. Having a woman prostrate in front of your member is the real rush." We were stoned and he really laid a head trip on her. He told her that in order to get our blessings convince us that she really believed in dominance she had to get naked, get on all fours and bark like a dog. She did it. After that Les owned Linda.

Les started to write all of Kellor's copy and found that she was good at memorizing it. And, since Linda believed in what he wrote for her, she read it with a passionate sincerity. She got what he wanted and she got what she wanted. Unbeknownst to her, Les took a picture of her giving Quentin head. He kept photo above his desk for months.

Les stole a lot of the ideas for Women for Womanliness from the magazines Vogue and Cosmopolitan as well as other checkout line fashion magazines that already populated the female mind. "How to get a man in 24 hours," "25 ways to please your man," and like agendas were adopted. The most effective place to drop poison into society is to, like a Trojan Horse, slip it in with the pre-existing state of the mass mind.

Women for Womanliness' overall philosophy centered on the double standard. Men had un bridled perrogatives that needed recognition. The prerogatives Woman for Womanliness suggested you allow men included Men for Manliness' standard demands like beer, sports, and the acceptance of extramarital affairs. Unmarried women were encouraged to use their sexuality to manipulate men. But married women had to exemplify marital fidelity.

Linda helped push though some of Quentin's other ideas. Restaurants should offer "Manly portions" at the same cost. Naturally restaurants wanted to charge more. "No," Linda announced on a music channel "you absorb the costs by giving women smaller portions." No one could deny his legitimization that men are bigger. But it took Linda's organization to get women to say that women want smaller portions because they need to and should diet to be attractive to men. Smaller meals showed that they understood their place; it was good etiquette.

Linda pushed society to be "man friendly" and "woman friendly." She denounced our "gender neutral" restaurants and public policies. In her editorials and media appearances she often presented issues in the form of gossip columns. She told American that many women would rather have men go elsewhere than to have to continue with the duty of sex. Academia had long championed the empowerment of sex workers. Some of Kellor's columns helped wives become more comfortable with the use of sex workers in such situations.

The definition of a good wife changed. Women's magazines asked if could you allow men their fantasy of having another woman in bed with you and your husband without negatively impacting children. The double-standard required fidelity for married women, unless the man approved of kinkiness. Then women's duty required following her husband's sexual lead. Some women, American acknowledged, wanted to farm out the sexual duties. Others wanted to increase the numbers of people in their bed. The point was to find a husband who shared in your lifestyle aspirations.

Expecting "physical fidelity" was viewed as unscientific in such discussions. Studies with mice and statistical norms bolstered these arguments. "Emotional fidelity" became a common phrase and thus the popular mind began to separate the physical and emotional. Agreeing with many feminists and post-modernists, Women for Womanliness argued the unnatural and artificial nature of the institution of marriage laid behind the high divorce rate. Conservatively, Kellor assumed that society required strong families. The family structure just needed to accommodate men's uncontrollable need for sex.

Les arranged for Linda to get a television show. Demographically it was an easy sell. She had huge followers in the under-thirty female age group. But much of television aimed at reaching these women. Kellor's shows also appealed to married women and divorced women over thirty-five. This demographic group had money. This group intimately understood the damage that sexuality could do to marriage. And they were sick of being marginalized in real life and media. They wanted to share in the fun of sex instead of always being pictured as its virtuous victims.

With this motherly and grandmotherly demographic, Linda initiated a bit of a sexual revolution. With their children and husbands gone, they no longer needed to be seen as staid matriarchs. Daughters, mothers and grandmothers bonded over their conquests on Kellor's couch. Her television show explained how all women could manipulate men for free meals and vacations. They had several episodes where women with Women for Womanliness t-shirts went into malls, approached random men and got them to go home and sleep with them. Though largely rooted in sex, Kellor's shows presented a model of women's empowerment.

Nearly every segment of Linda's show centered sex. She constantly told women that casual sex without commitment for unmarried women was desirable. "That's a woman's prerogative too!" she'd chirp. Married women, we learned, often wanted their men to sleep with strangers to maintain emotional fidelity. But Kellor explained that many women simply slept with men to get ahead in the office; office sex wasn't emotional. While married women had to have husband approved sexual expression, Kellor encouraged single women to "use all of her weapons" for maximal professional advancement.

Men loved it. Their dreams of casual sex without expectations had gone mainstream! And herein Les had miscalculated. For once he overestimated the morality of Americans. He had thought that we'd have to intimidate women in order to allow men to speak their minds. We would have to use the fear of men's violence and the fear of losing men to get women to agree to the explosion of macho values in society. He didn't realize that generations of television programs and feminists selling men's values to women had already set the stage for this revolution. Kellor understood women better than Les did.

Behind the scenes, our personal lives got way more dangerous and insane than nearly anyone realizes. Sleazy Sindy was the conduit of our insanity. Wherever that tramp is, let it never be said that she didn't have impact on the world. The eternal temptress, the dark side, the Eve; she brought us the apple of our desires.

Quentin and I rented a room in Weston hotel. Our 'headquarters' (as they were called for various implications of the name) were just about half a mile West of the Skybar and a half block South of Sunset. We chose that hotel because of its lounge. In the Weston lounge, the swank of the business class and the skank of Hollywood congregated nightly. The lounge is kept dark for purposes of intrigue. Cocktails being sixteen dollars a pop limits access. Its full of what we started calling 'Players.'

Becoming a player is a title that one has to earn. Quentin, Les (of all people), Sindy, and her friends had been trying to get me to become a full player for a while. And I was doing pretty well learning the ropes. But my eyes were fully opened to the real meaning of being a player on around October of 2021.

We had done a radio show on KLOS. That is Los Angeles' most powerful classic rock station. We had become quite a hit with the older rocker set. I'd say we had honorary rock star status in the music world. This demographic wanted no ethical debate with us. They were fans. They just wanted us to plug our event and their radio station. We gave away ten free tickets to Prison Wars that night.

I had been slowly acclimating myself to the art of "hooking-up" from other players. Players are clear about what they want and what others are offering. At the station there was a beautiful young woman named, I think, Julie. The most attractive thing about her? It looked as if her lips had been augmented.

Anyhow, after a minimal amount of small talk – players don't invest too much before they see if they're wasting their time – I popped the question. "Hey, we're going to go hang out at the bar at the bottom of our hotel. Do you know the Weston off the strip?"

"Yeah, I know it. I've been to that bar before." She probably had been there, having some connection with the music industry.

"Would you like to come along?"

"Sure."

"Right on Julie," I said checking that I had her name right, "we'll have fun." Each time I did a successful transaction of that nature I blushed heavily. It was so not me. I mean, before meeting Quentin I would have had to have known a girl for a long time and gotten a lot of positive hints before I could ask her out on a date. Needless to say, that hadn't happened many times.

Now I was become a player. I could hardly believe it myself.

Anyhow, we took the limousine back to the Westin. We went into the bar with Quentin and Sindy, but quickly lost track of them. That wasn't unusual. The nights always had a spinning characteristic. You would spin and be in one conversation. Then you'd spin and you'd be in another. Then you'd spin and you'd be at someone's house. Then you'd spin and be back at the bar. That was the normal course of an evening.

Julie was one of many girls hungry for adventure. Like me, and others in Los Angeles, she had come from some smaller town. Whereas I had worked my way into this scene, most of the female small town girls in such scenes are only there because they have the looks to get in. After no more than three drinks of spin and chit-chat, it is the duty of a player to move the party upstairs.

When we opened the headquarters door we saw Quentin and Sindy sitting on the couch in front of a mirror covered in white powder.

"Marty!" Quentin looked startled. He didn't get flustered easily. Looking back on it, I think that his being flustered at all was a result of my association with Melissa, as much as my friendship with him. I often thought that there may have been some element of blackmail, or fear of my giving him away, that kept me in the loop. At any rate, he was definitely panicked at that very moment.

"Marty! We're uh..."

This was another moment of decision for me. Another moment where I wish that my upbringing, my conscience, my college . . . something would have retrieved a stronger sense of right and wrong out of me. What was I to say? I was drunk. I had a hot woman on my arm. Was I to look like I was shocked at their behavior?

"What are you doing?" I asked this casually in an attempt to hide my ignorance.

"Leeners!" Exclaimed Sindy in lame scenester slang. I looked quizzical. "Speed. Marty. Speed." She offered as a correction for my puzzled face.

"Can I have a rail?" Julie's asking took care of my feeling that I may have offended her sensibilities.

We were up for three days. It was a bonding experience. We didn't leave the room. We ordered up food, and picked at it. It turned out that Quentin had been doing this drug for a while now. He had been going since the first night after prison games. Looking back, his darting energy when he busted into my room and told me of his spying plan should have alerted me to something being amiss. But I was so naïve I didn't even suspect this sort of thing.
Looking back, I could also say that it might have been a key to Les' domination of him. Les had been there when Sindy and he did it for the first time. I even suspect that Les set up their use. Les was around less and less during those days. He was riding high with leadership. His visits were like business meetings meant to keep Quentin, Les' figurehead and claim to legitimacy, in the loop. What a smart and sneaky worm that Les Christensen was.
That night I stepped off the ledge. I took the final step to being a player.
Through out all of this, unbelievably, Quentin tried to maintain a family friendly image. More than Les' culture mission, Quentin wanted Prison Wars to succeed. And he was trying to

keep his family together for its own sake too. The illusion of having a family life to return to, the idea that he was just on a business trip and soon to be back home, kept him from seeing what he'd become.

But his advocacy of things that went against what Melissa believed in, not to mention his secret life, made maintaining this illusion increasingly difficult. Moreover, Melissa wasn't buying it. We made less and less visits "home." They were too painful.

I remember one fight they had on one of our increasingly rare visits. It was typical. We arrived on the day a report had come out saying that there was a rise in crime for a week after the first Prison Wars game. As usual, Quentin's responses were Les' response.

Quentin told Melissa, "Men are trying to get into prison because it is the last bastion of manliness. Don't you see, men want Prison Wars. They need it. They try to sublimate our aggressive energy into study and work, but it doesn't satisfy our manly need to kick fuckin' ass on others."

I don't think he was ever entirely conscious that he was evading what she was talking about. Les' justifications for Prison Wars had become the totality of Quentin's reason for living. Quentin's values were Les'. With people other than Melissa, his living up to the Prison Wars ideals made him important. His success and social circles protected him from scrutiny and conscience. No one really challenged Quentin's identity and actions in public. But with Melissa this game didn't work.

"Quent, your language."

"Don't start with that again. Men . . ."

"Yes men, men, men. You're talking to me, Melissa, your wife. I know you. Such language and arguments aren't you, they're gross. What you are going after and valuing these days is totally foreign to me."

"Well it isn't foreign to me." Look Prison Wars has raised nearly a billion dollars for education. Don't tell me that it is bad for children. If it was, would the schools take the checks?"

"Anyhow, my spiritual trainer says I have a right to fulfill my…"

"Your spiritual trainer. I know what you did to your spiritual trainer."

"Yeah, guess he's sorry I found out what my true self was." Quentin chortled, his new chortle.

Melissa still loved Quentin, but he missed her point. Whenever she saw him she tried to talk him into staying and being with his kids. She harbored a ridiculous hope that his staying in the house for a few days would bring him back to sanity. She didn't want to talk to this man, but she harbored some hope of someday seeing her husband again.

But Quentin's addictions wouldn't let him stay. There was always a reason he had to leave. There was always a fight about his leaving. I always had to take Quentin's side with an apologetic look to Melissa.

She always said the same thing to me when we left, "Take care Marty and take care of Quent." My apologetic look convinced her that at some level I still inhabited my body. Every time I left there I had to go through the anguish of feeling the distance between who I was and who I had become.

Those days weren't all bad by any means. Melissa, if you're reading this, you should be touched by how long he hung on to you. We got what many men would consider to be every dream they've ever had. We were rock and roll personified. He wouldn't have even visited a less spectacular woman. She had to have a huge place in his heart to compete with our social calendars.

I remember the scandal and squawking that happened when we showed up for the academy awards in old t-shirts and jeans, unshaven and drunk.

But it is a sign of something when you stop dressing appropriately for occasions. On one level it shows that you're out of kilter. When we wore t-shirts and jeans to award shows and business meetings it was because we were just partying and oblivious.

On the other hand it shows that you are so hot you're above the rules. Towards the end we had no idea where we were going anyhow. Party, meeting, interview, publicity shoot, negotiation session and four more parties in one day. How do you dress for that?

Getting dressed up can be fun, but usually it is done because you have to. We didn't have to care anymore. We were bigger than that. "Players deluxe!" as the phrase went. Furthermore, we were expected to scandalize. Had we shown up to any event in normal clothes people would have been disappointed.

I guess the worst part of the clothing scandal was that I did wear some embarrassing clothes. I definitely didn't dress my age. As we got more outrageous our clothes did too. I mean, I'm in my mid thirties. I really shouldn't wear unbuttoned polyester shirts. But it all seemed so cool then.

I thought I looked good. We were good enough for fashion magazines to regularly feature us. We established what the Malibu, Sunset set wear. If you don't look strung out, it looks like you have to work for a living. It is an irony of tinsel town that you demonstrate that you are powerful by dressing like you don't have to work anymore. It is emblematic of a generation we were appealing to that we looked like we just woke up after an evening of partying.

We did a lot of partying in those days. By early May of the first year of the Prison Wars, speed and women were what partying meant to us. I achieved the party look by going days without eating or bathing. Both the women and drugs were bad for us. But I was happy to be so skinny that I could fit into clothes that were, as we said, 'stripper-chick hot.'

A lot of that look was due to the looks of the stripper chicks we hung out with. They all dressed to the nines. None ever looked like they had ever done anything but contrive to avoid public obscenity laws. They were hot wrapped candy.

Quentin became obsessed with his image. He would stop parties to see himself on TV. The whole party would be rapt and so would he. He would tell anyone who would listen, "You don't get hot looking by takin' it easy. The hot look is a result of the hot life. And WE ARE HOT!"

Quentin loved the attention we got and so did I. Can you imagine going to parties where powerful men cower to you, all the women want you, and all bounds and definitions of respectability are yours to determine? Can you imagine going to a party where everything you said was fabulous and witty? Drugs and power both aid that sort of reality.

And the overwhelming thing about it was the spectrum of people kowtowing to us: Businessmen, MTV types, intellectuals, celebrities, politicians. Everyone wanted a piece of our ear. No one was saying anything but "Yes, we'll talk."

Barriers are things that keep people in line. We had no limits. No one denied us anything we wanted for months at a time. I don't think that absolute power could have corrupted so absolutely back in the days of kings. The king had to pretend to be decent. We were admired for our flaunting of decency.

No wonder God doesn't show up anymore. All the adulation and power available these days would probably corrupt him beyond recognition. But that was not our problem. Quentin got into the habit of saying, "God I love being a God."

CHAPTER TEN – PARTY ON !

My being complicit in the drug abuse, the destruction of America, and the murderous sport of Prison Wars all showed corruption. But it wasn't my worst compromise of decency. That happened on one of our rare visits back to Malibu.

With the outset of Prison Wars it was amazing how quickly going to Malibu went from heaven, to not being fun, to being hell. Malibu was the same, but we had changed. We really didn't belong there anymore.

Melissa's attempts at intervention always came as a sort of pleading. It was ugly. She was trying to let Quentin see that he was over the edge. I knew it better than I would let on. My reluctance to fill her in on the juicy details of our madness was, of course, because I didn't want Quentin and I to get in trouble. But I was also trying to protect her. It hurt me to see her in such pain.

For Quentin's part, he went from lying to defending his actions. He did so out of a feeling that he could get Melissa to appreciate who he had become. But our becoming more and more deranged not only failed to win her over, it convinced her that we shouldn't see the kids anymore. Not being sane, her telling us we couldn't see the kids didn't register and we kept coming.

For my part I kept a lame balance between the two. I would support Melissa's arguments to the point where I felt I was in danger of being associated with nagging. I would back her up on the idea of spending a couple of nights there to relax. But Quentin's addictions were now talking. He was going back out for more. There was really no point in protesting.

The final night of our residence at the Malibu home it was raining. We had been up for days, doing interviews, rallies and organizing events. We were practically living in the Skybar and other similar venues. Quentin all of a sudden decided that he needed to see the kids. He needed to sleep. He needed to see his wife.

More and more often our infrequent discussions happened with her in the driveway with her blocking our limousine from entering the driveway. On that final day, she didn't meet us in the driveway. Happy about our luck, we decided to go into my guesthouse and do a line before we spoke with her.

When Melissa came into the guest home, Quentin was doing that last preparatory line of speed.

"Don't you understand?" Quentin's level of hysteria being tantamount to hers, "I am happy. For the first time in my life I am doing exactly what I want all the time!"

"What about the kids?"

"What about them? I want them to be happy. God, if they could find their power and have half the moments that I've had, I'd be glad to know them. I am bigger than anything the world has known because I have accepted myself. I wish that you'd do the same."

"Quentin you're sick!" This was Melissa's common, accurate and useless observation.

"I'm healthy. I'm finally healthy! You remember that weak-ass quack motherfuckin' spiritual trainer I was seeing forever? He was right. I needed to find out what the real me was. I got in touch with my inner self."

"Quentin, why do you always bring up your spiritual trainer. You are . . .

"My inner self isn't pretty. Oh no. It wasn't easy to look at. I'll admit that. But now I know who I am. Did you know that weak motherfucker, my trainer, couldn't even have sex with his wife, let alone do a strange woman he wanted to have sex with."

"But you have sex with strange women as often as you . . . " Melissa seemed near breaking. It was apparent that her distress had gotten to the point where our behavior was going to break her. Again, it was ugly.

"I am a man. Can't you see that baby? You should respect me more. Respect me for the man I am!"

She didn't say anything, except, a nearly inaudible, "Oh." Then she turned to leave the room. Then she hesitated and stood in the half open door red as a beet, but not crying.
"Quent," she was staring of him so vacantly that I don't think she could see him. And yet, Melissa had so much love as she said it that I nearly cried. "You aren't Quent anymore. You're not the sort of person I want around my kids or in my life. I've told you that before. I'm going to get a restraining order on you."

Quent yelled. "Then you're rejecting me. You're rejecting the real me. Remember that! I didn't walk out on you. You kicked me out."

She was still stony and cold as she said one of the most generous things I've ever heard said, "I loved Quent and when he's back I'll take him back. But I don't want *you* to come back here anymore."

"My spiritual trainer was right." Quentin kept screaming. "He always pointed out a discord between myself and my potential. Now I see that you were the..."

"No, don't!" She finally screamed with a shrieking rage that released a thousand demons. We were stunned and silenced by her scream. Then recomposing herself she bid her final salutations with dignity and love we didn't deserve. "Good-bye Quentin. Good-bye Marty." At that she left.

My thoughts were blocked out with a buzzing sound in my head. I was somewhat relieved to hear her being able to show a sense of calm at the end. She needed to end this. I hoped she would find peace. I hoped she would heal from all this. I really cared for her. Seeing her upset wasn't easy for me.

"Wow." Quentin said moments later. "I guess I'm really free now. I want another line. I need a drink. That was too much."

Then he asked something I'll never forget. He looked up at me with a sullen boyish curiosity and asked, "Did you see the way the wind chime behind her sparkled right when she yelled?" My stare couldn't have given a hint of a response. What was he talking about? Was he completely out of touch with the magnitude of what had just transpired? Had he no more empathy?

Reeling and stunned, I just agreed, "I could see it reflected in the table."

I was silent for a while. "What!" Quentin said in annoyance. "Why are you giving me this silent treatment?"

"No. Nothing." I gave a blasé shrug. I didn't want to alienate him during this time of tension and potential trouble. But I was still overwhelmed by the end of his marriage and what Melissa had to be feeling. Each of these encounters with Melissa hurt me. I cared about her. But this one was so over the top that I was dizzy and in pain.

"No nothing? No not at all," Quentin replied with a little energy. "You're my friend so I'm going to tell you like it is. I am not playing around when I say that I am a devotee of Les Christensen. It takes a lot of courage to believe in what he teaches. Maybe more than you have." I gave him a tough, hurt and challenging stare to claim my resolve. "Women and men are fundamentally different."

"Can they live together then? Or must we kick them all out of our lives and leave our children to be authentic?" I was showing my muscle.

"Wow! I can't believe you've understood so little. But I know you respect me." He hesitated and looked me over as I nodded. My affirmation was enough for him.

"You'd better respect me. I've done great things." Now he was a little hurt. "And I honor you for being honest with me and standing up to me and not being a peon. That's a reason I like you. But get me straight. I am not insane and not an idiot. Men and women can live together. But somehow we have to renegotiate the terms. We have been over feminized and the men's movement has been coming a long time."

"I've gotcha and I respect you Quentin. I think you know that. What stuns me is just how strong you are and how much you've changed. This was a mixture of accusation and honest admiration. "For me to be macho requires very little. I'm single. There is no one for me to hurt or be accountable to. My bravado has a lot of bravado in it. Yours is real. You stuck to your philosophy even though it really hurt someone you love." He checked my eyes for sarcasm.

"I'm completely floored and convinced of your sincerity and toughness."

"Good. Stay that way. Let's not be half-assed about our true sentiments Marty. Let's be honest and feel our power."

"If I can live up to it, it sounds righteous."

"Believe me you can. If I didn't see that in you already, I'd have dropped our friendship a while ago." At that Quentin slouched over and did a line. "You used to be a timid nerd. How many women have you had in the last three weeks?"

"I don't know, uh..."

"That's right! You don't know. You know what that means don't you?"

"Uh-hu. I know *exactly* what you're talkin' about."

"Uh-hu. You're a player!"

"Player deee-luxe."

"Player dee-luxe WITH GUSTO!"

Our ritual fun bond was back on track with the obnoxious 'player' language we had started using. We both had to move out of the Malibu home permanently. Quentin was off the leash and over the edge.

Immediately after the big blowout with Melissa, we went back to the Skybar and picked up Sindy and a few of her friends. She was happy to be with us. She asked little except to be used at our discretion. And she gave that most essential ingredient to men's well-being, touch.

About two nights after that Sindy got dumped with much less turmoil than Melissa had occasioned. Quentin simply told her that he was bored of her. The management at every bar told her to stay away from us. He was the paying customer. Such establishments take care of their exclusive clientele.

On some level I think leaving lots of women helped Quentin feel like leaving women was no big deal. This helped assuage his guilt over Melissa. Sindy reminded him of his infidelity, and that put a damper on his fun. On another level, he was just getting everything he wanted. And if he could have threesomes or foursomes or whatevers, with totally new women every night, why would he limit himself to just one tramp?

After that, we spun down with double the ferocity. It wasn't just that we were after fun anymore. We were running from our consciences. We used drugs and women to this end.

And the women were as bad for us as the drugs. This was due to the type of women we spent time with. Their type, unfortunately, confirmed our dark image of humanity.

The women we chose were always nihilists at the same level we were. Nearly all had issues of abuse in their backgrounds: Little stripper-chicks and the like. None had the intellectual power to ever challenge our abuse. None had even half a notion to do anything but plead for another line or another limousine ride. As I have said before, the users that got used were already tragic users.

"You know all women are whores." I remember Quentin cryptically announcing to me one night. When he said this he had a woman on his lap! She shot him a dirty look but said nothing.

I was in his world and completed his thought, "Especially those that want a home and children - the ones who want a quality pimp daddy." We were reading the same pages. We both did our obnoxious "Uh-hu. You know *exactly* what I'm talking about."

"But as long as you are paying for everything, they don't mind giving it all up whenever you want it." Quentin was smiling broadly when he said this to her. They immediately started making out.

I smiled and gave mine a light and tender hit on the chin and said to her, "that is as long as you don't call them whores." I didn't think Quentin heard me. But at that, while still making out, he shaped his hand like a gun, pointed it at me, and shot it.

Our corruption had to do with drug abuse and it also had to do with women. As soon as I finished saying you can't call them whores, I dropped the one on my lap off to do a line. But both problems were ultimately ones of morals. You can see it in the fact that a man who was once married and happy with a family made the statement I quoted above. You can also see it in our relation to women generally being about physical stimulation.

Quentin and I started binging and womanizing like few debauched public figures in history. If you live like this without a sense of caution, like we did, you eventually have to get caught. Our first bust turned out to be quite lucky from our perspective. Had we been caught with the large amounts of serious drugs we were regularly doing, all of our lives would have turned out much differently.

We got caught in a car, leaving a party, with pot and mushrooms in the glove compartment. We had left the home just in time. When the police entered the party they found even more illegal substances. The arrests resulted in really heavy lawyer fees and jail time for some folks. Since we used a lot of cars that we borrowed from our many friends, and this car was not ours, we successfully denied that we had any knowledge of the mushrooms being in the car. We said that we hadn't been inside of the party that we were outside of. We got out on bail.

We were sure that Les would be angry as hell at us for compromising his big world view encompassing agenda for the enjoyment of a few sordid drugs. Being a hero of druggies, most people would never guess that Les hated drugs. Though he kept his severe hatred for drugs from us at this time, we knew he didn't hold them in high esteem. His strategy required that we believe he was sincere in his admiration for the life we were leading.

Right after getting out of the police station, we went to meet Les at the hotel. We were shocked when we entered the room. Les was sitting on the couch behind a large mirror with numerous large lines on it. Les even did half a line. He said it was only half a line due to the fact that he'd been up partying for days. In retrospect it was obviously a lie. He didn't really party unless it was necessary. It was a bonding gesture. Like pigs at the trough, we appreciated it.

We were prepared for Les telling us that we had messed up the movement, that we were not taking it seriously enough. We believed that Men for Manliness was important, but it was his program. We were determined to continue with our partying. And we were prepared to tell him that if we were going to be an embarrassment to him he could control Men for Manliness himself and we would otherwise cease to publicly associate ourselves with him.

When we finished our lines, we were surprised to find that not only wasn't he angry about our drug bust, he was really fired up about it.

"You guys should be allowed to do whatever you want to do and I will never be ashamed of you. It's the system that is persecuting you that should be ashamed of itself."

Les was a rebel rouser. And he used his logic and mediocre acting skills well. We were both aware that he was manipulating us as if we were a crowd and we were proud of it. Besides, we wanted to be told doing drugs was all right.

"That's right Les. We're not the guilty ones. They are!" Quentin was a big fan.

"And now," Les announced, "we start our revenge on the system that wronged you, that limited you."

"But how are we going to do it Les?" I wasn't sure what he was thinking about, but also aware that I was now playing a role in some scheme.

"You guys know I'm all about democracy. Let's turn the hypocrisy of drug laws into the basis for a democratic revolt."

"Democratic revolt! I like it." Quentin enthused.

"And that looks like?" I cautiously queried.

"Crowds. Crowds. Crowds. We're going to have a smoke out tour called the 'Days of Wine and Smoking' tour." Les was beaming.

We spoke about it all night long. If we get enough people involved, there is no way they could arrest or issue tickets to everyone. We decided that we'd like Freddie to be involved. 'No one fucks with Freddie's posse!' and 'Let's have a revolution!'

were two things I said that night that became slogans of the movement. Freddie got credit for those popular catchphrases, but I made them up that night. I was scared, but excited. I was out of my mind.

Les brought tons of media to our hearing. Our sentencing day for marijuana possession was hot news. After receiving and paying our fines, we held a press conference in which we all admitted that we smoked marijuana right outside of the courthouse. We did it with glee. We made standard arguments for legalization and then we announced our tour.

The tour was incredible. We did sixteen cities. In all of them we had lots of bands and lots of parties and lots of drugs and lots of women. I remember one night in Cleveland I had two females sucking me off as I did a line and smoked a joint. In Vermont I had sex with four bisexual women in a hot tub with a view you wouldn't believe. We were always in the private rooms of the most exclusive clubs.

Furthermore, our political successes were unparalleled. More than the Prison Wars, our smoke-out tours gave us a national mainstream following. Celebrities spoke and smoked at all of the shows. We were on every television show. We were the news and entertainment media.

At a preordained time in the show (usually nine pm) everyone in the park would have a pipe loaded or a joint rolled and in their mouth. And we would all smoke simultaneously.

It was always an amazing feeling. It was a spiritual space totally separate from the rock concert itself. It would, of course, be dark by then. Then some of the greatest musicians of our generation would start tittering on their instruments in a way that never failed to cast a spell of incantation. And as we approached the pre-ordained moment, Quentin, Les and I would go on stage. Quentin would start things off with the ritualistic, "Its coming, its, its coming. Three, Two, One, smoke!"

At Quentin's command huge billows of smoke would be released from various sources into and through the crowd as everyone smoked simultaneously. Then the light show would kick in.

I developed some weird squeals along the tour. About two minutes into the smoking I'd introduce the squeals. They were very primal. They were sub-lingual murmurs meant to mirror our deepest common nature. I was never sure what would come out. It was as if I were channeling. As a result of this, some people on the tour started to call me 'Sub' for subconscious.

Finally, after about ten minutes of smoking and trance, Les would take the microphone. His speech was studied but it flowed with the mood really well. Someone had to take us out of our space gently. He was surprisingly adept at this for an essentially drug-free guy.

"Friends...fellows...your breath is your breath is your breathing into the possibilities...we are here...start with dreaming...know you're free...know you can...be...live...be...live...we can be free...control yourself. Control your own self....control yourself...control yourself, yourself...we can be what we want to be...free...no limits...free...to...be...who...we...breathe...like a wave...that will...we...shall be...what we will to be...we...can...be...free...we..can..be..free..we, can, be, free. We can be free."

Often the crowd would join him in what could have been a chant but by way of mood ended up being a chanted whisper. At this point we realized that every breath was a breath of liberation and defiance and self-government. Then Les would blast us out of it by yelling with the crowd, "1, 2, 3, THIS IS DEMOCRACY." Quentin would then grab the microphone and say, "Ladies and gentlemen, the Clone Dolls."

And at this, Freddie, Les, Quentin, the band the Clone Dolls and assorted musicians would start into a raucous version of an old marijuana anthem. It was Dylan's old hit with the chorus, 'everybody must get stoned."

This made the updated old hit (no pun intended) a hit on all the music stations. And, as much as that hit has been a popular anthem before, no one who wasn't there can gauge the effect that song had when we sang it on that tour, in a group, in defiance. Young and old, black and white, successful and lower class; we were all united. It was a great feeling of brotherhood.

We made huge amounts of money on this tour. The DVDs were huge. T-shirts boasting "We can be free", "Be free", "Breathe", "Control yourself", "This is democracy," and "We can" were big sellers. And the television rights to the live finale brought in over 45 million viewers. We had advertised, "come be a part of the revolution." And now the revolution was televised.

On the final night, we played on the lawn of the main mall in Washington D.C. At the bewitching hour people all over the United States turned their televisions up loud enough that they could be heard outside. They grabbed a pipe or joint and headed outside.

In some areas, people were alone, except for their neighbors that witnessed them. In some areas it became a block party. Many were recruited to smoking the weed for the first time. Many were feeling the thrill of being able to smoke publicly for the first time after a lifetime of hidden smoking. All around the nation people smoked together, listened to Les and sang the anthem.

Again, it was a bonding moment for many of the citizens of our country. These people felt like they were part of a community again. They had collective power to remake their nation without appealing to Washington types with big bucks. We could have the life we wanted.

The powers that be were bested. There were too many of us. There weren't enough cops in the country to stop us. Out of the closet and proud, Marijuana finally gained its rightful mainstream place in our national life. Marijuana smokers had had their revolution.

Les was a genius. It had happened.

To indicate his true character, I will tell you something Les said during the Days of Wine and Smoking tour. All around us party lifers were constantly laughing, screaming and giggling. Les would have none of it. He hated people that did drugs! Most of you won't believe that psychedelic Les didn't like drugs, but he didn't. He once said that, "Fun is for people that don't have meaning."

If you were going to talk to Les it would have to happen early in the evening. On off days he was nearly always gone by five o'clock or so. He drank a taste of liquor and faked inhaling some intoxicants in order that he might mingle with those he needed to mingle with. After that he'd go to his hotel room to sleep the effects off. His goal was always to be sober in the coffee shop by 7:30 so he could read until midnight. We'd often see him there reading as we went up to our room. We didn't bother him as we knew he was trying to hide from us.

I also remember him once announcing that, "No original thoughts come from this crowd." He made snide remarks like, "Ahh the accumulated wisdom of humanity." "You won't find half a thought in this whole room." Comments from Les such as this were common. Books had, I suspect, always come between him and relationships with other people.

But the discussion I most remember having with him, reflected ideas that I think are pertinent to the purpose of this account. I know they reflect the main themes he was reading about as he built the movement.

"Les old man, whatcha drinkin'?" I often used that appellation when he seemed to be off temper or isolating himself. It was a gentle chiding to get him to be more sociable. Sometimes, it shocked him back into sociability. On this occasion it did not.

"Drinking? Drinking? You know what I'm drinking? Coffee. And, I know what you're drinking, cosmopolitans."

"No. No. Les. That was last week. Now I'm drinking Daiquiris. Cosmos are so very last week. That's why I'm checking in with you, for an update. You haven't been very sociable lately."

"Oh. Sorry. I've been working on the documentation of a theme and it's sort of obsessing me."

"Okay then. I correct myself. Hey old man, whatcha thinking?"

Les smiled and began. "Marty, do you know the difference between Buddhism and Christianity?"

I shook my head and did what I had learned to do in school: I took a stab and waited to see if it was right or not.
"Different Gods?"

"No. No. The word 'God' doesn't even translate across cultures. You can't use that word in relation to both religions. Actually I shouldn't even use the term 'religion'." Les proclaimed in exasperation.
When Les sensed that I was being put off by his gruffness, he often modified his tone, because, I think, he liked me. He liked me because I was the guy that had the patience to try to understand what he was thinking on the tour. I was the only one of the entourage who had (at least at one time in my life) taken ideas seriously. And, I think he, like many scholars, was a bit lonely. He relished having someone to teach.
Realizing I was being nice in talking to him, he got patient again.
"No. One is prescriptive and one is descriptive. That is Christianity describes what one should do and Buddhism prescribes how one should do things."
Seeing us together always made Quentin appear. It wasn't jealousy. It was a chance for camaraderie that made him appear. He'd probably been making his excuses and his way over for minutes.

"Hey guys, mind if I..." Les' eyes made a slight roll by way of lowering his head in a way that I only think I've seen Les do.

"Quentin." I said, perhaps smiling too brightly in an attempt to keep the gel of our triad from being strained, "Do you really think you have to ask? Les was just telling me about the difference between Buddhism and Christianity. So put on your thinking cap."

"It's on firm." Quentin said this with a wiggle of his head. He was quite a comedic drunk. His looseness of jaw as he wiggled his scalp told me he had gotten off to a running start with his evening of drinking.

"Yes. The difference that interests me is their structure in terms of being manuals. If you were to look at them as manuals, Christianity has very little in the way of specific instructions."

"Jesus came to get rid of the old laws didn't he?" I exclaimed. "Score one for the bar heads.

"Precisely. He reduced the whole structure of the religion down to vague commandments, "love thy neighbor.' Yes, but how?"

"That's the sexy commandment!" Quentin's interruption was inappropriate and, worse yet, he was stealing my material.

"Precisely again. This commandment has no content. It is telling you what to do, but not how. Theravada Buddhism, and to a lesser extent Mahayana Buddhism, really give you precise guidelines to achieve parallel aims. How to work on ones breathing and thinking processes is spelled out in great detail in their texts and traditions."

"There are kinds of breathing?" Les' reaction to Quentin's first comment was kind enough that I hoped this one would be received well too. But it was clear that Quentin wasn't following the thread here. The astonishment was ad hoc. He never wanted to know much more than the action plan. As I've noted before, Quentin was adverse to theory.

"Yes Quentin, my boy, there are kinds." Quentin didn't like people speaking down to him. I guess this had happened a lot in college. His not reading much and perhaps his success had likely informed his negative reactions to condescending tones like the one Professor Christensen had just displayed. I predicted a bad reaction.

"Well that's all nice and all, Professor, but what has that got to do with a hill of beans? Where's the beef and show me the money! My time is money and my money is time. And I have a lot of money, but not enough time." Les and I both cocking our heads at the same time with impatient glares put Quentin back into his seat.

"Without history one has no sense of time. Your life is short, nasty, and brutish." Les announced proudly.

"But, as you were saying." I intervened loudly to forestall this getting ugly. "You don't think that Christianity gives us enough in the way of practical guidelines for living."

"And the result is the hill of beans we're sitting on." Not expecting that to make sense Les continued. "The reason that we are so able to manipulate the public is that they have no mooring. Christian civilization is pliable because it has no roots, no instructions."

"That has historically been a good thing." I countered showing a challenge to bolster Quentin's interest via sparking confrontation and opposition, in addition to demonstrating some interest for Les' sake.

"It has been a good thing, in terms of our being fabulous inventors and protean – able to change easily. It has been destructive in terms of our being open to manipulation by demagogues. There are no established reasons or even traditions, especially in Protestant countries, that act as brakes on such mob behavior." Les' point was simple to understand really.

"This hearkens back to Jesus just saying 'do it!' Without reasoning." I checked to see that I got his story correct, as a good journalist should.

"Christian methodology. Christ's saying, "love someone," without reason, without a realistic possibility of or method of application, is a weak palisade against those who would twist the popular imagination."

"Yeah. So I never could understand what the hell it was that Christians would have me do. And now I see why. It was Jesus' fault as a teacher. God I love this guy." Quentin put his hand on Les' hand and Les blushed.

"Yes and that is why we are so successful. We're in America, the least traditionally bolstered culture in the weakly bolstered West. In Asia, they would have deep reasons and understandings of their place in nature and the family structure that would mandate against such behavior. Aristotle was right about the training of a person via molding behaviors. But he was wrong about that being a sufficient basis for building a moral civilization. Reasons, assumptions, matter."

"You really believe that cultures have histories that make them who they are and do what they do?" I asked.

"Of course! That used to be common knowledge. Now days people…" He started into his anger mode, but didn't want to go there. So he became calm and moving his hands out to his side with his palms up, he changed moods. "Yes. That seems fairly obvious and basic to me."
"I was researching a comparative study of the frequency and cause of mob violence in different cultures when I heard of Prison Wars. My research aimed to show that our culture has

more mob violence and different reasons for it than other major cultures.

"In fact, I'm still researching it, but thanks to you boys, I have, as Quentin would say, something more productive to do."

As Les finished his sentence raised his glass in a successful attempt to turn his last sentence into a toast. I could sense the subtle sarcasm in Les' statement. He had disdain for the circles he was running in – even for the world he was running in.

With that Les announced that he was getting tired and going upstairs. We tried talking him into one or two more drinks. But he, per usual, protested that drinking too much would interfere with his morning reading.

Les often used a confusing subject to forestall our attempts to keep up with and, thereby, stay with him. In this instance he said he was reading Dostoevsky's Brothers Karamazov for confirmations on his observation about the need for enslavement created by Jesus' love of chaos.

What would a couple of drunks say to that? His brushing us off in such a complicated manner wasn't necessary. We always got distracted by some mischievous situation after a drink or two with Les. Then we'd naturally go our ways and he'd go his.

As Les shuffled away, Quentin said, "That was fun," with a slight edge of insincerity. "Let's go up to the room and see how the party is running."

I said "yes," but then hesitated, as something was still nagging me. "Quentin, I'll be up in a minute. I want to catch Les to ask him a couple more intellectual questions." The word 'intellectual' was meant to dissuade Quentin from joining me. It worked.

"Have fun! See you upstairs." Quentin said as he stumbled away.

Les was very surprised that I had pursued him. "Marty!" To what do I owe this encore?"

Somewhat scared, I asked the million-dollar question. "Les. I know that you don't respect or enjoy the party scene. It makes you sort of miserable."

"No Marty, no," Les said by way of apology, "Only I have so much work to do in the morning, so much reading and so little time these days. I love your party scene."

"Les! For once, be real about this. I'm drunk and I probably won't remember what you say in the morning, so just be honest. You don't like what we do! It makes you impatient and cranky. So why? Why are you involved in Prison Wars? Really."

"Really?"

"Really."

"You're right. I am against partying and all things Dionysian. It reeks of sacrilege. I am very bitter about the state of the West, which you as a 'partier' represent."

I was sympathetic and trying to pay attention, not get offended, through my drunk. "But, then why?"

"Because my studies have led to conclusions concerning dynamics in Western history. And I still have a love for the West - if only for what it was. And, I see the extremes, the weakness of our culture. But I also see its strength. And I want to help it."

"By planting seeds of chaos?"

"Yes. I have looked at the timing of mass movements. I have looked at the fall of decadent Rome and Athens. We need muscle to survive. And it may take a temporary destruction or disruption of our culture, if we are to get back to a macho- a war like, competitive state.

"And if Prison Wars pushed our current enervated ridiculous parade of a celebrity consumer culture over the edge, if it destroys it, well hopefully it will have happened while the culture still has the strength to recapture itself.

"If I pushed this culture to its final conclusion ten years from now, the culture wouldn't be able to recover. People need to stop being idiotic and ruled by politeness and bureaucrats and televisions, by remote control, while we still have a semblance of memory."

"Wow. That is a big plan."

"Yes, ironically, via inoculation, I am trying to save Western civilization.

"Look, trust me, I am an historian. Don't step outside of your role. What you're doing, the partying and all, is very important."

I buried that exchange. He left to his room and I stumbled off to a party. I was amazed to learn what was really happening. It brought up a lot of questions. Verifying his calculations should have become an obsession. But I didn't have the patience or inclination to pursue them. I was often high and intellectually lazy.

Anyhow, if I brought it up again upstairs, who in the party room would understand what he had said? Besides that, I knew that if I told people, it could undermine this fantastic voyage. So I decided to trust Les, and to do my part with more gusto than ever.

Perhaps I just took the easy way out. I know I did. At this point I wanted nothing more than to keep surfing on this hedonist wave.

I primarily considered myself late for the party upstairs. And clawed my way back to the party like a drowning man trying to board a lifeboat.

CHAPTER ELEVEN – WIPE OUT

Prison Wars made us famous and important. The 'Days of Wine and Smoking' tour made us ubiquitous. It brought us to the attention of a whole other demographic. Now there was nearly no age group or type of American who hadn't heard of us.

Quentin and I were mostly on mainstream celebrity gossip type shows. But we were also regular guests on Freddie's show and other youth style shows.

Les was rarely on trash television with us. He mostly went on serious broadcasts. Les was much more comfortable designing and holding debates about cultural policies and his lack of a love life did not make good titillation.

Yet, via his bombastic and outrageous style, he actually managed to turn formally serious news shows into trash talking venues. And this spread. More and more of the thinking class pundits traded in insults and outrage.

And, though Les became a vocal and highly public spokesperson for Prison Wars and Men for Manliness, he always publicly held that he was representing the views of Quentin, Prison Wars, and the drug tours. He often used our antics as illustrations of his points. Thus he worked trash and political editorial broadcasting simultaneously.

But even when he wasn't on gossip programs with us, I got the feeling that he was somehow involved; he was watching over us, writing the script for our appearances.

One memorable appearance we had was on the Woman for Womanliness founder Linda Kellor's television show. One appearance in particular, many people have told me, may have been the one that most marked her transition from run of the mill advocate and host, to a full-fledged trash advocate. Of course, being transitional, the show started like just any other of her celebrity interviews.

Linda was asking me about Prison Wars and its morality when none other than Sindy Lieberman jumped up from the recesses of the audience. I was totally stunned. Quentin seemed a little angry, embarrassed, and shocked.

"You're a son-of-a-bitch! You won't even return my phone calls anymore. I thought I meant something to you Quentin." Sindy reeked of sleaze.

Linda, not moving from her heavily cushioned chair, was the first to respond. Her fake reaction of astonishment made it obvious that she knew this was going to happen. "Were you betrayed by Quentin?" She guessed with apparent surprise and concern.

Sindy, like the rest of the people that Les put into media was angry and adamant about the injustice of not having her desires met.

"Did you just play with me? We were faithful lovers for nearly a year. Did that mean nothing to you?"

"A year? We're you faithful to her for nearly a year Quentin?"

"We'll, no."

"You said you were." She pleaded.

"Marty," Linda addressed me, "Did he say it?"

At that time I could remember thinking to myself that this whole thing had to be a set up by Les. Within a second the question, "Why did Les do it?" was quickly replaced with the question, "what would Les do?" Then it hit me. I knew how Les wanted me to play it.

"He said it!" I revealed as if it were a reluctantly divulged admission. Quentin shot a hurt look at me.

That's when I shocked him, the audience, and myself by getting into the spirit of things.

"He says that to lots of women. That's why Quentin, my brother, is a player. Player Number One."

I put my hand up for the acceptance of the high-five coronation.

Quentin put his hand out and I slapped it.

"Uh-hu. Uh-hu. Player dee-luxe number one." Quentin chimed in, both relieved and realizing that we had rewritten the rules of the discussion.

"With gustovation." Quentin slanged.

"With gustorado." I upped.

That encounter marked a turning point for me. After that time, I found myself being like a little mini-Les. I imagined that Les created the situation with Sindy as a sign of faith in me. Whenever I could, I put a little of the intellectual backing, drama, and spin I thought Les would appreciate on the moment. I made my responses deliciously witchy. I felt the power. I became way more vocal. This gave me a feeling of belonging that I previously hadn't had. I had a role and it was important. I was sort of Quentin's private Les by proxy.

"Quentin you bastard. You betrayed me?" Sindy again pleaded.

My having taken the offensive, Quentin now took the offensive. "You got played by an expert player little girl."

"Ya!" I chimed in, "You didn't get betrayed, you got played!"

"Uh huh, uh huh." We affirmed in victory.

Up to this date Linda's show had been like all the others. People were accused of being bad people and the audience joined the accuser in righteous indignation.

Most of these shows featured a somewhat respectable host and guest that were shocked to find out what happened. And, aided by the host, the respectable type led an inquisition against the immoral person using the judgment of the audience as a condemning jury.

That's why Linda's next action was such a shock and a turning point in our culture. She, the hostess, took the side of the evildoer. Linda Kellor took Quentin's side.

"Girl, you look a little too old to be shocked that a big time player like Quentin Longus wouldn't play with you."

"He said he loved me." Sindy pleaded, expecting the typical audience sympathy.

"And that you'd live happily ever after?" Linda jumped in, "Somebody get the retarded little girl her Daddy. Quentin how many were you playin' when little miss innocent was getting hers?"

Quentin looked at the camera with a seriousness that was meant to hide the fact that he'd been largely faithful to Sindy when they were together.

"Dozens. You know, I don't even really remember her."

"My God, but you are a player. You probably could service a lot of women at the same time." Linda looked at him with the look of a salivating madwoman. It was the only time I ever thought of her as attractive.

"Was your name Sindy?" I was being mean and hurtful. "Sindy, you're a little cup skank. You're welcome for the party. I just hope that you gave enough to deserve it."

Linda piled on, "I hope you did - A chance at Quentin Longus. Well, well, well, you are a lucky little girl. But you're an ignorant little girl. You should be thankful and instead you show resentment? I can't say I feel anything but a sense pity and sense of amazement at your ignorance and ingratitude. You're a whore and you don't even know it." Hosts had not previously spoken like this.

"She's not alone." I created humor by donning a mocking news anchor editorial voice. "I just wish that people would grow up and mature and be hypocritical about being whores - no more." As I knew les would want, I tried to work a slogan into the conversation that could spread throughout society.

"You're too kind and too funny. To be blunt, she's evil and a kill joy." With that Linda led the first ever audience booing of the moral party on a television talk show.

Deep in my heart, somewhere, I'm sure I felt bad for Sindy. She'd been betrayed and used. I'm sure that Les talked her into airing her grievances publicly. Linda's reaction being so perfect seemed proof. The boos of the audience were prompted, after all, by a sign in the studio. I had done Les' bidding without any prompting. Sindy was a pawn in a big game and she got hurt.

After that show, Linda's shows often featured laughing at people that had been victimized and cheering the victimizers. Those who ripped people off, who hurt people intentionally, got high-fives and accolades. What had been a source of audience censure received praise. From that time on, much of morality was reversed on television. And while life imitates art, this was television, so it was even more powerful.

We thought that we had really accomplished something. We had had a profound effect on the country. Our party lives were legendary. No one could tell us 'no' as nearly all of the culture now supported us. It was an amazing adventure for a boy from Nebraska. It was the highlife. I was the highlife.

Walking down the streets you would often see 'Number One Player' and 'I am democracy' shirts. For a short time "hypo ho no more" even became a t-shirt. We thought we had reached the pinnacle, but it didn't stop there. We were also a part of another televised revolution. We had, in fact, just started.

Freddie, taking a hint from Les, announced the start of Bacchanalia Fridays. Every Friday, when announced on his show, people were to go out into the streets and do whatever drug they liked.

This was a step up from the hippy dippy marijuana tours. It was time for civil disobedience with hard drugs to happen nationwide weekly. We weren't sure if it was going to work. We weren't sure that Freddie's network would air calls for mass drug use. But Freddie told Quentin and I that he was doing it regardless of what the networks thought.

Freddie said we should go on his show and have a long conversation about the drugs we liked and which ones we were going to do immediately after his announcement. We joked that our being on his show would give the movement a "big shot in the arm."

Freddie claimed the Bacchanalia Fridays show as his idea. But, I'm not so sure. Such strategic choreography was trademark Les. But Freddie was sharp. And it was becoming hard to tell where Les' philosophy of excess and releasing the desires of society left off and the culture's autonomous momentum began. Perhaps Freddie was just following in the spirit of the evolving times.

Freddie admitted to doing the hardest drugs on air. He reminded the audience that he was already under arrest and so had nothing to lose by saying everything he wanted to say - Prison had made him free. Quentin admitted occasional psychedelic use and using amphetamines (without specifying which) for work. I played the straight man. I said I only smoked marijuana. My using the term "marijuana" was a nice bit of sarcasm. Every indulgent drug user knew that no person who smoked marijuana called it that.

One of the first callers to the show, probably a plant, after our announcements set the tone with, "Though I don't use hard drugs, I respect your right to do what you enjoy."

Freddie replied, "Right on Sub. We all got a freak. I respect your respecting my freedom and rights. And now," said Freddie turning to the camera as to speak directly to the home audience. "We have a special guest. A friend of mine and of ya'lls, Professor Les Christensen. Professor Les, what up?"

"Hi Freddie." Les was beamed in. I saw him in the monitor. He had one of his tweed professorial smoking jackets and a matching dark brown tie. "Hello, Mr. Longus. Hello, Mr. Sanger."

Les' surprise visit on such a lowbrow show confirmed his having had a hand in this idea. We were surprised, but not shocked. "Hello Professor." We said in unison with broad smiles. It had been a couple of weeks since we'd seen him.

"You and I done rapped about this here idea before I announced it. And you got some interestin' insights that I totally agree wit'. So lay on the folk what choo tol' me."

"Well Freddie, we have to realize how racist all drug laws are. Forty percent of black youth are incarcerated for drug crimes at some point in their lives."

"My first time to jail was for that shit."

"And that is wrong. And the drugs that the courts penalize are chosen on the basis of the races that do them. White folks, I know you don't do crack, but you do smoke pot and do hallucinogens. You do cocaine. But those drugs are not as heavily penalized, not coincidentally, as hard as crack cocaine is. All drug laws are racist.

"You white folk that do just as many drugs and were a part of the Days of Wine and Smoking Tour, yet you are not in jail in the numbers that the minorities are."

Les did not talk about the counter argument that relied on the heavy sentences for meth amphetamine that mostly white users used. We had discussed this very subject with him, so I know he knew about this literature. He was engaging in conscious demagoguery. He was ensuring minority participation. And, at the same time, he was framing it as a social justice issue for liberal sympathizers.

"And viewers, even if you don't do hard drugs, I think that you should do whatever it is that you do in solidarity with your minority brothers that have been penalized for enjoying their lifestyles. And while you may not use the same drugs of choice, you certainly appreciate diversity. Stand against the oppression that unjustly imprisons the black man and oppresses you. Standing up against racism is standing up for your rights."

"Right on. We appreciate the solidarity." Freddie seconded.

"We're all men." Les was not done. "I am worried about this action however. We are standing up for our freedom absolutely. The police, because they are racist, hate diversity, and don't understand rights, are against some drugs, may not turn a blind eye to this party. They may come after you because of your solidarity with the black man."

"I am not worried about the black men so much, as they are already tough. But I want the white man to get tough enough to defend himself. For this reason I instructed all of the Man for Manliness branch leaders to instruct their squads in the use of firearms and some martial arts."

"Damn. That's a plan you've got goin' on there!" I said, sporting a hint of white boy black talk and thinking that it would be what Les would have me say.

"We are men. We are not going to be bullied. We, as our brothers incarcerated for their choice in drugs, will have to get tough to protect our freedoms. We believe in non-violence, but as our most macho and successful president, Teddy Roosevelt said, you should walk softly and carry a big stick."

Les was a master of propaganda. He had used the light hippy-esque drug tour to warm the nation up. With guns and hard drugs, this was a considerable escalation.

"But don't worry about anything. If we have solidarity, the cops will be totally outnumbered and our party can go ahead unimpeded. There is strength in numbers." Les concluded.

We all said goodbye. Freddie did some shows where he showed his fighting techniques. Gun sales soared. We repeatedly publicized our hope that no violence would erupt and thereby surreptitiously put the idea that violence was possible in the minds of the police and the people. We hoped that the media barrage and gun sales being in the news would quiet the cops into submission. Quentin and I had camera crews follow us into a West Los Angeles firearms store and into martial arts training sessions. We were with the program.

It worked. Again, we relied on our old crutch of there being safety in numbers. Police cannot enforce laws against mobs that greatly out number them. But we also felt that our new militant feeling was crucial for our success. People were doing all kinds of drugs and nearly no one went to jail. Everyone had a great time. In the one place where the police tried to bust up a gathering, California's Berkeley – Oakland area, the police got chased out by repeated gunfire that caused them to entirely evacuate the area. In one night we had accomplished the local sovereignty that the legendary Black Panthers had failed to create in decades.

Liberation!! It was a night to remember. Quentin and I were joined by lots of celebrities. When the news of our squad's success was added to the realization of our national success, the nation had a party. We were empowered. Democracy felt great. We had our rights back. We were free!!

The level of our penetration of the American cultural scene was now undeniable. Bacchanalia Fridays became huge popular street parties. But, it wasn't just about the drugs; the people of America were also changing. Whereever you went people now aggressively talked about rights, freedom, the tyranny of laws and the smallness of the government.

Beyond the raw empowerment and freedom that people were starting to feel, there was also a sense of public unity that was sweeping many in America. This seemed to be a great thing to us. Americans were going from being passive consumers to being active citizens – active in public.

And to the extent that there was unity in America, and the groundswell wasn't all bottom-up. We were its acknowledged leaders. Whenever a city needed a boost for its anarchy, we would announce we would be there that Friday.

We had the times of our lives. We would go from city to city and be met at the airport by the famous and their entourages. They would take us to exclusive parties and we never lacked for anything. We'd be celebrated publicly at the witching hour. And this would launch the night into more parties that ended up in us being given all the free drugs we wanted and having large orgies. We never had to carry drugs. The world was our party.

When we did interviews it was mostly about our interactions with other celebrities and our adventures. Our party life and credentials gave a sense of realism to our interviews. Everyone wanted to know us and who we knew. Our lifestyle was our message. It was the envy of the nation. We were only too happy to lead by example. We knew that Les couldn't do our job – so we did it.

But this started to become too dangerous for us. Everywhere we went, airport security would check us and recheck us. This was okay, as we didn't ever need to carry drugs. But it did become a hassle. In the center of the celebration, any cop that tried to touch us would have been lynched. But the police intrusions into our hotel rooms and having our limos stopped all the time began to wear on us.

It didn't matter. We were public figures, and the public itself had woken up to its strength and dreams. Huge bacchanalia parties were going to happen weekly in nearly every city in America with or without us. Large parts of many cities were becoming anarchistic zones of lawless freedom. We started to back off on our public appearances.

One place of long standing retreat for Quentin and I was a specific home in Pacific Palisades, near Malibu, from back in the old days. It was the home of Stephanie Hirsch. This still good looking woman was in her early fifties, wealthy, and divorced.

Stephanie had cultivated a circle of young musicians that she was promoting as rock stars. It was a somewhat strange scene. She and her other middle aged friends wanted to be teenage groupies. But not knowing any real rock stars, they went to Hollywood and found aspiring young studs to cultivate.

These young guys would sleep with their patrons and lived great lives, mostly funded by the women's ex-husbands. Everyone was hip. No one worked.

Some of the aspiring rock stars were just disgusting. Casey was one such kid. He had the look of one who had only partied for years. Though twenty-five, he looked thirty. That was *the* look. He had dyed his hair so many times it seemed to be a wig and his clothes were expensive but uncared for. He screwed old men for the clothes that he had and the cars that he drove. He literally smelled. But he was good looking and sang for a band. He was in.

Others in Stephanie's circle were actually talented. There was Stevie with the big red afro for example. He had some songs that seemed to be hit material. They were catchy. But he was aging and he never wrote anything new. He didn't have to do that until he was famous, so he just lived off the songs he had written in his teens.

This was a scene of promise that kept folks from growing up. Slowly time was making these dreams unrealistic, but the old women provided enough enthusiasm to blind the rising star struck men as they deluded themselves. Drugs added to the illusion. It was a creepy and self-deceptive mutual admiration society.

I think that Stephanie's being older and having all these kids around, kind of made Quentin feel like he was in a home. And this home accepted him unconditionally. The women that came through were a little older than our normal groupies. Stephanie didn't like the competition and the reminder of her age that younger women brought. Though immature, these divorced women were not as vacuous as the younger groupies. But the women were into being used just the same. They were stabilizing without being intimidating.

Because Pacific Palisades is located next door to Malibu we could have worried about running into Melissa. It was so close to Quentin's – or Melissa's - home that he could have gone over there in minutes. But that wasn't much of a concern. Except for high profile parties and media excursions, we left the house less and less.

This home probably saved our lives. It slowed our partying down. It gave us stability. We had everything we needed there. Quentin started playing saxophone with young Stevie's band. We swam and used the tennis court to convince us that we were healthy. We were taking a lot fewer drugs than we took on the road. But not a day went by that we weren't very high. We had lots of people over to watch Freddie's show with us every week. Every day was still bacchanalia day for us.

Meanwhile, Les hit the airwaves harder than I had seen him hit them in a long time. He was everywhere. He was doing the same work we were doing, but he was doing it on a different level. He appeared on news shows with men in suits. We hadn't seen him in a while, so it was good to see him when he was on.

I remember the first news show in which he tangled with Senator Burke. His nemesis had come to debate the morality of public drug abuse and lawlessness. It brought a smile to my face to see Les still had a razor sharp ability to use his favorite technique: the element of surprise.

"This is a nation of laws, not of men." Burke proclaimed. "If we do not have laws, chaos will ensue, power will be king."

"Senator who built this country? It was heterosexual men." It was quintessential Les.

"What does that have to do with anything?"

"What you are proposing is a deliberate attack on the heart of the traditional prerogatives of male individuality. You are arguing for a weakened, emasculated, order following, passive view of the citizen."

"I'm not talking about any such thing." The Senator should have been advised that trying to bring Les back to the topic was only ceding the floor to him.

"We're tired of it. We're tired of the attacks on heterosexual men. We built this nation! Our macho nature is what got us free from England. It wasn't effeminate law following, clean men. This country was founded by rough and tumble heavy drinking heterosexual males."

"What? You're mad. You ought to . . . " Burke's outrage only made folks listen harder to his logic.

Les continued and the camera followed him, "You lawyer types want us following orders and staying cute and in control. This country wasn't built by laws and lawyers and will rot if it's taken over by such men. I say it is the prerogative of every male to take what he wants when he wants to."

"Sir there is a sense of community standards." Burke made the mistake of using an argument he'd used before.

"Community standards are to protect women and I will protect my women myself. But, you want a country of genteel little rational half-men that are protected as if they were women." That was the first time in modern memory that the phrase 'half-men' had been used. Freddie's famous song using the phrase came later.

Then Burke used an argument that had been gaining credence in liberal circles. "Without law we will have lynching again. Do you want that?"

And whereas Burke recycled the past, Les came up with new arguments.

"Lynching had its merits. It sure as hell was better than keeping criminals on the street forever and giving them rights who eventually get off to enrich lawyers like you. And yes, innocents were hung. But how many people get hurt by criminals you've gotten off?"

"Fink? Colakov? Anyone? These are white-collar criminals you've gotten off. And let's not mention Garcia. Defending a man who sodomized and beheaded . . ."

"This doesn't have anything to do with those cases. We are here to talk about the lawlessness you encourage."

"I am the true advocate of community standards. Not your pussified version controlled by shyster lawyers like you. If someone does something I don't like, I take care of it myself. And if you want to stop me, you try. But, I will kick your ass if you try to come between and my prerogatives. If you keep defending pigs, I will kick your ass and you will *know the law of my foot.*"

"I won't speak with you anymore, you're insane."

"Run away coward. Go tell someone else what they can do. But I tell you, street justice is good for the community."

"Well I guess that ends our interview." The man in the metallic suit said.

"Well he's probably gone to get the big bad men in the law to protect him. He is going to sue me for violating morality codes. His kind sickens me. Do you let people tell you what to do?"

"Well, I try to stand up for myself." The announcer said defensively.

"Damn right you do. I respect you."

"I respect you too." The announcer ended.

Les was a bad ass. How much of one I hardly knew. I thought that all was fun and games and that we had completed our story. We were back in Pacific Palisades and having days of fun and parties and resting on our laurels when Les came to visit.

To the extent that his efforts were successful, Les found more and more reason to be self-confident and arrogant. Cranky and impatient with small talk at the best of times, he was getting to where he resented nearly everything anyone said to him. But he was still haltingly nice and respectful to us.

When we saw Les in the corner of the coffee shop we nearly galloped to him. "Hey Les! How are ya' man?" Once we were fully seated, I said what Quentin and I were both thinking. "Man you look like shit."

"I'm tired. I'm tired from working so hard."

"Why? Why are you killing yourself? We've got everything we've ever dreamed of. What could you possibly want that you don't have?" Asked Quentin. I had had a hint about the answer to that question.

"I'm missing my two big guns. I could fight better with help from you two. Where have you guys been?"

"We've been resting and enjoying our spoils. Les, you're relentless. Don't you ever just stop and enjoy?"

"Yes, come partying with us for a night. Relax."

"Partying is immature. It's embarrassing for men to act like boys." I know no one who knew the public Les would imagine he'd talk like this, but he did. The public arguments were part of a calculated act. We had known the real Les for so long that we didn't even think to bust his ass about the disconnect between his public and private thoughts.

In fact we respected Les for it.

"I guess people are maturing later these days." Quentin took Les' remark personally, as he should have. And it was interesting to notice that, of all people, only Les could really scold Quentin like this and get self-reflection rather than attack. Les was like a father figure to Quentin.

"Or not maturing at all." Les had too little tact for his own good.

"Oh Les why are you so against having fun and relaxing? You're so hard on yourself." I tried to calm the rising tension between the two.

"Fun is for people that don't have any meaning." Wow! Had Les come to fight? He was on fire. Something was wrong.

Quentin asserted himself, "How do you know that meaning isn't for those who refuse to have any fun?" He would have gotten wild approval for such a clever turn of phrase at any of the parties he'd been to in the last months. Not here.

"Because I have read. I have been through history. I am not of this age. Fun is a very recent and unsustainable basis for values – for a society. I am a being of wide perspective. My world is a world of historical battles. Haven't you figured that out? I know enough to know. And, frankly, I'm disappointed that so few others know enough to have any common sense or sense of the big picture.
"Parties are stupid and meaningless. The people who engage in them are mutes. Marty, you remember our talks, certainly you know what I'm talking about."

"Sure Les, sure." And then after a bit of Les staring down at the coffee shop table, I tried to reach him again. He was so sad that we forgave his antagonism. "But Les, I'm worried about you. We're going to a really good party tonight in Malibu, come with . . ."

"Parties won't help!" Les exclaimed hitting the table "Your parties are no longer doing anything for us on a theoretical level. If you don't understand that participating in your culture makes you passive and stepping outside of it makes you active, you're lost. Individuals don't create cultures, cultures create individuals.

"I need to think, not drown my ability to think in booze and chitter-chatter. That way is death. Parties are not an idea that I find worthy of entertaining at a time like this. The answer will only come through thinking. And it seems that you guys can't help me with that at all." Les was screaming. He seemed on the edge of a breakdown.

We hung around with a lot of sycophants. Les was one of the few people we felt we really knew. As corrupting as he was, as insane as he was, he himself was not corrupt. We always trusted him to tell us the truth. Quentin would have stormed out of meetings with anyone else that was as direct as Les was to us. As the only other true insiders to Prison Wars, we were very intimate with each other.

"Les . . . Buddy." Quentin offered compassionately.

"I'm sorry guys. I've been over worked lately. I love you guys and appreciate everything you've done for me, for the movement. But we've barely begun. We've gone nowhere."

"Really?" I asked with a self-satisfied grin that quickly turned to curiosity.

"Really." Les replied with bemusement. "Really and my top guns seem to have gone AWOL on me."

"Come by our house," I offered, "so we can discuss our next plan of action."

He nodded happily. Les knew people and played them well.

The third round of Prison Wars games was a total surprise to us. We knew only that it was going to double as a Bacchanalia night. This was done in order to unite the three groups of followers we had thus far assembled.

The first Prison Wars crowds had been republican-style macho yahoos. Marijuana smokers weren't really the type that went to sporting events. But, starved for an event after the month of silence that followed the end of the 'Days of Wine and Smoking' tour, the second Prison Wars games had been filled with stoner, slacker youth types.

But it was Freddie and his gangster followers that made Prison Wars demographically explosive. A mix of red necks, stoners, and gangsters can explode. To help stop problems from brewing, we made posters that showed our three demographics, with their vices smiling together. The captions said, "Don't judge, party."

During the third Prison Wars game, Quentin, Les, Freddie and I recreated our Smoke out act. It was phenomenal. Drugs bonded all the categories.

The contest was amazing. The contestants dressed as Cowboys and Indians and used bows, arrows and hatchets. The lack of modern guns meant that there was a little less blood than there had been at the first two contests. Les had told me, "Extremes aren't yet average." Our being joined at the end on stage by the new criminal stars made it look more like an award show and even less like something of consequence.

In front of the crowd, Freddie plugged his television show and said that the victorious criminal stars were going to be on his next show. Rather than participate, Freddie was an MC at the third Prison Wars games. At the end of the event, in this capacity, he made a surprise announcement that brought democracy to a new level. He was reading from a piece of paper that I later found out he and Les had typed together.

"We meet here without any problems. Black, white, Latino, Republican, Democrat, rich and poor. People would say that we would have some problems with all of these people here together. One hundred police, not including the normal one hundred Prison Wars guards, are here watching and guarding you. But they didn't need those pigs. There wasn't no problems from the crowd.

"We kin govern ourselves. This is democracy.

"We kin govern ourselves. This is democracy.

"We kin govern ourselves. This is democracy.

"We kin govern ourselves. This is democracy.

"We kin govern ourselves. This is democracy." The crowd cheered.

"But during the contest, there was a problem. But it wasn't our problem. The police arrested seventeen people on drug charges."

"I stand with 'em.

"I stand with 'em.

"I stand with 'em.

"I stand with 'em.

"I stand with 'em.

"I stand with 'em." The crowd laconically followed the chant in suspense.

Freddie, was getting into it and lifted his arm up in the air and made an angry face as he made the final repetition.

"I stand with 'em."

"We as a people are sick of this oppression. I'm mad as hell and I smoke green. I demand my right to control my own body. I'm mad as hell and I smoke green. I'm sick of this oppression.

"They took those people into their police state. But I say ain't none of us free unless we all free. As ya'll leave this stadium, my friends and I are going to walk the six blocks to the police station on 21st and Leroy and demand the release of our friends and get them out.

"Are you with us?" Freddie didn't get enough response and so asked again.

"I said, Are you with us?"

"Yes." This time the whole crowd yelled.

"Are you with us?"

"YES."

"ARE YOU WITH US?"

"YES!!!" This was unity!

"Let's go. Let's go. LET'S GOOOOOOOOO."

With that the crowd went wild and the evening went off in a direction that I had not anticipated. The crowd marched to the police station. There were at least ten thousand of our people there. Les, Quentin, and I, all watched this on television from our sideline stadium suite. What everyone wanted to know was if the police would attack or not. But they hadn't had time to gather a sizable force together.

In front of the station stood one obviously shaking and nervous policeman with the seventeen suspected drug arrestees. As our crowd approached the station, the policeman spoke over a bullhorn. "We are releasing the seventeen suspects and don't want any trouble. There are men with weapons on this roof but we don't want any trouble. Please disperse, we don't want any trouble."

The camera covering this event panned up to show about thirty policemen hanging over the top of the building's roof. Then a man whom I never saw again, took the bullhorn from the policeman. Les didn't speak along with this man, but I am sure that he could have. "Prison Wars is a war against all unnecessary prisons. Drug laws are not necessary. You better start releasing all those on drug raps or next time we'll storm your prison walls and let everyone out. And don't you fuck with any of my friends here tonight or there will be hell to pay! We don't want to see your pig asses for the rest of the night."

"Let freedom ring. Let freedom ring. Let freedom ring."

With that, the crowd joined him in the chant and then left with the suspects without resistance or shooting from the police. People were elated. The crowd walking away smashed quite a few windows. And some looting took place, but no policemen were to be seen.   In some cities more looting happened than happened in ours, where the event had actually taken place. But, again, no police were to be seen.

This evening scared the hell out of me. The stand-off had been intense. We saw it on television, but could feel the power in the air. I had become afraid of democracy. I expressed my concerns to Les.

"Jesus. That was huge."

"Historic." Was his reply.

"Yeah!"

"We'd better get out of the building. I'm shaken."

"Why?"

"Can't they get us for starting a riot? Won't they shut down Prison Wars? Won't this destroy everything we've worked towards?"

"We, my friend, had nothing to do with that riot. Freddie started it. Freddie can't be arrested, he's already under arrest."

"That means that he's free to do whatever he wants." Quentin explained the obvious.

"The irony."

"And don't you worry your purty little party head about nothing. They won't stop Prison Wars. You know why? Cause we're not the only ones with an addiction. There are too many big players gettin' too much out of Prison Wars to shut it down. The State needs this money to pay off their massive debts. There'll be controversy and hand wringing by politicians. But they're all hypocrites. Sitting ducks for attacks, cause in the end, there is no way they'll get in the way of this big of a money maker. They literally cannot afford to.

"Being broke the State really has no choice but to continue to support Prison Wars. We'll throw them an extra 5 percent of the revenue and they'll shut up. This strapped government is our whore. We don't have to fear going under now. No. Now we go on the attack."

And while this speech could have been delivered with the passion of Dr. Frankenstein pleading with nature for the monster, Les said it all in calm deliberation. A laconic, 'check mate' would have followed perfectly.

Never resting, that week Les started his foreign policy.

"We must be strong. If we don't get used to killing, we cannot maintain our liberties. Liberties come at the hands of violence. War is a necessary component of a free society."

Les was always ahead of where I thought I was. He was saying that our military could take on and dominate any country we wanted to. It would solidify our country, give our men back their sense of power and enrich us. We could start off taking over a country that had oil and thereby lower our gasoline prices.

"Wars of conquest will erase our deficits, they will pay for everything. But they will do much more than that.

"Those who do not embrace violence are slaves to the powers they cower under. We must break limits just for the sake of breaking them. The destruction of smaller countries will be the start of our omnipotence. One must hate other countries because by their very existence they implicitly challenge you to a fight. Men understand that. With our military there is no reason we should not dominate others. They would do the same to us if they could. We can't let them. Why don't we fight?

"Are we not men?

"Are *we* not men?

"Are *we* not men?"

Les led his television audiences in chants that I am sure they mouthed at home.

"War has always been the key to economic freedom and power. Don't let the mealy mouthed bankers tell you otherwise.

"That is why they launch us on wars. But they do it for nation building and to stop bad people. They never do it for conquest. Why? Because that way they get to keep all the money. And rather than identify as killers, our military identifies as do gooders of the nanny state. They get the money and they control us.

"We want to go to war for our own reasons, for our own wealth, for a sense of common national power. We want conquest!"

"Are we not men?"

The following week Freddie announced that he was going to start monthly sex tours. "We goin' city to city on Freddie's party train." Freddie's party train was going across country, city by city, and ignite public orgies. The sexual ethos was starting to seep into the drug filled weekly Bacchanalia nights as well.

Les had come to see us, to get us out of semi-retirement, to lead these tours. Along side Freddie, we were the headliners. This brought in black and white demographics and kept the tours from being about race or divisive. The sex stops were amazing. Even I, grand partier that I had become, had never seen so many naked bodies.

The police were too uncomfortable to go into the areas where the orgies were. This movement was unstoppable. The first city the police showed up in the participants removed all of their clothes. Of course, it was caught on tape and played over and over. But why watch the tapes when it is coming soon to a city near you?

People tried to stop it. Senators spoke of amendments to the Constitution. Church groups complained. And when they did Freddie had them swarmed by orgiastic naked folks. The fruition of Les' aggressive tactics had become second nature.

Freddie's first television show after his sex tour featured an unusual set. Freddie still sported one of his sweat suits, red this time, and gold necklaces, but he was in a newsroom set. Instead of the couches, he was the anchor of a news program.

"Ladies and Gentlemen. Thank you for tuning into the greatest show ever, *your show*, the show of the people, Freddie's democracy.

"We gots ourselves a news format today because we have a superstar trio, me included, assembled to talk about very important issues. Lotsa people been attacking us. They've been sayin' that I'm aginst women. They've been sayin' that my show, our new movement isn't healthy for women.

"To talk about this I have assembled the two smartest people I know. They are the representatives for movements I truly believe in and good friends too.

"Les Christensen represents Men for Manliness and is also, as you know, a co-sponsor of Prison Wars. Linda Kellor gots her own television show and represents Women for Womanliness.

"We gonna talk some talk and we gonna talk about some action too.

"Welcome."

"Thank you Freddie."

"Thanks Freddie."

"So what do you think about what's happenin' in our society with the men and women and all...?"

Les began, "Men for Manliness is a political movement and we demand that the people are recognized for their power and rights. And amongst our rights is the right to do what we want to do with our bodies."

"Linda, what about this claim that women are against this new movement?"

"Well Freddie, its crap and my ratings prove it. Women don't lose power by this new movement. They gain it. Prostitution is a legitimate way for us to make money.

"Men are horny, maybe I take advantage of them. But if men want to pay me for sex, I'll take it. Of course I'm rich now. So I buy men.

"But I like sex either way. And sex with drugs, it's my birthright."

"You go girl." Freddie cheered.

Then Les took over as anchor and announced, "A Senator Ed Burke has started calling for a halt to all Prison Wars activities. He wanted to outlaw Men for Manliness as a revolutionary group."

"I'd like to see that." Linda snickered in her airless style of laughing.

"He ain't the law," Freddie said, "We the people are the law now. He got nuthin'."

"You know," Les put on his angry macho tone, "You know, Burke will try to cut off our balls with law to make us genteel and weak men. But we kicked the crap out of that type of man with the birth of Prison Wars. Men are becoming tough again. We are taking back our freedoms."

Freddie added, "It's like the fear that the power structure's got of the black man. They always trying to control him and talking about his sexuality and tryin' to keep him away from white women." Freddie and Les had been having some talks. "We're sick of this sort of racist fear and control."

"Exactly, Freddie," Les riffed, "And that is the same reason our nation is so in debt. We are afraid to fight other nations because these wimp politicians want to keep us in cages. They are scared of our power – people power. They know that if we win wars against other nations, the men who fight the wars will be hard to control. We'll fight for the booty and get the booty."
"Fight for booty, get booty." Freddie sloganeered.

Les continued, "We are sick and tired of these moralistic suits passing laws and pushing cops in our faces. Who are these people? These are the folks who have ruined our nation with lawyers and debt; their debt not ours. We don't need to be controlled by them. They built the debt to control us. With war we can get our credit back and take the nation back. Its time that the government trusted the people – of the people, by the people, for the people."

Linda concurred, "And we are sick of the attacks on the manliness of our men. Real women have nothing to fear by having powerful men around. The macho warriors will bring us things. Soldiers are hot. We have fun together. And no pinstripe or badge should tell our men what to do. Our men will take care of us with booty. And our conquering heroes deserve a little sex when they get home.   Men who fight in wars are hot!"

"We have identified several Senator's offices in each city that are fighting our movement. These people will not push us around anymore. We will not stop doing drugs and we will not stop expressing ourselves, and we will go to war with anyone we damn well please and take the booty. We will not be held down by these pinstripes anymore."

"Go to the Man for Manliness website and find your local target. On the next Bacchanalia night we'll attack these Senators and TV and radio stations that are trying to stop us."

Les pushed hard for crosspollination. He pushed hard to get Freddie's hit "That's what men do" to be Linda's television theme song. His efforts brought generations, genders, and races together in a way that they'd never been before. They could all agree on pleasure and freedom being good and Les knew it. And, the new promises of wealth and power through war brought the entire cauldron to a boil.

At the Fourth Prison Wars Senator Jim Kirk announced the Freedom Act. It removed all television censorship, eliminated obscenity and drug laws, and removed of all restrictions on the hours that alcohol could be sold. For good measure it even made prostitution legal. Such a law would have been totally unthinkable only a few years early.

And he announced that he'd be running for president as, a "War and Party" candidate, in the 2024 elections.

Between Freddie, Prison Wars, Women for Womanliness and Men for Manliness, and the new war theme, Les had transformed the culture. Men had become more debased, more leering, and stupid. Women that didn't dress sexily were likely to get their clothes ripped off for being hypocritical whores. And no one was arrested or confronted for such things anymore. People were having sex in the streets, snorting and smoking drugs publicly. People used the word 'war' more and more often. And violence pervaded men's very posture.

Les was speaking more and more like a prophet on his television appearances. And he still pursued small subsidiary goals like having three day weekends and making it harder for women to get into college than men because they will work fewer years and contribute less to the economy.

But, beyond his particular ideas, Les was becoming more and more mad for power. Since the day that he met Quentin and I in the Pacific Palisades coffee shop, I could see the small flourishes when he seemed out of his mind were growing in length.

On one of the final days I ever saw Les, I told him that I was scared of what was happening and what he'd become.

Les grew enraged as he yelled, "I am the prophet of liberty. I have rekindled the violent bloodlust that sparked Achilles revenge for Patroclus – that set the West on fire. I am the lightening out of the sky man come to shatter the weak puss-filled minds of the legions of blind consumers who suckle like so many blind slimy baby rats at the teat of mass media."

"Only the lobotomized army of mass man fears pain and death. They alone run into the womb. I will bring pain that will bring life. Man must again grapple blind in chaos, do war with his destiny. All must endure Prison Wars as modern man's suffocating prison of comfort swaddles him death in a soft glow more horrific than any fire. Hate is a truth we need to be alive. We need conflict in order to think again.

"Apocalypse now or death! Rivers of blood must wash the trash and trifles from the eyes of the shadows. Rivers of blood must sweep the blinders away. Storms of blood are needed to thin the herd! Real blood must flow.   Death will bring life. Torrents of real red blood must drown modern man! I am an ax murderer and it is time to wake up!

"I want to invade your home. I want to kill your family. I want blood. Real blood! Does that scare you? Great! Go with it. Don't look for comfort or escape. Don't run from the power. I used to think with my head, now I think with my blood!   I used to know what I was doing, now I have given over to my potential!"

Those of you that only know Les from television have seen him be humorously rude and snide, but not really angry. We all know he is an extremely intemperate man. But after this diatribe, I was sure that Les wasn't just angry, but mad!

Quentin and I were fueled by drugs and parties. Les was propelled by concepts. His years of solitary study had given him an underlying bitterness. Success made Les ever more obsessed with his ideas and intolerant of dissent. And his fame added a sense of power to his thoughts. Increasingly his innate cruelty and certainty of purpose propelled Les, and all of us, toward a rendezvous with destruction.

CHAPTER TWELVE – JUDGMENT DAY

The Culture Wars didn't start with Les. That phrase was common coin for a decade or so before Prison Wars. But Les adopted the term for his own means. He played the Culture Wars game in a way that no one else had. Other professors had noted the dearth of positive powerful male role models on television. He took it to a new level. He understood that you had to bring men to a boil slowly. He couldn't have started with sex tours, war, and intimidation. He had to back in slowly.

Taking up Christian issues was a part of his strange-bedfellows strategy. He managed to get gang members and Christians together. The Supreme Court decided that it couldn't get in the way of community standards (ie, hatred). Most Americans were rubbed the wrong way by the idea that a community (mob) wasn't free to determine what was in its own best interest. And though Les had Christians and gang members unite against portrayals of gay men on television, specific targets ceased to be the issue. The Christians liked Les' macho rhetoric, and now they had a target they could perform their masculinity on.

Les was always folding the momentum of his previous movement into the next one. The smokers, turned into the druggies, turned into the freedom mobs that then went for total social liberation based on being macho, then war. He then organized marches on politicians that tried to stop him and television studios that portrayed men as weak. He then pulled large segments of the Christian community into the movement over gender normality.

"Real men are macho" shirts should have scared me. But I somehow wasn't totally scared until the attacks on gays started. It intimidated all of those on the sidelines. He had attacked politicians and police and the system, but he'd never attacked a particular demographic before.

Of course it started with politicians. Politicians that wanted a spot on television's number-one shows were quick to repeal all hate crime legislation. Those who went against the current got attacked, physically, for being anti-male. Now the true horrors were emerging.

My first hint concerning our ultimate destination came when Les stopped talking about liberty and freedom and started talking about hate. The idea of not being able to have a gay-free religious boy scouts bothered a lot of people. Les was the first to say that gay men were an insult to real men everywhere. "We straight men created this country and deserve to determine what it looks like."

And then Les' debating on the basis of the historical record just turned violent. "Why do we have to look at the embarrassing and humiliating specter of faggots all the time? We straight men built this nation. Straight men are superior and I'll punch the shit out of any fag that wants to argue that. In fact I'll punch the shit out of anyone that says they are gay." And then he unleashed the mobs on media that didn't comply.

By that time the road was clear. Anybody that didn't help was suspicious. Everyone marched to Freddie's new cat calling hit song, "half-man." Anybody that didn't hurt others was considered a source of weakness in the culture. War was the future. Violence was inevitable.

History is a lesson to those who think. And World War Two let me know that scapegoating doesn't usually stop with its first victims. First they came for the gypsies, etc. Safety was already only to be found in conformity.

Les was educated. When he started using the disease models he knew what it implied, "We need to keep our country free! Having our boys constantly exposed to gay role models weakens us. Effeminacy is a disease. Every boy should fight. We need to ready for war. We have to guard our culture against infection." He was taking all his material from Goebbels. Unfortunately, no one remembered Goebbels anymore.

To my credit, I resisted following Les once I saw that he was starting to fold hate into the concept of manliness. The attack on gays, though popular, threatened people I had known. I told him I couldn't be a part of his campaigns anymore.

Les then told me that he had always known that, deep – down, I was a half-man. "I'm sure that is why you are against this movement. You've never been as tough as Quentin and I." Acting like he had the power over life and death, he continued. "Don't worry I'll protect you half-man." It was one of the creepiest things I've ever heard. It let me know that I had to get out of his sight quickly.

Our triangle broke at its weakest point. I was able to pull Quentin away from Les. Quentin was less turned off by Les' new moves than I had. I didn't ever really confront Quentin about the ethics of Les' new violent tactics. We just disappeared together into drug use. Drugs were the excuse I used to get away from the mess of everything. Quentin floated away with me because we were attached by history and, even more so, our common drug habits.

And, frantic to escape the anarchy that had enveloped us, partly driven by guilt, I went head long into another nihilist tailspin. Only this one didn't have a soft landing.

We went back into days of fucking and doing drugs night after night in party after party. We found twenty-four hour clubs that we pretty much never left. Nothing around us challenged our view of life. In fact, the general culture encouraged us. From advertisements to media, to the general mores of society - all told us that we were the crème de la crème. We had the good life: Parties, women, all of it. Only this ride was not televised. We had fallen into a black hole.

The things we were looking for were hollow and boring. It was all based on sensory stimulation. The rush of seeing a woman sucking your private member, the rush of a drug, of crimes gotten away with – what it all speaks to is an emptiness that needs to be filled. Complicating matters was the biological fact of rising tolerance levels: Seeking rushes leads to satiation and ever-greater escalations into darkness.

I never studied ethics, but I think I now have a deep understanding of corruption. Once Melissa's name came up. Quentin was barely able to walk when it did. He said that he wanted to play saxophone. Then somehow he transitioned to Melissa just before he passed out. He said that he had outgrown her, "boring ass." Families can be boring. Families can be boring. But they also provide caring and connection. Fun had become the only thing that mattered.

Near the bottom of my personal corruption pit was the idea that all people are just objects to be used. They exist for your pleasure and fuck 'em if they can't get you off. And you truly hit bottom when you realize that you yourself are just an object to be used for stimulation. If you are only something that gets stimulated, are you not a lot like an inanimate object? Getting of for what? Nothing. For whom? No one? There is no one there. Three are only a series of physical sensations to be had. Shocks. Jolts.

Our crew became unsavory. It seemed that they got younger and younger and sleazier and sleazier. They reflected our character. Casey, who we knew from Stephanie's home came back into our lives. The more he looked like a male version of the beaten whore, the more attractive he was to the men that supplied him. He never had a job, always looked like he just woke up and always drove a car valued at over $80,000. The American dream had found its personification in him.

Benny Beats stands out from this time because of the films he made. He always had dried drool connecting the sides of his upper and lower lips and a fedora hat. He was a heavy consumer. He used to take lots of acid and watch his own films. He was handsome. You'd never guess that he was under thirty-five years old: he was twenty-five.

Benny's films were massive creations of modern collage. Ducks and men with capes in deserts filmed with negative exposure. Modern thought is full of unrelated images signifying nothing. Society is said to be post-literate. He had a secret frustration that he explained to me; he could never be big because he could never find a story. He was unable to concoct an argument.

I remember Les speaking about this very topic. He told me with great interest, "Modern art is much more paralyzing than fascist art. Do you know why?"

"No, but I have a feeling you're going to tell me." I snarkily replied, showing a very low level of interaction skills.

Les would not suffer fools. It made him angry. "Okay lazy boy you want to play dead? Fine. But first tell me, which leaves less room for thought, fascist art's total certainty or modern art's complete failure to commit?"

I took conventional wisdom's side. "Well I think fascism is worse. It tells everyone what is wrong and right, while modern art gives options."

"Wrong!" Les exclaimed with irritation. "At least fascist art modeled argument. But the illogical nature of modern art paralyzes the ability to even concoct an argument. Fascism restricted rational thought. But surrealism causes the total death of cumulative knowledge and rational thought. It is a lacuna, a black hole, from which no mental construct can ever find grounding.

Then, spitting in frustration Les concluded, "Fascist art killed men, modern art kills man!"

Only an hour or so after Les said that, I put a hit of acid in my mouth and watched one of Beni's always-short films twelve times. I remember noticing that I saw objects that had previously escaped my attention in it every time. There was a flying birthday cake that hit a man in the face. That seemed very funny at the time. But I finally got bored. I remember resenting that Les didn't have a sense of humor. Life was fine and the film was funny.

When the realization hits you that all you know is trash you only have two choices: Go for a stronger rush or kill yourself. We charged with a ferocity that blended the two options.

The boredom of decadence consumed us. Perhaps twenty pages of details of nights of debauchery would convey the sense of ennui. But I am in the midst of the meltdown of society and so don't have time. Anyhow, you've seen it all before, if not in real life then on television.

I guess March 15th was the luckiest night of my life. Quentin, Casey, and I were approaching a party in Malibu. As we approached the driveway the creepy guy who had really upset Melissa by being in front of Quentin's house, who I had seen at the first Prison Wars, but who I hadn't seen or thought of in a long time, appeared out of nowhere. He had a camera. He spotted us and quickly got in a position to take a picture.

Quentin screamed, "Hit him!!" I was driving. When Quentin grabbed the wheel I was still stunned by his scream and, being drunk, didn't have much power to resist. The car swerved and the photographer went about three feet off the ground, hit our car again, and then went under our wheels before we hit a stone wall.

I woke up in the Emergency room. They had to sew this skin over my slightly fractured jaw back up. I kept waiting for Quentin. I kept thinking that Quentin would visit me. He didn't.

Quentin and Casey ran away from the scene of the crime. They must have been taken home by our limo service. Sam our driver and the limo people, as well as every taxi company I tried denied picking them up. The bar owner said I came in alone and that they weren't there. The dead photographer's camera had no film in it.

I was charged with homicide, not manslaughter, as it was shown that I had veered off the street and onto the sidewalk to get my victim. After knocking him over I had apparently tried to get back onto the road and might have made a quick get away if it weren't for that damned electrical pole. Attempting to leave the scene of the crime and driving under the influence of a controlled substance were also added to my list of charges.

When I hit the electrical pole there was a blackout for a 2-mile radius. They said I was lucky that the car body hadn't been touched by live wires. I'm not so sure.

I remember waking up once in the interval as I was being lifted into the ambulance. In my incoherent state I can remember thinking, "fun...this'll be fun, I've never been in an ambulance before." The next thing I knew there was a thread going through my face. I had the similar reaction of thinking about how neat the thread felt being pulled through my skin. The next thing I knew I was in a hospital bed. I didn't fully recover consciousness for a day.

The next months involved seemingly endless transfers from the hospital to the courtroom. There was never a time when I didn't have two guards stationed outside of my room. In retrospect, I guess I can understand why they'd consider me a high risk for flight. At the time, I resented my jailers.

I was truly alone in prison. My mother and father flew out from Nebraska. Not having contacted them for a long time, their presence just made me feel guilty. Anyhow, my parents are working class folk. Not having money, they had to return home after just visiting for a few days.

Not once during my stay in the hospital did Quentin, Les or Casey visit me. Not only that, the Prison Wars credit card was cut off. They were completely distancing themselves from me. That realization hurt. What hurt worse was that I deserved it. Where had I been as Quentin abandoned Melissa? I had been on the side of the deserters. So it shouldn't have been a shock and I really had no right to complain when I myself was deserted.

I had become Quentin's shadow and so had to kill his other shadow. I figured that the man I killed had been blackmailing Quentin a long time ago when he was still clean. Maybe he knew Sindy before I did. At any rate, I couldn't demonstrate any previous connection between Quentin and him. He was dead and not available for cross-examination.

Quentin's lack of shame had long removed him from susceptibility to blackmail. Still I think the sight of the photographer must have revived some deep ancient connection to a corner of conscience in Quentin. The sight of him probably also reminded Quentin of his betrayal of Melissa. This was a reminder of the limits of conscience that, at a subconscious level, probably dogged him. The bonds of conscience, in my experience, are never totally severed. Then again, Quentin might have thought that killing the stranger was a fun idea at the time.

In my nightmares Quentin and Les discussed the importance of their work and the moral nature of their not sacrificing the progress of their ideals for me. They probably used my tragedy as a source of reconciliation. They got closer by commiserating over the need for my abandonment.

In my nightmares Quentin would say, "I'm sure that Marty would have asked us to continue." They did this in a way that implied that I was dead. Les would agree that they should continue in my name. Then they would toast to Prison Wars and laugh loudly as they drank. This, anyway, was my nightmare. The reality was probably worse. They probably didn't mention me much at all.

At first, on my lawyer's advice, I plead not-guilty. That was just a way to get closer to a plea bargain. But from the first day of the trial I could see that this sort of positioning was a lost cause.

During the arraignment there was one bright spot. I was completely stunned when I saw her in the courtroom. It was Melissa. She looked stoic. She didn't smile at me. Tears escaped from beneath her dark sunglasses. I was generally too ashamed to look at her. My expression showed no sadness. I had no right to put that burden on her. I was guilty. She had endured enough.

During the trial Quentin was called to the stand. He had Les and other witnesses saying he wasn't with me that night. It became their words against mine. A professor and a mogul versus a hanger-oner. Furthermore they had the corroboration of the bar owner and several barmaids that I hadn't been with them that evening. I was going down without a pillow.

The judge would not listen to my lawyer's insinuations that there was a connection between Quentin and the dead photographer.

"Martin Sanger alone is on trial." The judge said with annoyance when my lawyer tried to raise such angles of attack for me. "We are not interested in circumstance, or conspiracies based on alleged relationships between others, only your guilt or innocence." The judge was right. I alone was on trial. No one else was by my side.

It was during the trial, as my anger at Quentin was nearing obsession, that I got my kamikaze idea. Prison Wars got me into this situation. Prison Wars would have to get me out. I dropped all defenses. For me to get real justice, I would have to get into a hardcore prison. From that realization on, I went against my lawyer's advice at all times. I switched my plea to guilty.

I stood up in the middle of the courtroom and admitted that I had done it because I thought the man looked gay. I admitted to the substance abuse, but claimed that should be used in my favor. I told them that I often enjoyed swerving at pedestrians, but that when I was on uppers I could always pull out in time. I must have drunk too much that evening. For that, I admitted, I was sorry. Not because it had resulted in a death, but because I couldn't get away.

During the sentencing, I snarled at the judge. I gave him the nastiest glare I could muster. As a climax, during sentencing I ran to the bench and tried to strangle the judge, screaming, "Politician, pawn, you're not a superhuman, half-man!" It was beautiful theatrics aimed to get Les' approbation, except that I felt so much rage pouring out of me that I nearly did succeed in strangling the judge. It was a good thing that the third bailiff had a stun gun.

I was successful. I was given twenty-five years to life in the Pelican Bay State Prison, in Del Norte County, California.

I don't know if you, dear reader, have been a part of our prison system, but it is the most humiliating thing that could possibly ever happen to you. It has takes care of your every need. Beds are provided, the guards wait for you during your medical check ups and your food choices are made for you.

By this careful preparation it strips you of all initiative. You are enmeshed in someone else's design and you can't choose otherwise. Moment by moment you are simply there to fulfill the mandates for you set by the logic of the system. I obsessed on the fact that I couldn't meet the designer of the system. It had no living designer. No human component, no individual thought was allowed in. It was inhumane. Prisons run on their own inertia, by their own internal logic.

I finally completely understood what was meant by the idea that suicide was the last gasp of freedom coming out of a man. The humiliation of being an automaton, from waking, to showering, to sleeping, was nearly all I could stand. It gave me insight into the motivation of the Prison Wars contestants. My feeling of not existing fed my obsession to fight in Prison Wars. Already being dead I had nothing to lose.

The only person I really did meet confirmed my hatred of everything. His name was Hector Las Casas, he was in for armed robbery and he was my cellmate. Hector never referred to women as anything, but "beeches." And he talked constantly about killing "Neeggers." And "Fukeen" was, as far as I could tell, a part of every English sentence he had ever uttered.

The only time I saw an expression of anything but hard dispirited concrete from Hector was when I mentioned the possibility of us having Prison Wars games at our facility.

"That's right. I'm going to get me some fukeen beeches deyn. Go out like a fukeen man do homie." He finally had an idea to smile about. People like that make me shudder. As dead as I had been, I least had an illusion of having once been worthwhile. I wasn't vindictive or mean. This man seemed to be a total cipher. He was the personification of all reasons humanity should end. I had to live with him for months.

I was lucky in prison. It could have been worse. Everyone knew of my association with Quentin, Les, and Prison Wars. The inmates had watched me on television for years and had been exposed to the televised coverage of my trial. They had dreamed of being in Prison Wars and were grateful that I had helped create it. They all admired my celebrity lifestyle. To know me provided some kind of vicarious glamour. People wanted to be my friend. My lunging at the judge also got me some respect.

Many newcomers to the prison system are withdrawn and reclusive. Their shock conveys their fear and dispiritedness. For this reason they are targeted. Not because they remind the inmates of their powerlessness – criminals aren't that sentimental - but because they are easy targets for the sport of humiliation. Despite my look of victimization, my celebrity protected me.

But I was unprotected from the insults of the immediate and all encompassing environment surrounding me. Hector's attitude was repeated in a thousand other incidents. The inmates were brutally hard, the guards were brutally hard, and the walls were brutally hard. I didn't see any smiles that weren't given for the appreciation of cruelty for months. Soon I forgot about freedom and altruism. Soon I forgot about myself. The entire world was enveloped in darkness.

My plan of revenge gently faded. If the entire world was hard, why did I expect anything else of Quentin? Even I had treated Melissa similarly. Why should I bemoan a fate that I deserved? Why should I try to stop consequences that all people deserve? The universe is a perfect reflection of itself. It is cold, hard, and impersonal. I had done enough. I decided to let it be.

We live and try to get some joy and respite amongst the degradations we all have to face. That is all. Work and eating have always been mandatory. Love and kicks are the only areas of freedom. We live and die in a machine. As I became more aware of reality I lost the need to escape pain. My commitment became a stoic one. The only way I could survive these harsh prison walls was by commiserating with them, by becoming one.

Justice is a concept. It isn't a deity or other type of material entity. I finally reasoned that it was a figment of the imagination that it was better to ignore. Fairness meant nothing. Fairness punished me. Fairness didn't exist. These thoughts cancelled each other out. Thought didn't exist. Only reality existed. Non-acceptance was illogical and would hurt me. I didn't live in a fantasy world. Adjusting to reality became my overriding concern.

I gave up all of my plans. I was going to spend the next twenty-five years of my life in prison. That was reality. If I could get used to it, I wouldn't have minded spending the rest of my life in prison. What else was there but pain?

Though less interested than ever, I was still able to keep track of Quentin and Les' actions via television. The prison inmates loved them because of how brutal they were. Everyone knew that Les was behind the Freedom Act. Quentin's theme that we should release every person being held in jail due to drug violations made him especially popular. Though mostly in for violent crimes, a large proportion of those incarcerated here were first sent up for drug crimes. If they hadn't gone to jail for drugs, they might not have learned the prisoner lifestyle. They might be free.

The alpha-males were given pride by Prison Wars. Les, with Quentin, had invoked the dichotomy of female and male. Quentin was constantly photographed with several women. Les seemed to be a better influence on him than I had been. He became an avatar of Dionysian sex and partying again. He was back in the spotlight. His partying became less dark. His uber male consumerist lifestyle was once again the goal of a generation.

But even more meaningful, to those incarcerated, was the rise of Freddie as the first criminal celebrity. He had what Quentin had, but he was also revered as a killer. The middle-class whites first aspired to be Quentin. But, it was soon evident that Freddie and his possie represented the ultimate in manliness. And, while Quentin did all they dreamed of, celebrity criminals completely validated their lifestyles.

And then Les took another step. It was something that I should have foreseen: He went racial. Of course, he picked the easy target as an appetizer, as a warm-up act.

"We have to fight if we are going to be a strong nation. Hate is a feeling we can't let go of. And even if that weren't true, it is time to start purifying our nation of foreign combatants. The Muslims know that we've been at war for over 1400 years. After 9 – 11, Mall Jihad, and the Los Angeles freeway bombings, they themselves have announced that they're our enemies. We need to get rid of every single Muslim inside of our borders."

On the day that Les announced his purge idea, Freddie announced that next Bacchanalia night would be directed at smashing businesses owned by Muslims in the United States. "They hate freedom. They tryin' to stop us. We gonna show them how real men protect their freedoms." The website promised locations near you. Jacksonian Enterprises was striking again.

That Friday night four Muslim prisoners were fatally stabbed. Three more were beaten to death with fists and chairs. The guards did not intervene. There was a new level of violence coming out of the Prison Wars. Furthermore, Muslim owned stores, and those were owned by people who looked Muslim, – namely Sikhs and Hindus – were burned down across the nation. These populations started to flee the nation in droves. The unfolding ugliness confirmed the wisdom of my resignation from this ugly world.

As a result of the stabbings, all Muslims were sent into a segregated yard; that is all Middle Eastern Muslims. The black Muslims largely disassociated themselves from their Arab brethren. This was interesting. I thought it a good omen for the nation. After four hundred years of being in America, even in prison, the black inmates were fundamentally patriotic.

In fact, as if by some sort of need to expunge their guilt or distance themselves, black ex-Muslims were amongst the first people to attack the Middle Eastern Muslims. Hate makes people take sides. They weren't leaving any dangerous ambiguities threaten their safety. They were with Freddie and America all the way.

As selfish as this will sound, the stabbings resulted in positive developments for me. After the stabbings we weren't allowed to watch television for a week. Prison officials knew from whence the agitation was coming and they stopped it. Unfortunately, the ACLU threatened a lawsuit to get television back on based on our first amendment rights. Though violence was the inevitable and obvious outcome, prison lawyers ordered the State to turn the televisions back on. Council warned wardens that there could be no censorship. Television programming became a government protected right.

The time of the television ban was a time of reflection for me. Being alone made me feel a little less like a victim. The prison was obsessed with Quentin, Les and their now violent legion of democratic clones. This legion had been like a thousand shouting devils mocking me and tormenting me non-stop. When the television was off, a sense of calm returned to the prison. My brain started generating its own topics of discussion. I noticed it again.

I started to understand my oppression. The voices from the television had drowned out my own voice. It was as if I was Gulliver being brought down by a million Lilliputian stones. Each word pummeled me down a little more until I could make no sound at all. The week without television allowed me to realize that I had lost my voice. It was during this silence that I realized that I had become a member of the living dead.

But there wasn't total silence. Silence asks questions. Remembering who I was, who I had been, and who I had been before that, was painful. A lot of emotions that I didn't want to face were there. My crimes haunted me. I could barely stand to look back. My number one question was "why?" And the answer that I always came back to was the accusing mirror. There was no escape from my guilt.

As I said earlier, the prison strips you of your initiative. There is a state of mind you develop there that doesn't have a word, but deserves one. It would denote a total stupor. You can function, get through your day, and be completely shut down inside. That was the state I had gotten into. And this state was comforting. I had died for my own sins and that was appropriate. The numbness had protected me. As I awoke, I started to have a strange experience of nostalgia for that sense of numbness. But the anesthesia was wearing off.

Realizing that I had started to exist again implied that I had the possibility of coming back from the dead. Identity implied choices and those choices implied responsibility. I wanted to hide. Hell is knowing that you have a choice.

I knew I had a moral duty to reconstitute myself. But I was far from sure of who I was. I had enjoyed my Prison Wars years. I had enjoyed contributing to evil. Could the person I might become once again be as innocent as that reporter who had just landed a job with Fortune? Might that reconstituted me have an obligation, a debt to repay that I might not be able to repay? Might a reconstituted me be just as eager to enjoy power brutally as the old me?

The new silence the lack of television brought did not bring peacefulness. Not having television was torturous.

By fortuitous coincidence another transformative element also came into my life around the same time. After about six months of imprisonment I got a visitor.

The guards brought me into the holding cell behind the visiting room. They warned me that everything I said would be recorded and that I would have a fifteen-minute limit. They would still be in my head. This visit was not to imply freedom of thought or feeling. I was not to harbor the illusion that I was leaving the prison in any way shape or form.

When the door opened, I was completely stunned to see Melissa. She didn't smile when she saw me. For my part, my legs mutinied against my mind and turned back towards the door I had just come through.

"Jesus! Melissa!" I thought and tried to escape. During those seconds several things were warring inside of me. How could I talk to someone whom I had betrayed so badly? Feelings of self-hatred cut closer than ever. Perhaps my pain was just bullshit to make me feel like I was repentant and deserving of forgiveness. She would not let me hide behind a sense of persecution. She was my wrath. She was my conscience. The shame in me simultaneously pleaded both "beg" and "Don't you dare beg."

Facing the cell door, Melissa was waiting behind me, behind glass. It was impious to turn around. But she had come here to see me. My body had frozen. I had to garner all my strength to turn my head back around to look at her.

When I looked back, she looked more empathetic than she had initially. It was like her hard look in the courtroom, but with less of a hint of tears. Melissa motioned for me to the chair in front of the window with her steeled eyes.

As I sat down at the booth and put the receiver to my ear, my head spun with questions.

"Melissa." I ventured, "God. Melissa." I continued with my head bowed to where I only saw the counter. "God. I am so sorry." "I am so sorry." I started crying. Sobbing in fact. "What the hell happened to me? I am so fucking horrible. What the hell was I thinking? I am so sorry for all the pain I ha . . ."

"Marty, Marty, Marty." Melissa gently repeated trying to stop my momentum. "Marty, stop it. Stop it!" Her voice quickly went from compassion to anger. "I don't want you to do this! This isn't about you." I continued squirming until she firmly shouted, "STOP IT."

"Why are you here?" I spoke with empathy and looked up at her. I didn't want to lose her.

"I need to understand." Melissa was strong but plaintive. Both of us were having inner dialogues out loud. Both of us were grappling to reconcile ourselves to the events that we now confronted.

She repeated my questions, "What the hell happened? What happened to me, my life? What happened to Quent, to you? What the hell happened?" She was getting more tense and choked and frantic. She shook as she continued, "I had a life. My family, home. . . What..."

Melissa was beautiful in this moment. I felt like I was looking at her for the first time. Her slightly curled brownish hair, the wrinkles next to her mouth – I had never really looked at her like this. It was as if I was seeing her for the first time.

Nervous, I decided to ramble, to say anything, to fill the space to keep her there. "It is hard for me to make sense of all that happened too. You knew me. Oh God you knew me!" At this a rush of emotion took me over and I started to weep again. Melissa remained silent this time.

"I was a journalist. I had a job." I said through my tears. "I'm sorry to feel sorry for myself."

We both sat in silence for a while. Then I confessed to the stranger, "Melissa I am forgetting who I was. I am becoming a prisoner. I almost didn't realize how much I had forgotten who I am. I'm losing my mind in here."

Not wanting to lose her patience, I selfishly said what I had to say. "Thank you so much for coming. I don't deserve your company. Thank you so much for coming even though I don't deserve it, and if I never see you again, thanks so much for coming."

We sat in silence. It looked like the visitor was going to go. She looked away and started to push herself out of her chair. Then she stopped. She sat back down and looked at me. I avoided her eye contact.

"Marty. I've hated you for a long time. I've hated what you did. I've blamed you for what happened to me. I know that Quent is his own man. I know about Les and that you were his employee. But God damn it! You were our friend. You were a part, you were a part of our family. You're a fucking pig and I want you to know that!"

We sat in silence until I worked up the nerve to apologize. "I'm sorry I betrayed you."

"I'll bet you are." My confessor shot out with the angry smirk and stiffness of someone who has taken a hit off of a cigarette to keep their emotions in. I looked down and then, after some moments of silence, she angrily recanted with a sense of shame and contrition, "I'm sorry. I'm sorry for what happened. I'm sorry for you. I'm sorry for me."

More sheepishly than I had ever asked any question I asked if she had seen Quentin. "No. Not for years."

"How are the Justin and Sam?"

"They've been sent off to a private school. They were getting challenged to fights as Prison Warriors every day in public school."

At that Melissa looked up at me with a look of pure accusation. "I can't help you, not even just a little bit." At that she got up and left.

At first I found myself getting angry at Melissa. On one level she has every right to blame me. But she could have stopped Quentin. She tried, but not overtly or early enough. She provided the home in which the corruption fermented. She obviously wasn't motivated by money and fame as we were. But her main interest being the preservation of her home and family life also gave her a self-interested reason not to stand up to Prison Wars. She could have tried to stop Quentin before he started. She could have been more forceful in her attempts to get him to quit after it started.

But I concluded that Melissa's complicity couldn't compare with mine. She just continued her domestic life. She didn't ask to be put in the situation that fate threw her into. Outside of her not acting to save the public, she was an incredibly warm and kind person. She was a responsible citizen. I actively and publicly helped Prison Wars. I became corruption personified. No one is innocent. But there is such a thing as guilty and there is such a thing as more.

Sometimes I excuse the entire world. I wonder why I would expect better from people. We are, after all, animals. I love mankind because man created civilization. But the destruction of this country shows an unforgivable degeneration. Mankind needs a sense of unredeemable guilt. To totally forgive man is to leave him too free.

People should be more aware of the blood on their hands. Smug moral judges secretly judging others from the sidelines don't impress me. They are not forgiven by their private judgment of others. In fact they excuse one as a non-participant. Pretentions of being an innocent bystander stink. This line of thought ran over my absolving of Melissa. But then I would again think of her with love.

At first the lack of television gave me the inner space to have such dialogues. And Melissa personified the long gone good person that I had my inner dialogues with. These sorts of dialogues incorporated Melissa a day or so after her visit. But meditating on her as a real person made me realize my constant meditations on guilt were self-absorbed.

I decided that for words to mean anything they had to be connected to deeds. I recommitted myself to dying for the cause of mankind. Rather than musing, my actions would argue that, despite his sins, mankind was valuable. Just as Melissa's very existence, my act of self-sacrifice would be a sign that mankind was redeemable. I resolved to put my plan into operation. Melissa became the person I thought of as I worked to stop Quentin.

One result of this decision to act is the manuscript you are reading now. For all the reasons previously stated, I felt it necessary to write this document. I wrote it in haste. Please forgive its shortcomings. But I hope that it has solved some of the mystery of what happened to our country. I hope that it can serve as a cautionary tale to any culture or civilization that is trying to maintain itself in the future. And I hope that it can serve as a token of atonement for me personally.

When the television came back on they were reporting that a gay celebrity had been shot. Gay people and supporters congregated at the site of the shooting to plea for tolerance and civility. An angry mob of men showed up. There was a huge riot. One straight man and twenty-two gay men were killed. The news showed the footage over and over again. I doubt that there will be any solidarity vigils the next time a gay celebrity is killed.

After the break from television, the horror of such an event, and its publicity, seemed starker than ever. It wasn't just another part of the daily barrage. It wasn't normal. It was horrible and it reconfirmed my conviction that the Men for Manliness movement had to be stopped.

As a matter of strategy, I decided to first focus on what Les would want. I had to find out what his current agenda was. He was on television because of the anti-gay riot, but he wouldn't talk about it. Instead Les was talking about race hatred in the guise of racial solidarity.

"Hal," Les addressed the black news anchorman with a tone of someone giving an editorial rebuttal for the station, "Black and white people shouldn't be at odds with each other. After all, they both got to America about the same time historically. Black people and white people built America. We define it."

Hal was no pawn. "That is horrible. You are saying that other groups don't belong here? This has always been a nation of immigrants. Immigrants built this nation."

"That's a lie. Everyone our age can remember when Los Angeles was a black and white city. White people were 83 % of the nation and blacks, as the largest minority were about 13 %. We have not historically been a nation of open borders. And the bummer is that white and black people had finally started reconciling, and black people were finally rising up when the Latino came in and messed it up for you.

"The blacks fought for minority access to schools, and the Latinos have overcrowded them with Spanish classes.

"White people tried to do the right thing by giving black folks civil service jobs, now you can't get those jobs if you don't speak Spanish.

"In fact all of the old jobs that blacks had from busboys to nannies, have been stolen by the Mexican invaders.

"We've got to take our country back." The night of this broadcast, thirty-two Mexicans were stabbed in our prison alone. Freddie announced that the next Bacchanalia night would be a day of black and white unity. There would be marches for borders, for taking the nation back. Neighborhoods were torched and over two hundred Latinos were killed that night.

I called Freddie on his cell phone and told him how Prison Wars could help. "We should have a Prison Wars game that featured blacks and whites together on a team against Mexicans." I repeated Les' arguments about needing to take the nation back. I knew Freddie backed this program of blacks taking back their place in the nation.

But most of all I begged Freddie to remember how bad the pen was. I told him that we needed to have a Prison Wars in which we all chanted, "We want out." He could lead the chant and then lead the crowd into prison and release all the prisoners. Disingenuously, I told Freddie that the public understood that most people were in jail for drug crimes (that certainly wasn't the case at my high security prison). If we held the next Prison Wars games at a prison site, I pleaded with Freddie, the crowd could just walk in and free the prisoners. It would be like when he freed the suspects at the last Prison Wars games, but going straight to the prison to release all of them.

And here was where I made it personal. I told him that I'd like to help him lead that chant. My being in prison after having been a known favorite with the public, would demonstrate just how wrong it was that our friends and neighbors, our fellow men, were locked up. With the public behind us, surrounding the walls, the police wouldn't dare stop the prison breaks. It would work. It would be a great day for freedom. I asked him to talk to Les and Quentin about it.

I reassured Freddie that I wasn't mad at Les or Quentin. They had to keep going for the good of the cause. No good would have come from their going to jail. I appreciated what they were doing. I told Freddie that his and Les' race theories were great.

Three days later I got a call from Quentin and Les on speakerphone. I repeated that it was ethical for them to lay all the blame for the homicide on me: it was for the good of the cause. I let them know that I wasn't angry with them. I understood that the movement had to go on. Moreover, I had been following their work and was really proud of them. Vicariously, their actions filled me with pride because of knowing what I had contributed to Prison Wars and Men for Manliness.

I repeated my plan to them. As Les would have planned, I told them about the "We want out" chant. I told them that having the games at the prison would provide the perfect opportunity for the biggest day for freedom since the Soviet Union fell. I repeated the logic that it should be at my prison so that I could represent the incarceration of those the public loves. Instead of the weak argument that most were in jail for drug charges, I gave them an argument that Les would actually buy. I told them that the release of so many violent offenders into society would immediately increase the toughness of society. It would help provide the nation with a shot of testosterone.

For added measure, I told them that I had an idea that I knew Les would love. I told him we should start a push to get prisoners to lead the nation's troops into the wars of conquest he was advocating. This would solidify the ethic of criminal as macho hero, as the ultimate patriot. And, if any violent crimes took place after the release of the prisoners, the bad results would pressure politicians to agree to commute prisoners' sentences into military service.

As I thought he might, Les went ga-ga over these ideas. They said they appreciated my dedication to the cause despite all that had transpired. The next Prison Wars would be at my prison. They agreed that it should feature me, were I still alive, leading chants for the prisoners' freedom afterwards. In fact they told me that as soon as Freddie relayed the ideas, they had started negotiating the details with my prison. They told me to start organizing a black and white team to fight the Mexicans.

The sons of bitches didn't even apologize. They sounded happy and even carefree. I could see Quentin's noxious smile and Les' face of serious consideration as we spoke. How I made it through that conversation without showing my rage I'll never know. The important thing was that my plan worked. They bought it. I was to have my chance.

For a brief period I again became a spokesperson for Prison Wars. The show was back on. To recruit I had to spout a belief in the whole Man for Manliness doctrine again. Of course, now it was in an advanced stage of development.

It was easy for me to cop our old cadences. But my rap got snagged up as I used the new racial and hate filled parts of the creed. I got choked up because I didn't believe in them, but also because these political angles, the idea of leading men into war, gave one a bigger rush than being the head of the emerging party nation had.

I would get engrossed in the power of my own sadistic voice and then stop in mid-sentence and remember. I knew the power of evil. I had been ruined by it. Every posture, every word brought back memories of corruption borne of omnipotence. Feeling the power of being a playmaker, a mover and shaker, came back again. I liked it and it scared the hell out of me.

Before, I had been playing a role to be a part of a game. Now I did it as a game with deadly purpose. I had to carry on as if I were an actor no matter what my inner inclinations.

I used Freddie's shows and Les' appearances to mobilize the prisoners. As a former national leader of the Prison Wars movement, I was automatically chosen to be our team's leader. Moreover, Les and Quentin started talking about me on television again. My leadership got bolstered when Les and Quentin announced my idea of having prisoners fight foreign wars and gave me the credit. The prisoners started to look up to me as a hero.

During this time I thought a lot about how far Les had taken television. TV used to be a source of passivity. Les got people riled when he got Kellor to make shows side with moral transgressors. But her shows still weren't directly calling for radical political changes and popular action. Les had made media a source of constant collective violence and action.

The people were on fire. Passions of the mob aren't pretty, but they are popular. And the bottom line of Les' new reality was ratings. He realized that they are more important than votes. He transmuted ratings wars into having wars for ratings. It worked. Les had instituted a new democratic sort of nationalism. The revolution was televised and it got more viewers and audience participation than any show in history.

I hated Les, but I couldn't deny the accuracy of his insight. No one could. His was must see TV.

I tried to select participants who would go into a killing spree given a moment of anarchy.

Prison life was hard. Cement walls give no love. The inmates give none either. But as cold as they were in terms of human sentiments of warmth, the prisoners still had the passions of hate and greed inside. Their desire for the good life was often based on the same hatred of the dreary lives of desperation many shared. It was a common dream of revenge that never left most people's minds.

Prison life is regimented. It has been made full of mechanical restrictions on purpose. The men caged here couldn't be trusted with freedom. They all wanted everything advertised now and were easily angered by their frustration. These men were in prison for acting on pure desire. They wouldn't settle for anything less than total freedom.

Had they had souls once? I could ask this about all of society. Their final test, unbeknownst to them, happened when I watched them watch Freddie on television. I could tell who the most desperate folks were. These were the ones who stared down to the pixel level of the flickering images with desire.

All society had become members of Les' team. My squad was a small sample of society. But it was elite in its willingness to give that last full measure of devotion. These contestants were willing to lose their lives and gain the world on the world's ultimate game show.

This is the last installment of my testament. My team knows nothing of our plan to free the prisoners via a peaceful takeover. Instead, I have told my squad that the plan is to start a riot and break out in the confusion. By way of pep talk I told them that tomorrow was our big day to break everyone out of prison. Tomorrow was our day to be men. Rather than fighting other prisoners, we would be fighting the system that made them prisoners. We were going to take on the world. Reckoning. We will be free as men or die as men. On my signal three team members were to attack nearby police and the rest were to run into the crowds and start fights. The police, I reminded them, would never shoot into the crowd. On my signal, we were finally to bring real freedom to America.

My real hope is that I can kill Quentin and possibly also have an opportunity to kill Les. If I only kill one, perhaps the other will be killed in the ensuing mayhem. Spectators will die. I feel bad about that. But then again, people that would watch or support a program like that . . . Hopefully, the guards will be able to bring order before the chaos gets too out of control. With the riot quelled and the leadership decapitated, I hope the movement will die. Les' mass purges and wars will have been averted.

I hope that after the leadership is cut down cooler headed leaders will then once again prevail. I hope the mobs will disperse and go back to being individuals. I hope that television goes back to being a sedative. Hopefully tomorrow, I can atone for what I have done; I can stop worldwide catastrophe. I can roll the clock back.

Before I go to my ultimate fate I wish to express my disappointment with myself. I should have been a better investigative journalist. As a citizen I should have known more. When Les mentioned thinkers he admired, such as George Sorel (I think that was the spelling, I'm embarrassed to say I didn't even do an internet search on him), I should have researched them. I should have been more immersed in political philosophy in order that I might find out more about Les' ultimate aims.

Even when I had 'journalistic ethics,' it just meant getting the facts right for the story, getting an accurate portrayal of whatever happened. There were no morals or judgments in my work. I covered issues, I didn't take them on. Being a passive mimeograph machine, I wouldn't have even thought to research morals. My corruption came from being an idiot.

I never studied enough history to realize what was happening. But, hopefully this intimate depiction of the rise of the Prison Wars movement will serve as a source of history for those that come after us. Hopefully tomorrow will give me the chance I need to redeem myself and our society.

Thank you for reading this.

CHAPTER THIRTEEN – BORN AGAIN

I can't believe I escaped! The chaos you know about. I killed Quentin! Well let me start at the beginning. I think I have all night to write.

On the final day, my march was like that of any other day. Everyday when I woke up I had to go through the horror of my story and situation again, realizing anew what had happened, where I was and how I got there.

Yes, I was locked up for a crime I hadn't really committed. Yet I was compliant in crime and knew I deserved my incarceration. Me! An ex-reporter for *Fortune magazine*. Me, my parents' son. Re-assimilating these realizations took the first five minutes of every morning. But was especially dizzying in the first moments of waking. Moreover, my guilt haunted me throughout the day via my very situation. There were no moments of escape from this reality.

Like all the other days, my retelling ended with the realization that I was really in prison. But today, I also had my redemption to think of. It didn't fill me with joy, just obsession. Likely scenarios played over and over in rapid succession. Some of them got all the way to my killing Les. Others just ended in my killing Quentin.

As a Prison Wars participant, I knew I would be on the field at the same time as Quentin. The middle of the field was to have dangerous objects in it. But would I be able to pick one up after entering? What would I do with a broken bottle, a screwdriver, a knife? At what moment would I make my move? I knew we'd both be on the sidelines at the beginning of the games. But I didn't know if we'd be on the same sidelines. There was a good chance he would be taking part in the opening ceremonies. Likely . . . scenarios rattled through my head.

The hardest obsession to rehearse was the one done for resolution. Would I actually be able to kill him? What kind of hardness would this take? What would his expression be like? I was afraid that after seeing his actual face I would not be able to carry out the murder. He was a wasty party boy and I had been working out. Physical strength was not an issue. But I had to do vision work to toughen myself mentally. I trained mentally so that seeing his face could not result in the slightest hesitation.

I repeated the same sentences over and over. "He is not my friend. He is my enemy. He is an enemy to mankind." I imagined scenarios where he was an alien disguised as a human. He was the devil incarnate. He was not the Quentin I had loved so dearly. If I was to do what I had to do, our hours of playing tennis, drinking, family pictures, all of that had to be out of my mind at the appointed moment. This was war. I had to condition myself.

But my months in prison were my main source of comfort. They had turned me into a very tough person. My body was now rock hard. I was sure that I could kill any civilian that looked at me the wrong way. I convinced myself that my body reflected a hardness of the heart I could rely on. There was no doubt that prison had, in fact, made me a tougher and more callous person.

I was really glad that this was to be the first game played after dark. It would greatly aid me in my attempt to conceal a weapon. I never rehearsed scenarios of my escape. There was no way of controlling the way things would turn out.

On the final day, just like every other day, the alarm that wakes us prisoners and get us out of bed, rang. For some time now my normal morning rehearsal of my history and regret had been augmented with a rising sense of mission. This was to be a different day.

"Let's do this thing!" My new roommate told me as I rose. After Les turned anti-immigrant there had been race riots in the prison between whites and blacks and everyone else. We actually got to this via a two-step process. At first the Mexican-

American gangs from America had sided with the Americans against the gangs from Mexico. Then there were so many accidental attacks on Mexican – Americans that they switched. At that point, it just became black and white versus brown.

Prisons were not the only institutions affected by Les' racial turn. Schools had become battle zones. Just one inter-racial fight was enough to cause everyone in the schools to take sides. Peace between races, we found out, is only really a cease-fire. Businesses, inhabited by adults, had less actual fights. But only a couple of fights in a business could permanently ruin the harmony, the stalemate, needed for the focus on productivity. Street brawls erupted widely. When push came to shove and shove came to punches, bystanders backed up their own race. The colorblind society was getting its vision back.

In the early days I had the idea that Les might have had a positive agenda. Even though he was doing it in a twisted way, he had convinced me that he was trying to strengthen America. The drugs, the macho posturing seemed like it could strengthen us. But it was now clear that his agenda was purely negative. He inflamed racial tensions within our country at the same time that he was using his platform to drive us to war. This was ugly stuff.

Our country had become a scary place. At Les' insistence, lynching came back (Blacks lynching the remaining Mexicans became common), women were scared to go outside unescorted, the whole nation was hooked on watching blood sports, and both of the promising Presidential contenders, from both parties, based their campaigns on a willingness to take us to war.

Perhaps in the future, if our nation becomes a nightmare nation, the new breed of macho historians will vilify me as the killer of America's savior. Anyhow, I prey that the nation goes back into domestic tranquility and that what I have done will be regarded as positive. You know what my motives were. Anyhow, what's done cannot be undone.

My new white and black partners and I went to eat before show time. Blacks and whites united. Honestly, it made me feel great and safe. Having a team made me feel comfortable. I had never had one before. While the multicultural society model taught ethnic pride, it just taught us white guys guilt and individualism. It felt good to finally belong to a group. We waited for the next bell and turned right, down the stairs, through the double metal doors and walked into the mess hall like kings.

This morning we had a special presentation during our meal. It was done from a small riser with a weak microphone and speaker just under the sole window in the whole hall. That window was amazing. I often thought of it. It brought in light. But I think its real purpose, the impact it had on me, was to reinforce the thickness of the walls that kept us from the outside light. Our prison's walls were about two feet thick.

"Ladies and gentlemen, boys and girls, eh hey ha." Warden Calhoun's lizard like joking did not convey warmth. "Men!" He nearly startled us as he went into a marine like voice. "Men," he said by way of motivation, "we are about to tear some shit up. The Mexicans..."

Then he went into some American history rant that celebrated the accomplishments of whites and blacks together. I wasn't really paying attention. I had helped him write some of it. And, besides, that whole line of thought just saddened me. It saddened me for humanities' sake. What the hell had we come to? This was America's glorious story turned totally ugly. Interestingly, it was the first time I had seen wardens united with any of the prisoners.

"Man, how noble in his reason..." I knew how this Shakespeare soliloquy had started, I wasn't sure how it ended. But I knew it was Hamlet despairing of the worth of mankind. Even so, I was very glad to have thought about the speech. Even though it was a dark speech, the creating of it reminded me that men had created beauty. It seemed a reverent and ennobling topic to ponder on what might be my last day on earth.

Anyhow, I had a mission and I had to keep on rehearsing it in my head. Warden Calhoun went over plans and signals. But he didn't know the real plan. My squad knew that they were to start a riot when I gave the signal. How ironic. I was thinking strategically, like Les.   He had taught me a new way of approaching the world. I think he'd be proud of my deception and scheming.

My mind also wandered back to when Freddie had startled everyone by calling detailed plays in the first Prison Wars. Plays didn't seem to win contests though. They made for an effective beginning. You could gain better position with them. But the exciting and decisive battles took place between individuals. Teams with superior individual talents won. That said, people had to be aware of where their teammates were and to look out for each other.

The point being that individualism, within a loose collective framework, was vindicated in Prison Wars. Capitalism was vindicated in Prison Wars. Superstars were created. The supremacy of guts was reaffirmed. The over reliance on command controls just showed that Americans had watched too much football. The breakfast pep speech unconsciously highlighted such themes. Anyhow, it seems meaningful speeches before a fight are part of the ritual that bonds us. Calhoun did a good job of it.

Nationalism does not have to be ugly. Groups do not have to be ugly. I don't know what to make of all of this. After breakfast I returned to my cell. I needed to be alone.

The prison yard had been retrofitted into a stadium. When the time came our team was gathered and shackled together like a chain gang. We walked down corridors we had been down infinite times before. We finally got to the last door before the yard. We had arrived. As we took off our shackles a guard barked some threats that didn't apply to men about to fight to the death. No one heard what he said. And then we were allowed to emerge into the noise and lights with minimal protection.

As I emerged I scanned the sidelines and was happy to see Quentin on our sideline. He was just behind the front row with Les and Freddie. Unfortunately, my targets were in a special protective box. Quentin looked at me and gave me a smug two thumbs up. They reminded me of the thumbs down motion that was supposed to take off with the first Prison Wars. His head turned purposely and I followed the direction of his stare. My God. Mellissa was there. She waved at me and I turned pale. I didn't need to see that.

At that a fantasy ran through my head. I dreamed that Quentin would recover himself because of her presence. I dreamed that he would stop this madness. I dreamed that he'd grab the microphone and say that he was ending Prison Wars, freeing me, and going back to his wife. But these were dangerous fantasies. I knew it wouldn't happen. Seeing her and thinking such thoughts were, dangerous to my resolve.

I looked at Les. He didn't bother looking for me. The crazy son of a bitch was breathing heavily and blinking. He was on drugs. I could tell. Freddie gave me a wide smile. Quentin looked like shit. But he'd looked like shit for a while. Les' condition was shocking. He had aged decades in years. And his grin had become permanent, frozen on. Quentin looked more maniacal than ever.

As we walked the field towards the sideline bench, I knew that Quentin wasn't looking at me anymore. But Melissa was still following me with her eyes. There wasn't anything I could do about that. I had to pick up a weapon with her looking. I wondered if she would put two and two together and try to warn Quentin from a distance.

I passed hammers, broken bottles and other dangerous objects. I was looking for a knife. I thought about just picking anything up as we got closer to where we were going to sit. Only having the selection of the last few yards would suck. But I was patient. And there it was. It was as if it had purposely been placed there for me. It was a long sharp blade. I purposely tripped and grabbed the knife. I stood up undetected and our line continued to our seats without notice.

At the end, of the spectacular music, laser and fireworks display and the national anthem Quentin started making his way to the middle of the stadium. My thoughts honed in on a final mantra. 'I am a crazy killer. I am a crazy killer. I am a crazy killer.'

The lighting situation couldn't have been more perfect. This was the time to act. The stadium went dark except for a single spotlight on Quentin. As he started his announcements, he didn't notice me running from the sidelines.

"Welcome to the fifth Prison Wars. Today we see the Mexicans dressed as terrorists, fight the American Army. And it will be a great show. But to wet your appetites, I have a special announcement of an upcoming August event. There are two small cities next to each other in Africa...

Quentin turned to see what was causing the disturbance and didn't even have time to try to deflect my attack. At the very last minute he didn't seem startled. It may have looked to people on television like he was raising his hand to block my knife. But I can tell you that he was raising his hand to wave at me. He had no idea what I was doing. He just reacted as if he were seeing his old friend again. My resolve was even tested by the fact that Quentin was getting ready to hug me.

I stabbed him in the side of his Adam's apple. The knife went all the way in. There is no way he survived. But in the middle of the stabbing bullets started flying and I started running. The teams knew that this was the signal for the beginning of chaos we had trained for. The designated few took on nearby guards and the rest of the team fanned out and started brawls with spectators. Instinctively the other team understood what was going on and did the same. Shots from one of the guard towers went into the stands and people poured onto the fields in panic.

With the death of Quentin it was as if God himself had been killed. The angels of hell were let loose. Les' endless buildup of hatred towards police paid off. Guards throughout the stadium were attacked right away. And, as the police were, as always, greatly outnumbered, there was no hope of reigning in the chaos. And people started killing each other with the newly liberated weapons as they hit the field. Everyone seemed to want to be a contestant in Prison Wars. It was a bacchanalian outpouring of violence.

I turned around and started to run back towards the side of the stadium I had come from. The lights were still off. I had the dark of night protecting me and a lead on the growing crowd. I was looking for Les. He was target number two. Killing him would end any hope of Prison Wars, or at least his twisted agenda, from ever coming back. I spotted Les sprawled over the wall of his private box being hit on the head with what appeared to be a laptop computer. Perhaps I should have gone into the throng to personally see that the job of killing Les was finished. But, things were totally out of hand, and the man beating him was not being delicate.

I tried to see Melissa, but she wasn't visible.

I decided to run for it when I saw a police van without a driver in the distance. I guessed that the crowd attacking someone about ten feet away was attacking the policeman that used to occupy the vehicle. I got next to it, fought my way into the driver's seat and cranked the engine.

About fifty people were between me and the large gate that separated me from freedom. Many of them were prisoners. Prisoners must have overwhelmed the guards inside too. Once in the van I floored it. If the maggots didn't get out of my way, that was their problem. I can remember each of the ten people I hit as I drove through the crowd at full speed. Two of them were lying on the ground injured.

I drove into the gate at about forty miles an hour. The gate busted open and stopped the car. My head hit the steering wheel and I think I was out for about a minute. I woke up with the feel of liquid on my face. The front of the car hood was bent in such a way that seeing over it was difficult. But when I tried, the car started again. Like a mighty flood, prisoners were now flowing out of the prison. Aggressively, I drove the car to the front of the crowd. When I stopped hitting people, I knew I was in the clear.

Due to limited visibility, after twenty blocks I stopped the car and started to run. I thought that I would have escaped the chaos. I thought I was far enough away that I would have escaped the anarchy of the prison, but I was wrong. I could hear people fighting inside of their homes. I saw several people grab newspaper vending machines and throw them through store windows. People were running through the streets with flat screen televisions, computers, and other merchandise.

Soon more people were on the streets. People just started smashing windows everywhere. Then five white guys went by chasing two Mexicans. Anarchy was breaking out all over. A prisoner in a terrorist uniform turned a corner about a block away. The prisoners had all escaped. It was time for me to change out of my Army uniform.

I threw a trashcan through a window of a department store. Running through the store I saw a guard that saw me. I think for a second he thought I was real military and felt relief. Then I think he recognized that it was an irregular uniform from the Prison Wars games and ran. I ran up the escalator. On the third floor I found new clothes.

Going upstairs, I decided to stop on the 4th floor and watch one of the many televisions on in the electronics section. A very pale announcer with an incredibly metallic suit on was seemingly yelling without raising his voice, "Major fires have engulfed every part of our city. Unlike riots of the past, this one seems to be in every part of our city."

Our city wasn't alone. Over one hundred cities had reported widespread chaos. The police chief of Omaha said that he was holding back his forces. Other police chiefs made similar announcements. I watched in rapt attention. The country was disintegrating. In Tennessee the National Guard had been called out to ill effect. Within ten minutes of arriving in the riot zone the troops broke rank and joined in the rioting. The President was nowhere to be seen. Military personnel have been seen looting and joining in creating havoc in every major city that was still reporting.

Freeways were jammed with people trying to escape. Looting of those stuck in the gridlock resulted in the cars being abandoned. And then I saw an amazing sight. Someone set a car on fire on a freeway. It started a chain reaction of explosions that when down the freeway like a string of fireworks. Seeing as that the rioting was country wide, I'm sure many of you weren't watching television when it happened. The entire freeway became a huge ribbon of fire. I watched in total disbelief.

People in some cities apparently did what they had done in their previous mob configurations: they attacked television studios. I saw one station being taken over live by hooligans before the channel went to straight commercials. I switched to another station it had an announcer. Another channel featured people looting a studio. But one by one stations started broadcasting previously taped sitcoms. I can only assume that the stations had been abandoned.

As the stations went off air, I made my way to the electronics department and set up a computer. And here I sit, writing. As with killing Quentin, this is a part of my action plan.

Tomorrow, if at all possible, I shall make my way back to my prison. It is the Pelican Bay State Prison located in Del Norte County, California. I am returning to find a copy of the chapters of this book that preceded this one. For those of you reading this without them, there are twelve earlier chapters. All copies are in the Security Housing Unit. There is a copy hidden behind the lower bunk mattress of cell D-319. Warden Craig Calhoun also had a printed copy in his office. Finally, there is a copy on the hard drive of the third computer from the left in the prison library.

If this chapter is found without the preceding chapters, know that they contain a personal account of my involvement in Prison Wars. They document events from the time I met Quentin Longus to my decision to kill him. The manuscript now appears to have become a testament to the events leading up to the total destruction of the United States of America.

I just heard a loud crash. I don't think I have much time.

Those most guilty for the chaos now destroying America were Quentin Longus, Les Christensen and myself, Marty Sanger. But, in assigning blame, I cannot leave out all of you that watched Prison Wars, participated in the Men for Manliness events, attended smoke outs, enjoyed Bacchanalia nights, and listened to the music of criminal stars. And those who passively watched their neighbors take part in such activities, even those who judged them without taking action, deserve some blame too. I feel sorry for all of us. We are getting our punishment right now. But you should realize the extent to which this meltdown is your own fault.

You might think it hypocritical that I, as a main supporter of Prison Wars, am casting blame on you all for making Prison Wars and this social apocalypse happen. But I am bitter. I am angry. And the one lesson I have learned through all of this is that character does count. And perhaps I'm only deflecting attention from my own lack of character, but the character of your general citizenry is of the utmost importance. Without the public's corruption we wouldn't have gotten anywhere. The populace's character is the thin line that keeps the law of the jungle at bay. If the nation recovers, if you want to pay for your misdeeds, talk about the character of your citizens. And only speak of us three main promoters of Prison Wars as the worst kind of villains.

I have to print this and leave quickly. I hear men running up the escalators.

9 780978 577711